CRASH DIVE 500

NICK HAMILTON BOOK 3

EDWYN GRAY

WOLFPACK
PUBLISHING
— EST 2013 —

Crash Dive 500
Nick Hamilton Book 3
Edwyn Gray

Paperback Edition
© Copyright 2018 (as revised) Edwyn Gray

Wolfpack Publishing
6032 Wheat Penny Avenue
Las Vegas, NV 89122

wolfpackpublishing.com

Paperback ISBN 978-1-64119-547-8
eBook ISBN 978-1-64119-546-1

Library of Congress Control Number: 2018965400

AUTHOR'S NOTE

Although all the main characters and incidents are ficti-tious no story featuring the Royal Navy's antisubmarine school at Tobermory would be complete without Vice Admiral Sir Gilbert Stephenson KBE, CB, CMG.

I wish to make clear, therefore, that the words and actions attributed to Sir Gilbert are entirely the product of my imagination and that he was never involved in inci-dents similar to those described in this book.

Vice Admiral Stephenson was a very colourful char-acter and a gallant British seaman for whom I have the greatest admiration and respect. Anyone who would like to learn more about his career as Commodore, *Western Isles,* should read *The Terror of Tobermory'* by Richard Baker.

EDWYN GRAY

OPERATION TENFOLD

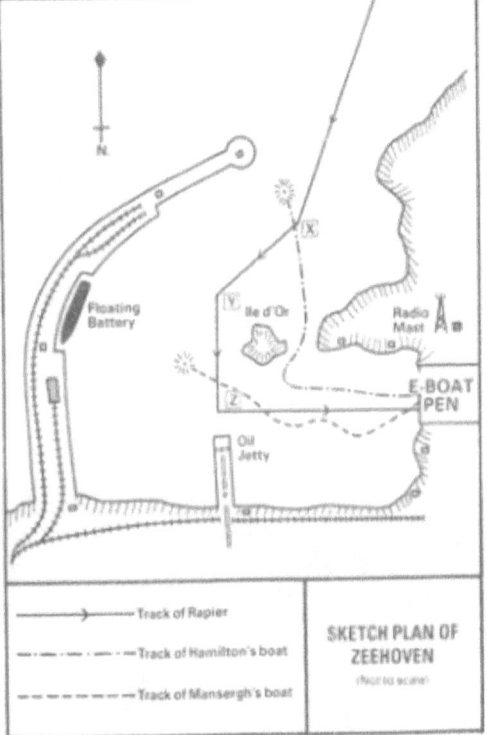

N.

Floating
Battery

X

Y   Ile d'Or

Radio
Mast

E-BOAT
PEN

Z

Oil
Jetty

—————▶——— Track of Rapier

— · — · — · — Track of Hamilton's boat

— — — — — Track of Mansergh's boat

SKETCH PLAN OF
ZEEHOVEN

(Not to scale)

To Vivienne with love

CRASH DIVE 500

ONE

Charlie Dobson wriggled himself deeper into the corner seat and scowled blankly through the window as the train ground to a clanking halt at the junction outside Queens-ferry. The London-Edinburgh-Perth Express was hardly living up to its name or its pre-war reputation. But what the hell did? It had been an hour late into York and, after being shunted into a siding to allow a troop train through, it was three hours behind schedule leaving Edinburgh. And to add to the miseries of the travel-weary passengers the restaurant car had been detached at Newcastle.

Not that such luxuries mattered very much to Dobson. As an able seaman on three shillings a day he belonged to another world to that of dining-cars. He stopped staring out of the window and shifted his gaze to the large green canvas kit-bag perched precariously on the luggage rack. And *that,* he reminded himself, was the only reason he'd volunteered for the Submarine Branch. Submarine pay brought an additional three shillings per day - a doubling of his wages - just for signing his name on a piece of official paper. There was, of course, the inevitable snag in the small print which laid down that, while under training, he only qualified for the extra cash on the days he was actually at sea and so, for the moment, it was largely a matter of expectation. But once qualified as a submariner the allowance was added to his rate *every* day whether he was at sea or not. And that meant he could marry Thelma this year instead of waiting another twelve months.

Taking the last of the dried-up sandwiches which the ration clerk had given him on leaving the drafting depot the previous day, he bit into the thick wedge of bread and sausage and started to think about the food he would be able to afford when he qualified. Next time he travelled north he might even have enough money to enjoy a meal in the restaurant car.

The express whistled a plaintive acknowledgement as the semaphore arm of the signal dropped to the 'clear' position and the sudden jolt of the couplings tightening as the engine began to move jerked the leading stoker in the opposite seat from his slumbers. The gestating snore choked in his throat, rasped like an angry rattlesnake, and was transformed into a startled grunt as he woke up.

Dobson watched the awakening with interest. The stoker had been asleep in the corner when he had joined the train at York and he had slept soundly through the ensuing four hours oblivious to the noise, the bustle and the succession of spine-shattering jolts each time the express stopped and started. Not even the party of chil-dren who had boarded the train at Newcastle disturbed his slumbers although Dobson noticed that the gentle rumble of his snore seemed to assume a more contented cadence after the same party of children had debarked at Edinburgh Central.

The two sailors were now alone in the compartment and as the train wended its way slowly towards the massive granite pillars, marking the entrance to the girdered span of the Forth Bridge, Charlie studied his companion with bored curiosity. The stoker weighed all of fourteen stone and he gave the impression of having enjoyed the good life and the flesh pots. His complexion, was naturally ruddy although his skin had a strange pallor that belied his robust physical appearance. A lurid tattoo on the back of his left hand proclaimed to the world at large that the object of his undying love was a lady named Maisie while the other hand displayed a flamboyant design of Asiatic origin. The red anchor sewn on the left arm of his serge jumper showed his leading rate while the three-bladed propeller on the right denoted his membership of the Stoker Branch.

Dobson's curiosity had to be content with this meagre harvest of facts. The stoker's cap lay on the seat alongside its owner but the ribbon was facing towards the rear and the gold lettering which might have provided a further clue was hidden from view.

Hawkins awoke with a start, rubbed his eyes, yawned, and turned his head to peer through the window as the train trundled out onto the span of the bridge. Queensferry lay below on his right and he watched a destroyer manoeuvring fussily to enter its berth. Then, lifting his eyes over the sun-speckled waters of the Firth, he checked the big ships snuggled at their moorings on the Rosyth side of the bridge. He seemed to be counting them as if to ensure that none were missing and, apparently satisfied with his roll-call, he turned his gaze away from the activity below and shifted his attention to his companion.

'Just joined the Trade, son,' he observed suddenly and without the usual preliminaries.

Charlie had been in the Service long enough to know that the Trade was the Navy's name for the Submarine Branch. But how the hell did the stoker smell him out as a newcomer? Following the direction of the questioner's eyes he saw his cap lying carelessly on the seat alongside him. The cap itself, after twelve month's wear, was no longer new. But the black name ribbon with its bright gold lettering *HM Submarines* was obviously a recent issue. He nodded.

'I've done a month at Blockhouse,' he said defensively.

Hawkins grinned patronizingly, pulled a packet of Player's cigarettes from his trouser pocket, and offered one to the able seaman. A match flared against the window glass and he held the flame forward for Dobson to take a light. Then, lighting his own, he drew a mouthful of smoke deep into his lungs and surveyed the young cockney.

'I've been in subs since '31,' he said complacently. 'And I'm still alive to tell the tale,' he added as an inconsequential afterthought. He paused. 'Which is more than I can say for most of my mates.' He looked at the able seaman searchingly. 'You'll wind up the same way I daresay - DD.'

'DD? What the hell's that?'

'Discharged dead,' Hawkins explained callously. 'It's what they write in your pay-book when your boat's posted missing. Keeps things tidy like.'

If Hawkins expected the young sailor to react he was disappointed. Dobson merely shrugged. 'You're too bloody cheerful by half, mate. *I* volunteered for submarines because I wanted to keep my feet dry. I've only been in this mob just over a year and I've already been torpedoed twice. You can have your bloody surface ships - just give me a berth where the U-boats can't get you.' He glanced questioningly at the stoker. 'You ever been sunk, chum?' Hawkins looked a trifle disconcerted. 'Reckon I haven't,' he admitted grudgingly. 'But that's because I'm in the Trade. When a sub goes down no one gets out alive. You'd better start getting used to the idea, son. There won't be no third time lucky for you.' The leading stoker savoured the expression on his companion's face. He twisted the knife deeper. 'I suppose you've done your escape training in the tank at Blockhouse?'

Dobson nodded. He could still remember his feelings of panic as the instructor had clamped the clips over his nose and tapped him on the shoulder to start the terrifying ascent to the top of the submarine escape tower. It was an experience he had no desire to repeat.

'I've been through the DSEA course,' he admitted. 'Waste of bloody time, son,' Hawkins confided. 'You might get up from twenty-five feet - but when a sub goes down it goes down deep. The DSEA kit's no good at two hundred feet. Not that it's much good anyway. Even if you get to the surface without bursting your lungs there won't be anyone around to pick you up. Subs don't sail in convoy. You're on your own, mate.'

The train was half-way across the bridge when it came to yet another sighing halt and Charlie could hear the wind whistling through the great steel girders of the span. He looked down at the mirror-smoothness of the Firth beneath and decided it was a hell of a long way to fall. He repressed a shudder and cursed the stoker. Thank God they weren't shipmates. Just imagine being cooped up in the claustrophobic confines of a submarine for days on end with a wet blanket like Hawkins. In an effort to change the subject Dobson nodded towards the dockyard in the distance.

'You for Rosyth?' he said cheerfully.

'Aye, that's right. Joining a training sub. They need a few experienced hands like me to keep it ticking over.'

Charlie felt his heart sink. He glanced around the compartment to make sure they could not be overheard. 'I'm posted to *Rapier* - perhaps we'll be in the same flotilla?'

The grin on Hawkins' face only served to confirm his worst fears. 'Same flotilla, son - we'll be in the same boat! Now ain't that lucky we met up together like this.' The stoker paused again. 'Mind you, I don't know what we're being so bloody cheerful about - she's a clapped out floating coffin from what I've heard. Just back from Australia. Had to tow her half the way home because her engines couldn't take it. I don't know why they bothered. They could have broken her up in Sydney and been done with it. Why they have to put these worn-out wrecks in the training flotillas beats me.'

The express resumed its journey with a clattering jolt and Dobson took the opportunity to gather his kit together. Surely there was *some* way of shutting the stoker up . . .

'You heard about the skipper?' Hawkins continued dolefully.

'No - who is it? Captain Bligh?'

Hawkins ignored Charlie's sarcasm. He revelled in gloom and regarded any attempt to lighten the atmosphere as a personal affront. 'The name's Hamilton. Old Nick they call him in the Trade and for good reason. Always looking for trouble. *And* finding it. Just the sort of bastard they always put in command of a training boat. He'll have you crying your heart out inside half a day.'

'Bad as that,' Dobson said casually. He was trying not to listen but it was difficult to escape from Hawkins' all embracing pessimism.

'Worse. He lost half his crew when he boarded that prison ship in '40. And you know what? They gave him a bloody medal. Just my sodding luck to get a bastard like him.'

Charlie heaved his kit-bag off the luggage rack and opened the carriage door as the express wheezed into Rosyth and came to a halt in a flurry of hissing steam. It was a relief to get away from the stoker and his woes even though the respite would only be brief. He'd been looking forward to the excitement of joining his first submarine but now, suddenly, he wasn't quite so eager. An extra three shillings a day seemed poor recompense for a ship-mate like Hawkins.

'What do you know about this Hamilton chap?' Danton asked as Mansergh changed down into third gear and drifted the Le Mans Bentley through the long S-bend outside Blair Castle.

'Nothing that's good,' Mansergh grunted. He brought the car to a screaming halt at the T-junction, glanced both ways for traffic, and then turned right onto the A985 trunk road into Rosyth. He checked the fuel gauge and decided they'd just about make it. Lucky he'd managed to find some black-market petrol in Birmingham or they'd.have been stranded high and dry somewhere in the vicinity of Carlisle. 'He got a rocket for disobeying orders when he was on the China Station so I heard. Nearly lost his boat when the Japs attacked Hong Kong.'

Sub Lieutenant Mansergh's sources of information

were impeccable. His father was a vice admiral and his uncle a post-captain. There was little he did not know by way of Admiralty gossip and wardroom tittle-tattle.

Peter Danton leaned back in the bucket seat and paused to admire the Scottish scenery along the north side of the Firth as the Bentley ate up the final miles to the dockyard. Despite the two gold rings on his sleeve his reserve officer status left him with a feeling of inferiority. Mansergh was regular navy. He'd joined Dartmouth as cadet when he was fifteen and he already had six years of sea service behind him and the knowledge made the lieutenant acutely aware of his own inexperience.

'I hear he's pretty tough.'

'Bound to be, old chap. Promoted from the lower deck. They're always the worst, y'know. Probably trying to cover up for his background.'

'I don't think it always follows, Toby,' Danton objected. I met a charming fellow at *King Alfred* who'd come up from the ranks. Damned fine horseman - he won the flotilla point-to-point.'

'That's just what I *mean*, old boy.' Mansergh swooped past an army convoy with dangerous abandon and blasted his horn as he tucked in behind the leading truck before streaking past with a roar of exhaust.

'Christ, Toby! Take it easy. You're not at Brooklands now.' The needle of the speedometer sank back to sixty and the lieutenant relaxed his grip on the crash handle thoughtfully screwed into the dashboard for the use of nervous passengers. 'And just what *do* you mean?'

'This chap Hamilton - doesn't ride, doesn't hunt and doesn't shoot. He thinks polo's something they play in the swimming pool at Chatham barracks. And,' the sub lieutenant added petulantly, 'he tilts his plate the wrong way when he drinks soup.'

Danton grinned. He was accustomed to Mansergh's petty snobberies and was disinclined to take him seriously. But as *Rapier's* newly-appointed executive officer the more he found out about his skipper the better.

'Come on, Toby. He can't be *all* bad. Didn't he get the DSO for something or other?'

Mansergh's mouth twisted cynically. 'He nearly got kicked out of the Service for that particular episode. It was only his friends in Fleet Street that saved his bacon. The War Cabinet wanted his guts but they decided it wasn't politic to courtmartial a national hero. Take my advice, Peter. If you ever get into trouble with their Lordships make sure you get your name in the newspapers and they won't dare touch you.' The Bentley slowed as they entered the blacked-out streets of Rosyth, and Mansergh lit a cigarette from the cigar lighter on the dashboard. 'And I suggest you don't introduce him to your sister either,' he continued. 'He's a bastard with women. God knows what they see in him - but you know what they're like.'

Rapier's new executive officer decided that Lieutenant Commander Hamilton was beginning to sound interesting. 'Stop whetting my curiosity, Toby,' he grinned. 'Tell me more.'

'Well, he's certainly not choosey if that's what you want to know. There was some scandal about a barmaid he picked up in London during the Blitz. And then he got mixed up in some mysterious business with a French showgirl. Mind you, he nearly got his fingers burnt when he started knocking off an admiral's stepdaughter. But he got away with it somehow.' Mansergh swung the Bentley into the entrance to the dockyard and stopped at the barrier. 'I heard he had some Portuguese or Chinese tart in tow while he was out East. Apparently the Japs got hold of her ... I wouldn't mention it in front of him. I gather it's a sensitive subject and it doesn't take much for him to fly off the handle these days.'

Danton searched for his pass as an armed sentry emerged from the shadows of the guard-room to examine their credentials. He found it in a side pocket and handed it over.

'No wonder the lower deck call him Old Nick,' he grinned.

Mansergh drew on his cigarette and savoured the taste while the Marine corporal checked their identity, returned the cards, and saluted smartly. 'I only wish he was ... I reckon I can handle the Devil. But Hamilton's different. When he's in command of a boat he thinks he's God Almighty. And religion's never been one of my strong points.'

Danton slipped the identity card back into his pocket and waited as the barrier rose into the air to admit the Bentley into the dockyard.

'In that case,' he said thoughtfully, 'perhaps we'd better start learning to pray.'

The sub lieutenant's reply was short, blasphemous and decidedly irreverent.

LEADING Wren Jackson always took a personal interest in the visitors to Captain (S)'s office. And the lieutenant commander certainly seemed worthy of attention. To begin with he did not have the usual unhealthy pallor she normally associated with submariners. His face was bronzed and he looked a picture of fitness; furthermore the gleam in his eyes suggested he was not a man to be trifled with. She noticed several other things as well: the ribbon of the DSO on his breast and the fact that the narrow gold ring on his sleeve stood out in bright contrast to the tarnished dullness of its two companions. She came to two conclusions. He had just been promoted. And he had recently returned from the Med or the Far East. With an intuition born of considerable experience she also decided he wouldn't take no for an answer. And she already had little doubt what the question would be.

'Lieutenant Commander Hamilton?' She paused for his nod of confirmation. 'Captain Rogers is expecting you, sir. I'll let him know you're here.'

Hamilton returned her curiosity as she flicked the switch and spoke into the internal telephone. Wren Jackson was the first woman he'd seen at close quarters for over twelve weeks and he thought she'd fit the bill nicely until he found something else. He would, of course, have to be discreet. The class barriers of the wardroom frowned upon naval officers consorting with ratings - male or female - so they'd have to book into a back-street hotel in civilian clothes. But that would be no problem. And in any case he couldn't stand those regulation service knickers. They were enough to put any man off - even after three months at sea. He studied her carefully as she spoke to Captain (S) and concluded she'd say yes. And that was before he'd even asked the question . . .

Wren Jackson smiled up at him as she put down the telephone. There was something about the set of his mouth that made her shiver deliciously. 'Captain Rogers is ready to see you. Will you go through, Lieutenant Commander?' She lowered her eyes fractionally but

Hamilton chose to ignore the secret message. He always believed in keeping the initiative in his own hands. Attack in your own good time and not when the enemy invites you to was his golden rule. It was a technique he had put to good practice on combat patrols on many occasions. And he'd learned to use it with women too. Not that the Wren receptionist was an enemy. If anything she was too friendly. And that could be equally dangerous.

The captain's office was situated at the western end of the administration block. The window directly opposite the door faced out over the submarine basin and Hamilton could see a number of grey rust-streaked U-class boats moored alongside the flotilla depot-ship. Beyond and to the right, across the smooth water of the Firth, lay the busy quays and crowded docks of the naval base with frigates, destroyers, corvettes and cruisers huddled in organized confusion. Standing high above the smaller vessels the massive superstructure of an *Illustrious*-class aircraft-carrier, undergoing a hasty refit before returning to battle in support of the Malta convoys, dominated the skyline.

Captain (S) had placed his desk on the blind side of the door where it was invisible to the person entering the office for the first time. It was done deliberately to put the visitor off his stroke and even Hamilton was momentarily nonplussed to find himself staring at the window instead of coming face-to-face with the CO as he had anticipated.

'Over here, Lieutenant Commander - port your helm and take a seat.'

Hamilton quickly regained his composure and turned to the left in obedience to the gruff command. The captain's desk was against the blank windowless wall behind the door and a pair of keen grey eyes appraised him carefully. Captain Rogers, an ex-submariner who had won a well- deserved VC during an early war patrol in the Kattegat, still sported his famous black beard even though it was now tinged with streaks of grey and tidily trimmed in accordance with the demands of his new seniority. Despite the captain's post-rank, Hamilton decided he was still well under forty years of age. Promotion could be rapid in the submarine branch - if you survived long enough to benefit. And, of course, providing your background was suitable. He came to attention in front of the desk and saluted.

'Lieutenant Commander Hamilton, sir. *Rapier*. Reporting as ordered.'

Captain (S) waved a casual hand. 'Take the weight off your feet, Hamilton,' he said cheerfully. 'And you can cut out the bull. I don't believe in red tape and formalities while there's a war on.' The ghost of a smile flickered beneath the beard. 'I gather you're tarred with the same brush.'

'So I believe, sir.' Hamilton decided to keep his own counsel. Senior officers had a nasty habit of turning chance remarks to their advantage when it suited them and he saw no reason to give Rogers any gratuitous ammunition despite his ostensibly friendly approach.

Captain (S) reached for his pipe and began filling it with a black treacly substance which the Navy euphemistically called tobacco. 'I understand you're just back from Aussie,' he continued conversationally. 'Are things really as bad down under as the papers say?'

'They're not good, sir,' Hamilton admitted. 'I haven't seen a newspaper since I left Sydney in April so I wouldn't know what they're saying. I picked up a few odd scraps of news at Simonstown and, of course, there were plenty of rumours flying around Gibraltar. I gather the Yanks knocked out several Jap carriers at Midway - but I'm afraid it didn't mean much to me. I was more concerned with our convoy losses in the Atlantic and the U-boat offensive off the American coast. If we keep losing ships at this rate it won't matter how many battles the US Navy wins in the Pacific. We'll have been knocked out of the war long before they reach Tokyo.'

Captain Rogers nodded gravely and puffed his pipe. 'Things aren't going too well,' he agreed. 'Doenitz seized his opportunities and exploited the lack of defences off the American coast as soon as the Yanks came into the war and the U-boats played hell until the US Navy got organized. Not that we're doing much better. We've been losing half a million tons a month since March and the figures for June are up around 700,000. And that's not our only problem. Ever since the Germans made their dash through the Channel with *Scharnhorst, Gneisenau,* and *Prim Eugen* our big ships have been tied down in Home waters in case they decide to come out in force. We know *Tirpitz* is ready for sea - and you know the trouble we had sinking the *Bismarck.*'

Despite his disclaimers of an up-to-date knowledge of the naval situation Hamilton was well aware of the tactical position. The Grand Strategy of war was something he left to the admirals and politicians - he was too close to the ground to concern himself with theories and a submarine commander's view of war must, of necessity, be limited to the immediate task in hand. But *Rapier's* lengthy return passage from Australia had given him time to think.

'I suppose we could try neutralizing the German

battle- wagons by a concerted submarine attack, sir,' he suggested.

'Don't worry, Hamilton, the powers-that-be are already working on the problem. *Tirpitz* has been hiding up at Trondheim since the beginning of the year and our Intelligence reports say she's low on fuel. The RAF has made several attempts to bomb her but she's too well protected and the armament experts seem doubtful whether we'll have any bombs big enough to break through her armour for another twelve months or so. The only way to sink her is to hit her below the waterline. The question is - how?'

Hamilton nodded. While *Tirpitz* lay snugly secure behind the booms and flak defences of her fjord with the other big ships of the *Kriegsmarine* close at hand in the Baltic or in north German harbours they posed a devastating threat to the Allied convoys supplying Russia with tanks, aircraft, guns and stores. And, all the time such a threat existed, the Royal Navy's heavy ships had to be held at Scapa Flow ready to support the hard-pressed escorts if a surface attack developed. It was a good example of the old theory of 'the fleet in being'. *Tirpitz* was the reason why Cunningham was being denuded of ships as he struggled to maintain control of the Mediterranean sea lanes and why the backbone of Somerville's grandiloquently styled Eastern Fleet was only made up of old R- class battleships.

'I suppose you've heard about the Japanese midget submarines at Pearl Harbor, sir?' he queried. Having just returned from the Pacific Hamilton was acutely conscious of Japan's latest secret weapon and he wondered whether senior officers at home realized its potential. 'One of them even penetrated Sydney harbour while I was berthed in the dockyard. Fortunately it only sunk a ferry but it could have been nasty. If *Tirpitz* is hiding inside a fjord I reckon a midget submarine attack could be the answer.'

Rogers stared down at the cold bowl of his pipe, struck a match against the side of the brass box on his desk, and applied the flame carefully as he considered his reply. 'What do you know about midget submarines?'

'Not a great deal, sir,' Hamilton acknowledged truthfully. 'The Australian papers had pictures and sketch plans of one the Yanks dredged up at Pearl Harbor. But I've never seen one in the flesh.'

Captain (S) tamped down the smouldering tobacco with his thumb. 'This is in the strictest confidence, Lieutenant Commander. But I'm sure you know when to keep your mouth shut. The Admiralty has already approved designs for our own midget subs and they're under construction at Portsmouth and at Armstrongs. It will probably be a year before they're ready for service but if *Tirpitz* is still stuck up that fjord when they're completed I don't give much for her chances of surviving.'

'I'd like to volunteer for service in one of them, sir,' Hamilton offered eagerly.

Rogers shook his head. 'I'm afraid not. The crews have already been selected and are under training.'

'I've been on combat operations without a break since the war started,' Hamilton protested. 'Surely experience counts for something?'

Rogers nodded and tapped the green-coloured file lying on top of his desk. 'I know all about your exploits - everything's in here.' He flicked over some of the foolscap sheets. 'Here's your rescue of the seamen from the prison ship *Nordsee*. And your gun action against the Panzers off the Belgian coast in 1940.' He continued to flip through the file as he read the report sheets to refresh his memory. 'I even have a secret report on your sinking of the Vichy French submarine *Gladiateur* - and not many people know about *that*. And that's the very reason why we don't want to employ you with the midgets. You're a very experienced submarine commander with a good record of success. We need *young* men on the *Tirpitz* mission - men who can adapt to the new techniques required. You old stagers are too valuable to waste.'

'I've no intention of being wasted, sir,' Hamilton told him bluntly. 'I've had a good rest and I'm ready for operational service.'

'I hear you had a rough time in Hong Kong,' the captain observed. He wanted to change the subject. He knew that *Rapier's* skipper wasn't going to like the job that lay in store for him and he tried to approach the matter obliquely. 'I understand you were the only British submarine in the Far East when the Japs launched their attack.'

'That's right, sir. Just *Rapier* and a couple of gunboats to save Hong Kong. We were the only major unit to get away. Mind you we only just made it. I was down to half a ton of diesel oil when we reached Darwin.'

'The full reports aren't in the file yet,' Rogers told him. He looked up sharply. 'Weren't you in Hong Kong in disobedience of orders? I thought the C-in-C had recalled you to Singapore?'

Hamilton made no effort to avoid the captain's eyes. He knew Rogers had a reputation as a fighter and hadn't been above turning the traditional blind eye himself when it suited his book. 'I was less than halfway back to Singapore when the Japs launched their attack. *Rapier* couldn't reach Malaya in time to be of immediate assistance and I knew that Hong Kong was virtually undefended from a seaborne attack. Wouldn't you have done the same thing in my place, sir?' Captain (S) smiled. He took care not to commit himself. 'I suppose everyone breaks the rules on occasions, Hamilton. The trouble is you seem to make a habit of it. At least no one can accuse you of running away from a fight.'

'I'm glad you see it that way, sir.'

'Good - and *I'm* glad we understand each other. Which, I'm afraid, brings me to the bad news. *Rapier* is being withdrawn from combat duties.'

The lieutenant commander shrugged. He seemed unsurprised. 'It was bound to happen sooner or later, sir. The old lady's done more than her fair share of fighting and the strain of the Far East operations plus that long trip home have just about finished her off. It's a pity though - she was a good boat. I suppose nothing can go on for ver. But she's still got some useful fife in her yet. I hope they're not proposing to scrap her?'

'No chance of that. We're not likely to break up a perfectly good submarine in the middle of a war. We're sending her up to Scotland with the training flotillas. She'll be acting as an underwater target for that bunch of pirates at Tobermory.' Hamilton's eyes wandered to the window and he glanced at the submarines moored in the basin. He looked at two brand-new T-class boats freshly commissioned from the builders and wondered which one would be his.

'Personally, sir, I'd like to get back East. I've a score or two to settle with the Japs. Perhaps you'll consider me when the new flotillas are being formed.'

'Naturally, Hamilton. But at the moment you're needed closer to home. As I said before, you're a very experienced skipper and you've had a great deal of combat service. Unfortunately there's not many of the original pre-war commanders left and people like you are worth your weight in gold. That's why it has been decided to leave you in command of *Rapier* when she goes to Tobermory.'

There was a bleak silence as Hamilton digested the captain's announcement. It had emerged so casually that it took several seconds for the full impact to sink in.

'A training squadron, sir?' He tried to restrain his temper but there was a tremor of barely suppressed anger in his voice as he put the question.

'I know it must seem rather a comedown . . . but, believe me, at this precise moment in time it's the most valuable job you can do. If you'd got more seniority I might have wangled you a flotilla command. But, as it is, this is the next best thing.'

'That's not the way I see it,' Hamilton said tightly. 'You've thrown my boat on the scrapheap and now I'm being sent to join it.'

'Try to look at it objectively,' Rogers said soothingly. 'There's very little our submarines can do at the moment. Apart from a few big ships Hitler's navy no longer exists. And Italy keeps most of hers in harbour. Admittedly we could do with a couple of flotillas out East to support Sommerville but with our limited resources the Admiralty has decided against it. And as you said yourself our biggest headache is the situation in the Atlantic. Make no mistake about it, Hamilton, we could still lose the war if the U- boats carry on sinking merchant ships at the present rate, and we need trained escorts if we're going to defeat them. And we won't get them by teaching them to hunt a clockwork mouse. They need to be up against experience and skill - a submarine commander who can exploit every trick in the book and still come up with something new. It's the only way they'll learn.'

'And I'm to be the clockwork mouse, sir?'

Rogers nodded. 'It may sound unglamorous but it's the most important job in the navy until we get the U-boat problem licked. I know you think this is a load of flannel but, believe me, it's the plain unvarnished truth.' The captain paused for a moment before delivering his final bombshell. 'You'll be crewing *Rapier* with trainees - most of your regular ship's company will be assigned to other duties. You'll be allowed a nucleus of skilled ratings but the rest will be raw recruits.'

'I suppose I ought to be grateful I'm not being sent on an operational patrol,' Hamilton said sarcastically. 'But somehow I'd rather be sunk by the enemy than a so-called friendly ship. How the hell am I supposed to handle a boat under combat conditions with an untrained crew?'

Rogers shrugged unsympathetically. 'That's your problem. But I imagine it's the quickest way to make the buggers learn! I hear you can be a damned hard taskmaster when you need to be.' He closed the file. 'There will be half a dozen new S-class boats ready for service by Christmas and we need six trained crews to man them. They've been assigned to the Far East.' He dangled the carrot temptingly. 'If you play your cards right you might get command of the flotilla. Naturally you'll get plenty of backing from Flag Officer (Training). And from me too. I know it's hard but you're the only submarine we can spare.' He grinned unexpectedly. 'After your experiences in Hong Kong I'm sure the rest will do you good.'

Hamilton smiled bleakly. 'Do I have any choice, sir?'

'None whatsoever,' Rogers told him blandly. 'You'll

have to make the best of a bad job. I'll do what I can to get you transferred to a combat flotilla but judging from your file, someone at the Admiralty wants you taken off operational duties and I'll have my work cut out.' Captain (S) was suddenly businesslike. 'You'll be leaving for Tobermory on the morning tide so there's no time to waste. If you'd like a night ashore it's okay by me- it's the least I can do.'

Hamilton thought of the pert little Wren in the outer office and nodded. One night would fit his plan very conveniently. If he sailed the next day it would put a stop to any entanglements developing. Love 'em and leave 'em - that was the way he liked it.

'That would suit me fine, sir. Thank you.'

'Good, I'm glad that's settled.' Rogers rifled through the papers on his desk with the zeal of a squirrel searching for nuts. 'Now let's look at this crew change. You can keep three petty officers and three leading hands - that's all. Flotilla will supply you with three petty officer instructors and a few leading rates for each department so that you have *some* trained men. But the rest will be trainees who've only done their basic training and an introductory course at Blockhouse. It'll be up to you to give 'em their sea legs and knock 'em into shape.'

'Am I keeping my officers, sir?'

'I'm afraid not. Mannon, your Number One, has been selected for his 'perisher' and we're replacing him with another RNVR lieutenant - Peter Danton. He's been in the Trade for two years and he's done a couple of operational tours as Number One to Smethers. I know he's Wavy Navy but he's a good officer.'

Hamilton said nothing. He had no high opinion of reserve officers although he was prepared to admit that he'd been lucky with Mannon. It meant that until he had measured Danton's abilities the entire responsibility for *Rapier's* safety would rest on his own shoulders and, broad though they were, it would be a considerable strain.

'Spears has been appointed as engineer lieutenant - he's adequately experienced so you should have no problems in that department. The third and fourth hands are regular Navy sub lieutenants. They know nothing about submarines but they've seen plenty of sea service so they'll soon knuckle down to the routine.' Captain (S) grinned knowingly. 'They'll probably be *too* keen to begin with but I'm sure you'll know how to curb their impetuosity. Any questions?'

Hamilton shrugged. 'No, sir.'

There was certainly *one* question he wanted to ask but he knew Rogers was unlikely to satisfy his curiosity even *if* he knew the answer.

'Good - then it's all settled. *Rapier* will leave in the morning. And don't be surprised by your reception when you arrive at Tobermory. Old Stephenson is a bit of a tartar and he likes to give new arrivals a good shake-up. His methods may be unorthodox but you'll find his bark is worse than his bite once he gets to know you.'

'I'll bear it in mind, sir. And do what you can to get me off this bloody hook.'

'I'll try - but I can't promise anything.' Rogers reached forward and shook his hand. 'For heaven's sake keep your nose clean and don't go stepping on anyone's toes. You've got a bloody great mark against your name for something that happened on the China Station. Don't ask me what it is because I don't know. You'll have to pull something out of the bag if you want to get back onto operations.' Hamilton remembered the *Suma* episode. He was under no illusions about the reason for his unpopularity with Their Lordships. Shooting survivors was hardly a welcome addition to the traditions of the Royal Navy. And his summary execution of *Suma's* Japanese executive officers would remain a stain on his record for a very long time. In the circumstances it was hardly surprising the Admiralty wanted to tuck him away in an obscure training base on the west coast of Scotland with an untrained crew and a submarine that had seen better days. But he had no regrets for what he had done. And he had no intention of explaining his reasons. It was no use fighting a war wearing kid gloves.

He recalled Admiral Fisher's bombastic threat at the Hague Peace Conference in 1899: . . . hit your enemy in the belly, and kick him when he is down, and boil his pris-oners in oil - if you take any - and torture his women and children. Then people will keep clear of you.

Well, Jackie Fisher was right. And if the Admiralty didn't like it they should have the guts to remove him from command and publicly charge him with his alleged crimes. Until they did he saw no reason for acting any differently if the situation repeated itself in the future.

TWO

The long haul through the swirling riptides and currents of the Pentland Firth in the teeth of a Force Seven gale did little to improve Hamilton's still-smouldering temper. His oilskins were streaming with water and his feet squelched wetly inside the flooded sea-boots as he braced himself against the rails to maintain his balance. Both the newly- joined sub lieutenants were sprawled on sofas in the wardroom fervently praying for death and, although Danton, the submarine's Number One, was still on the bridge alongside him, the reserve officer was retching noisily over the side at regular intervals as *Rapier* rolled and twisted in the tumult of the storm.

The submarine shuddered violently each time the heavy seas crashed over the bows and swept green down her foredeck. Then, venting its fury against the steel ramparts of the conning-tower, the angry ocean hurled a wall of stinging ice-cold spray high into the air before surging back to gather strength for the next assault. As Cape Wrath vanished in the gloom to port Hamilton ordered a course change to the south-west and moved to the weather side of the bridge as the Coxswain eased the bows round onto the new bearing. But the alteration of course brought no respite. *Rapier* wallowed into a trough with a twisting lurch, crashed down with a spine-shuddering jolt, and then groaned with the effort of straining for the top of the spray- flecked crest that followed.

A submarine is probably the world's worst sea-boat. Lying low in the water and lacking the necessary freeboard it is completely at the mercy of heavy seas. And because a surfaced submarine rides in ballast the resulting instability gives it an unpleasant corkscrew motion in anything of a seaway. Most commanders seek shelter beneath the surface and submerge when they encounter bad weather but Hamilton had decided otherwise. He had a 'green' crew and the sooner they discovered what it was all about the sooner they'd get over it.

Conditions on the bridge were bad enough. But below, beneath battened hatches, the interior of the submarine was sheer unadulterated purgatory. The duty watch on the exposed conning-tower, drenched by continual cold stinging spray and battered every few minutes by waves flooding across the narrow bridge, were at least breathing clean fresh air. Inside the submarine, and despite the efforts of the big deckhead fans, the air was stale and fetid. An odour of sour vegetables mixed with human sweat polluted the atmosphere and the acrid stink of diesel oil and exhaust fumes penetrated into every corner of the hull.

By the time *Rapier* had passed Cape Wrath and altered course to the south-west the mess decks were awash with fresh vomit that surged from side to side as the submarine heeled and rolled in the beam sea. For all of his boasting Hawkins was one of the first to succumb to the rigours of sea-sickness and, making his way aft to check a reported leak in the supplementary pressure fine, Charlie Dobson found the stoker huddled miserably against a bulkhead in the mess compartment abaft the engine room.

Not that Dobson was feeling much happier himself but the fact that he had something to occupy his mind enabled him to stave off the worst pangs of nausea. He, too, however, added his contribution to the bucket alongside the main fuse panel as he made his way through the motor room.

'Thought you'd been sent along to teach us new 'uns the tricks of the trade,' Charlie grinned at the hapless stoker. The memory of the train journey was still fresh in his mind and he found it difficult to resist the chance of getting his own back.

Hawkins groaned as the deck rolled relentlessly from port to starboard. His normally rubicund face was a pale shade of green.

'Why don't you piss off, Dobson,' he croaked.

Having checked the faulty air line and made his report back to the control room over the intercom Dobson paused to goad Hawkins again before returning to his station in the fore-ends.

'Cook's getting dinner ready, mate. How's your appetite? Bacon and eggs tonight - and fried tomatoes—'

The stoker gave him no opportunity to complete the menu. Bending forward over the bucket he brought up the remains of his stomach with a retching groan that evoked sympathetic reactions from the other off-watch engine- room ratings. Dobson's cheery grin lost some of its sparkle as his own stomach churned and he hurried through the watertight door into the reeking fumes of the motor room before similarly surrendering to the bucket he had christened a few moments earlier . . .

By the time *Rapier* had passed through the Little Minch the storm had lost the worst of its fury and as the Cairns of Coll light appeared to starboard Hamilton ordered a further course change towards Ardmore Point and the approaches to Tobermory. The wind had now veered to the south and as the submarine came under the lee of Mull the violent corkscrew motion eased to a gentle, almost soothing, roll.

Hamilton peeled off his oilskins and glanced around the bridge. The two lookouts seemed none too happy but they had stuck to their posts throughout the storm and they showed no signs of relaxing their vigilance now that conditions had improved. If Todd and Browning were typical examples of the new trainees he had little to worry about. But somehow he doubted it. He gave each man a quick word of encouragement and then turned to Danton.

'Everything okay, Number One?'

The lieutenant wiped his mouth with the back of his hand and conjured up a feeble grin. 'I've known worse, sir. Too much soft living while I was on leave, I reckon. I'll soon get my sea-legs again.'

Hamilton nodded. His new executive officer had at least passed his first test. The fact that he had been sick was irrelevant - even Nelson had been a notoriously bad sailor. The important thing was the fact that he had not allowed his personal misery to distract him from his duty. And that was all that mattered.

'I imagine things are in an awful bloody mess below,'

he warned Danton dispassionately. 'I want everything cleaned up before we enter harbour. The Commodore apparently inspects all new arrivals and I don't intend *Rapier* to lose her reputation for being a taut ship.' He raised the lid of the voicepipe and whistled into the tube.

'Control room, sir. Duty Coxswain.'

Hamilton smiled as he heard Blood's reassuringly calm voice. Ernie Blood had served with him as first coxswain and senior petty officer from the day of *Rapier's* commissioning and his solid reliable presence had been a source of comfort on more than one occasion. Perhaps if the chief had been at his side when the submarine's landing party had run the Japanese survivors to earth on Charlotte Island the story might have ended differently.

'Tell Sub Lieutenant Mansergh I want to speak to him, Cox'n.'

There was an almost imperceptible pause. 'Sorry, sir. Mister Mansergh is in the wardroom. He ain't feeling too well.'

Hamilton could picture the malevolent grin on Blood's face as he made his report. The Coxswain could afford to see the funny side of it but, as skipper of *Rapier*, Hamilton was forced to take a sterner view.

'Did he call the other Sub to relieve him?'

'No, sir. And the other gentleman's nearly as bad. I took over when he left the control room - everything's okay.'

'Thank you, Cox'n. I'll come down and sort them out.' Hamilton closed the watertight lid of the voicepipe and turned to Danton. 'I'm going below, Number One. Take over the Watch and call me to the bridge when we enter Bloody Bay.'

The executive officer acknowledged the order and

moved to the front of the bridge. He could see Ardmore Point five miles ahead through the evening mists and he passed a course correction to the control room as Hamilton thrust his legs into the upper hatchway and descended the ladder. Ernie Blood was waiting for him at the bottom and *Rapier's* skipper glanced quickly around the compartment to ensure that everyone was at their station.

'We should be approaching Tobermory in about an hour, Chief. Get the off-duty Watch to clean up. The Commodore won't want to inspect a ship that smells like a public lavatory. And when that's done tell them to shift into clean rig and relieve the Duty Watch.'

'Aye, aye, sir. Sea Duty men on deck, sir?'

'Yes - and you'd better make sure the fo'c'sle party know what they're supposed to be doing. I'll be in the wardroom if I'm needed.'

He ducked through the for'ard hatch, stepped into the narrow fore and aft passage on the other side of the bulk-head, and pushed the wardroom curtains aside. His humour was not improved by the scene that met his eyes. Jimmy Blake, the junior sub, was sitting miserably in the chair with a slop bucket beside him. He tried to get to his feet as the skipper entered but Hamilton waved him down. Mansergh, the duty sub lieutenant, was sprawled out on the bottom bunk, snoring noisily. He had neglected to provide himself with a bucket and had used the deck instead.

'On your feet, Mister Mansergh!'

The snoring stopped abruptly and the sub lieutenant moved his head warily to one side to see who was speaking. He looked at Hamilton but made no effort to get out of the bunk.

'Sorry, sir. I'm just about all-in.'

'Are you the Duty Sub?'

'Yes, sir.'

'Then why aren't you at your station, Mister Mansergh? On your feet! No officer is relieved from Watch without my personal authority.' He waited while Mansergh dragged himself reluctantly off the bunk and repressed a grin at the sub's horrified expression of disgust as his bare feet stepped into the revolting mess on the deck. For a brief moment it looked as if Mansergh was going to be sick again on the spot but with a supreme effort he fought back the urge and swayed unsteadily before the captain.

'Now get back into the control room and resume your Watch!' Hamilton snapped. 'And next time you *think* you're too ill to work report to me. *I'm* the doctor on this ship. I don't care a damn how ill you feel - you stay on duty until I order you to be relieved. Is that understood?' Mansergh looked slightly sheepish. 'Yes, sir. I'm sorry, sir. I thought it would be alright as you and the Number One were on the bridge.'

Hamilton eyed him coldly. 'You're on a submarine now, Sub Lieutenant - *not* a battleship. Each and every man has a specific job to do. And if any officer or rating fails to do that job he places not only the boat in danger but he also hazards the lives of his shipmates. There's no room for a passenger in a submarine. We're a team. If you ever leave your station again without permission I'll have you thrown out of the ship!'

Mansergh saluted, grabbed his sweater and sea-boots, and made his way contritely through the curtains to return to his post in the control room. Hamilton watched him go, rang the bell for the steward, and glanced at Blake.

'I hope you won't start taking a leaf out of Mansergh's book, James,' he said quietly.

'Not much chance of that, sir. I don't happen to have a Vice Admiral for a father. And in any case I can't afford to flop the course.'

Hamilton leaned against the bulkhead. Jimmy Blake looked bright enough to make the grade. And he was certainly keen.

'What made you come into submarines?' he asked suddenly.

Blake flushed slightly and his embarrassment brought the colour back to his pallid cheeks. 'My old man was in the Trade, sir,' he explained and then added half-apologetically, 'Lower Deck I'm afraid - Chief Petty Officer.' '

Hamilton nodded sympathetically. He could understand Blake's reluctance to go into details. No doubt Mansergh had already made the young sub lieutenant feel thoroughly uncomfortable over his humble background.

'Nothing to be ashamed of, James. And the CPOs are the backbone of the Navy. I'm an upperyardman myself so I know what it's like when you don't have the right connections. I certainly won't hold anything against you on that score.' He paused as something triggered his memory. 'Chief Petty Officer Blake . . . wasn't he serving in the *Sepia* when she went down off the Lizard a couple of years ago?'

Blake nodded. He hesitated as if unwilling to relate his story but something about Hamilton's presence inspired confidence. 'That's right, sir. He was the only man to escape from the for'ard section. Unfortunately a story started going the rounds that he'd abandoned his mates in the flooded compartment. Of course the rumour was fully investigated by the Court of Enquiry and he was exonerated from all blame. But they took him out of submarines all the same and he never really got over it.' The sub lieutenant paused at the memory. 'He went down with the *Royal Oak* at Scapa in 1939. I heard that he managed to get away from the ship after the torpedoes hit her but his mates told my mother that he deliberately let himself drown in case he was accused of the same thing again.'

Hamilton remained silent for a few moments. The Navy could be a hard place and he knew only too well from his own bitter experiences how malicious rumours could spread and fester.

'Thanks for telling me. But take my advice and keep it to yourself. If young Mansergh finds out about it he'll make your life a misery.'

'Don't be too hard on Toby, sir. I know he's a bit wild but he's alright underneath. He can't help bucking against authority - he was exactly the same on the training course. Once he settles down and finds his feet he'll be the best officer on *Rapier*. He just needs time.'

'Well, that's exactly what I *don't* intend to give him,' Hamilton said brusquely. 'He'll buckle down and do as he's told or he'll be out of my boat quicker than a flea's fart! I shall have a word with him in private this evening so that he understands the position. I know he won't listen to me - and I must admit I'm just as pig-headed when someone tries to give me good advice. But you're his shipmate, Sub. See if you can persuade him to take things seriously. He might listen to *you*.'

Jimmy Blake smiled ruefully. 'I doubt it, sir. If I know

Toby he'll tell me to get stuffed. I daresay he'll tell you the same thing - only more politely, of course.'

Hamilton leaned anxiously over the bridge screen as *Rapier* reversed motors to pick up her mooring buoy in Tobermory Bay. Most of the surface ships were already berthed for the night and he was acutely conscious of the silent spectators watching from the darkened bridges of the destroyers and frigates gathered in the crowded anchorage.

'Tender coming off from pierhead, sir.'

Hamilton glanced to starboard and saw a motorboat spuming through the black waters of the bay. It carried no flags but a sixth sense warned him that the Commodore was about to pay his customary uninvited visit to the new arrival. If so it was all the more reason for wanting *Rapier* to pick up the buoy smoothly and secure the shackle without fuss.

'Starboard ten.'

'Starboard ten, sir. Ten of starboard wheel on, sir.'

'Half astern both.'

'Half astern both, sir.' The repeater bell tinkled. 'Telegraph repeated half astern both, sir.'

'Midships . . . Port two.'

'Midships - port two, sir. Wheel on, sir.'

'Stop motors. Helm midships.'

Hamilton watched the bows glide gently towards the buoy as his orders were acknowledged and repeated. A seaman was standing in the bows with his boathook poised to grapple the buoy while his companion waited anxiously to jump across with the line. The fo'c'sle party was Mansergh's responsibility and, for once, he seemed to be paying attention to the task in hand. Crouched on the foredeck casing, he watched the mooring buoy draw level with *Rapier's* bows and nodded to the rating holding the line. The man hesitated nervously. Less than two feet of smooth water separated the submarine from the mooring canister but to the inexperienced sailor it looked as wide and impossible a chasm as the Cheddar Gorge.

'Jump, man!'

Hamilton cursed silently as Mansergh repeated his order for the seaman to leap onto the buoy with the line but the terrified sailor remained firmly rooted to the deck plating like a petrified statue. Time was of the essence when picking up a mooring. A few more seconds and the bows would have run clear and the whole tedious business of backing and filling would have to start all over again. The silent watchers on the other boats must be getting their fill of entertainment as they gloated over the submarine's ham- fisted efforts to berth. And God knew what thoughts were passing through the Commodore's mind as he witnessed their performance from the sternsheets of the approaching tender.

Mansergh suddenly realized that the buoy was moving slowly beyond reach and, with a snarl of annoy-ance, he grabbed the line from the hands of the hapless sailor, balanced himself precariously on the extreme edge of the fore casing and, while Able Seaman Evans held the buoy with his boathook, leapt across the void. He landed safely, slithered momentarily on the weed encrusted surface, grabbed for the ring, and held on grimly with one hand as he passed the line through the eye.

'Line secured, sir!'

'Well done, Sub!' Hamilton motioned his hand to the Coxswain. 'Stop motors.'

Rapier lost way as the propellers stopped revolving

and the submarine drifted down current to close the gap between the bows and the buoy.

'Pass the bridle!'

The seaman responsible for handling the mooring shackle had a more dedicated sense of duty than his companion with the line although the fact that he wasn't required to leap across to the buoy had more than a little bearing on the smartness of his reaction. He guided the cable to Mansergh and watched the sub lieutenant haul it in and secure it to the heavy mooring shackle.

Toby celebrated his success with an impromptu dance on the slippery surface of the buoy and then bowed theatrically in the direction of the other anchored ships as if to acknowledge their applause ...

'I can see the monkey - but where's the damned organ-grinder?' a voice bellowed from the foredeck. Hamilton did not recognize the voice but he had little doubt as to its owner and hurrying to the for'ard end of the bridge he thrust his head over the screen.

Commodore Stephenson was standing on the fore casing and glowering at Mansergh's antics on the buoy. How and when the Terror of Tobermory had come on board the submarine was a mystery and, at that precise moment of confrontation, Hamilton was not over-concerned at finding an answer. In the tension of picking up the moorings he had forgotten about the approaching tender and he cursed himself for being caught unawares. He was, however, in good company. Practically every commanding officer entering Tobermory for the first time found himself in similar disarray - Stephenson seemed to have a genius for surprising his captains at the most embarrassing moments. Hamilton pulled himself together and turned to *Rapier's* coxswain.

'Get below, Mister Blood. Make sure everything's shipshape. And tell the sub to open the fore hatch and stand by to receive visitors.' As the chief petty officer hurried down the conning-tower ladder Hamilton showed himself over the for'ard bridge screen. 'Commanding Officer on the bridge, sir. I'll be down in a moment.'

Swinging his leg over the side he started to descend the vertical steel ladder which ran down the outside face of the conning-tower. The rungs were still wet with spray and his heavy rubber boots made the descent doubly difficult. He heard Stephenson's sardonic snort as he missed his footing and landed on his backside with a resounding thump.

'Getting ready for the Christmas pantomime, Lieutenant Commander?' the Commodore enquired sarcastically as Hamilton picked himself up. 'Or perhaps you're our new entertainment's officer from Ensa - I must admit the fo'c'sle party certainly look as though they'd make better chorus girls than sailors! And what's that damned fool doing on the mooring buoy - practising a *pas de deux* ?'

'Most of the ship's company are straight out of basic training,' Hamilton explained more politely than he felt. 'They've only been at sea for thirty-six hours.'

But Stephenson wasn't listening. There was a mischievous expression on his face that, to the knowledgeable, betokened some imminent devilment and Hamilton held his breath. He'd heard numerous tales of the Commodore's unorthodox methods and he had little doubt that *Rapier's* inexperienced sailors would play right into the Terror's hands.

Stephenson removed his gold-peaked cap with a flourish and threw it down onto the deck. Then approaching the fo'c'sle party drawn up on the fore casing and standing stiffly to attention with their collars flapping in the evening breeze he surveyed them in silence for a few moments before carefully choosing a suitable victim.

'Imagine it's an unexploded bomb,' the Commodore snapped at the rating drawn up at the end of the line. 'What would do you about it?'

Charlie Dobson looked at the cap and gulped. He hadn't the remotest idea what he was supposed to do with an unexploded bomb - or any other sort of bomb for that matter. Standing like a ram-rod he stared out over the starboard side as he strove to resolve the problem.

'It'll go off in ten seconds, man! *Do* something!' Stephenson glared at the young able seaman and began counting with ominous deliberation. '. . . eight . . . seven . . . six . . .'

There was a sudden commotion as Mansergh leapt from the buoy onto the fore deck casing and hurried past the line of rigid sailors. The countdown had reached to 'three' as he confronted the Commodore.

'Bomb, sir?' he asked eagerly. 'Where?'

The Terror pointed to the gold-peaked cap lying forlornly on the deck. 'There it is - do something!'

Mansergh did not hesitate. Moving quickly towards the cap, he raised his foot and kicked it smartly over the side where it landed in the water upside down and proceeded to drift slowly astern. Hamilton tried hard to repress a smile. Much as he disliked the sub lieutenant he certainly seemed to know how to turn the tables on the Commodore. Or so it appeared. But Stephenson had not acquired his reputation for nothing. He stared down at the sodden cap bobbing gently on the surface and then looked at Mansergh. 'Well done, Sub.' He paused and watched the complacent smile of satisfaction blossom on Toby's face. Then he pounced. 'Now let's imagine it's a man overboard. *Go in and get him out!*'

The smile vanished in an instant. Mansergh swallowed back the reply that sprang to his lips and looked over the side. The water was black, cold, and extremely uninviting but he knew it would avail him nothing to argue. And the longer he delayed the further he would have to swim. Slipping off his shoes, he took a deep breath and dived in.

The Commodore watched him enter the water and then turned away. Having cut the sub lieutenant down to size he had no further interest in him. His eyes surveyed the foredeck in search of fresh mischief and he beamed happily as he saw *Rapier's* deck gun.

'Call the gun crew to action stations, Captain,' he snapped. 'Load with blank and fire six rounds rapid at the lighthouse.'

Hamilton knew all about the commodore's idea of fun and he decided the game had gone on long enough. Mansergh, admittedly, needed to be taught a lesson, but he wasn't going to see the rest of his men made into laughing stocks in front of the other ships.

'I am sorry, sir. I regret I cannot carry out your order.'

Stephenson bristled and fixed him with a baleful stare. He was too wily, however, to start an argument with an experienced captain until he was sure of his grounds. If the gun crew had made a hash of the exercise his comments would have been blistering. But the commodore knew that a responsible commanding officer did not refuse to obey orders from a superior without good reason.

'I will see you below, Lieutenant Commander,' he

said coldly. 'Perhaps you will be good enough to show me the way.'

Hamilton found it difficult to conceal his qualms about the impending interview as he led the Commodore to the fore hatch. The performance of the crew had been appalling and even lack of experience was an inadequate excuse for their ineptitude. But, as he followed Stephenson down the ladder, he felt almost too tired to care. The battle with the gale in the Pentland Firth had sapped his strength and the strain of finding a course through the dangerous waters of the Minches without adequate navigation marks had drained the last reserves of his energy. Normally he was accustomed to the back-up support of a highly-trained team of officers and men. But, with the exception of a few key men like Ernie Blood, he was now entirely on his own. Perhaps if he had enjoyed a good night's sleep before *Rapier* sailed from Rosyth he might have had the stamina to shoulder the additional burdens of responsibility thrust upon him by the crew-change. But Wren Jackson had been a demanding lover and it had taken him until three o'clock in the morning to satisfy her. And even then she'd insisted on a quickie before breakfast . . .

He closed the wardroom curtain behind him and turned to face the Commodore. The Terror of Tobermory wasted no time on polite preliminaries.

'Well, Lieutenant Commander? You refused to carry out a lawful order. I hope you have a good reason.'

'I think I have, sir. Apart from six men the entire ship's company are raw trainees. They only came aboard yesterday. If I had let them loose with that gun they'd have sunk half the ships in the anchorage.'

'You seem to have an unduly high opinion of their

capabilities,' Stephenson growled. 'From what I've seen they couldn't even fire at the sky without missing.' He smiled suddenly and waved his hand towards the settee. 'I suggest you sit yourself down and tell me all about it, my boy.'

Hamilton gave a brief resume of his interview with Captain Rogers and included a short but vivid account of the submarine's passage from Rosyth to Tobermory. The Commodore heard him out and then nodded sympathetically.

'You were quite right to refuse to carry out my order. If I had been aware of the situation I would not have been fool enough to give it. But that's the first and last time I'll let you get away with it.' His eyes twinkled as he issued the warning. Then, suddenly, he was serious again. 'I need a target submarine to train my escort commanders. Unless I can give them something to hunt they might just as well pack up and go home. You will therefore have exactly seven days to work up your crew and make *Rapier* an efficient unit. And whether you succeed or not your boat will be sent out on exercises immediately that period has elapsed. Is that understood?'

'I'll do my best, sir.'

Stephenson fixed him with a basilisk stare. 'Don't you *always* do your best?' he demanded.

Hamilton parried the attack with a disarming smile. 'Of course, sir. But on this occasion it won't be easy. Most of the men have only had their basic shore training - and few of them have been at sea for more than twenty-four hours at a stretch. I can't ask too much of them at the beginning.'

'Well *I* can!' the Commodore informed him decisively. 'And if they want to blame anyone for making them work too hard tell 'em to blame me.' His eyes suddenly sparkled with humour. 'I'm too old to worry about my reputation. Everyone who comes to Tobermory is warned that I'm a cantankerous old bastard. And by the time I've finished with 'em they know it's true.' Stephenson chuckled delightedly. It wasn't true, of course, but he liked to think it was. In fact once new arrivals had recovered from the initial shock and had become familiar with his unorthodox methods they quickly came to admire and respect the grand old veteran. Although he now held the courtesy rank of Commodore, Gilbert Stephenson had retired from the Navy as a full-blown vice admiral and, like many other senior officers, he had been recalled to service with the White Ensign at the beginning of the war. And, truth to tell, he was thoroughly enjoying his new lease of life.

'That young sub I sent over the side to recover my cap?' he enquired as he got up from the settee. 'Something familiar about him. What's his name?'

'Mansergh, sir. Toby Mansergh.'

'Of *course!*' The Commodore beamed as he recognized the name. 'Must be Chubby Mansergh's boy.'

Hamilton was not on nickname terms with flag officers but he knew to whom Stephenson was referring. 'His father is Vice Admiral Mansergh, I believe, sir.'

'Well, I'm damned ... no wonder the little devil had the nerve to kick my cap over the side. I was Sub Lieutenant of the Gunroom when his father was a snotty on *Ramilles.*' Stephenson sighed happily at the memory of far-off days. 'Many's the time I've had to tan his hide for insolence. Like father, like son, eh? I suggest you keep a close eye on that young man. He'll make a good officer if he follows in his father's footsteps. But he'll need to learn discipline.' The Commodore moved towards the curtains that divided the wardroom from the fore-and-aft companionway. 'I'll bid you goodnight, Lieutenant Commander. And remember, you have seven days in which to bring your men up to scratch.' He pulled the curtains aside. 'Don't bother to see me to my barge. It's not my first visit to a submarine.'

The Commodore vanished through the curtains before Hamilton had time to stop him. Moments later there was a clattering commotion outside as someone kicked a steel bucket and he heard Stephenson's famous roar of disapproval as he berated the unfortunate matelot responsible for leaving it in his path. *Rapier's* skipper smiled. The Commodore was going to be a hard taskmaster. But despite his formidable presence Hamilton could detect the reality of the man underneath that armour-plated exterior. And he decided he liked what he saw.

Clear Lower Deck. All hands to fore-ends. Clear Lower Deck. 'Another bloody pep talk,' *Hawkins grumbled to Dob*son as they made their way for'ard in obedience to the loudspeaker's braying command.

Dobson seemed unconcerned. 'After what happened this evening it's more likely he'll tear our bollocks off. And I reckon we deserve it. God knows what the Commodore had to say to him when they went down to the wardroom.' 'Well, it's like water off a duck's back to me, mate,' Hawkins boasted as he eased his bulky frame through the narrow oval hatchway in the transverse bulkhead. 'I've heard it all before.' He found a convenient corner and leaned back against a nest of pipes with comfortable lethargy. 'Wake me up when it's over, lad. I don't want to miss my supper.'

Hamilton stood with his back to the for'ard bulkhead

as the men assembled in the confined space of the fore-ends mess. Danton was at his side and Mansergh, with an expression of affected boredom on his face, rested his buttocks on a spare torpedo slung under the starboard rack and carefully studied his fingernails. Having checked that no one was missing Ernie Blood stepped forward and saluted.

'Ship's company present and correct, sir.'

Hamilton acknowledged the Coxswain's salute. The fore end's compartment was scarcely bigger than the carriage of a subway train and the forty men of *Rapier's* crew were cramped into the tiny space like city commuters in the rush-hour. He surveyed them in silence for a few moments before speaking.

'No doubt you will be surprised to learn that I am not disappointed in you,' he began. 'And, to put you out of your agony, I don't intend to give you a roasting. Many of you have never been to sea before and this was your first taste of rough weather. You can take it from me that you're not the first sailors to be sea-sick in the Pentland Firth and you won't be the last.' He paused for a moment while his eyes scanned the sea of faces. 'I'm afraid I can't offer any miracle cures for sea-sickness. If you're lucky you'll become immune. If not you'll have to learn to live with it. But in future, no matter how ill you may feel, you will remain at your posts and carry out your assigned duties. I know it sounds hard but you'll get used to it. Is that understood?'

There was a general murmur of assent and Hamilton turned a quizzical eye on the two sub lieutenants. Blake stared down at the deck and nodded while Mansergh merely grinned.

'The less I say about your performance on our arrival

at Tobermory the better,' he continued. 'However I fully appreciate that *Rapier* has had no time to shake-down and you are all unfamiliar with the boat and the equipment. In the circumstances, therefore, I hold no one to blame.' He paused again as his eyes searched the faces for signs of the back-slider or malcontent. He stared pointedly in the direction of Leading Stoker Hawkins before moving on to survey the others. Although he had had them under his wing for only thirty-six hours he had, like all good captains, already recognized where the weaknesses lay. 'But mark this carefully - this is the first and the last time you'll get away with it. Commodore Stephenson has given me seven days to get you licked into shape and I intend to succeed. In peacetime it would have taken three months. You have exactly one week. And if any of you fail to measure up to my standards by the end of that time I will personally ensure your discharge back to surface ships again. Do I make myself clear?'

The murmur of confirmation was stronger this time and Hamilton could sense that he was getting home to the young seamen crowded together like sardines in the cramped mess space.

'The Submarine Branch is a great Service and the men who serve in it are proud to belong to it. I want to see all of you inherit that same pride. But I warn you - you will only become qualified submariners by discipline and bloody hard work. During the course of the next seven days you'll curse me and your instructors from sun-up to sun-down. But take my word for it - it will be worth the effort in the end. When you put up your submariner's badge you will become one of the elite of the Navy. The elite of the Navy that's the finest in the world.' Hamilton waited for a few moments as he tried to catch the feeling of the men like a hound sniffing for the scent of a fox. He could sense an atmosphere of expectant eagerness to succeed.

'Finally let me say a few words about discipline. I know that many of you have volunteered for submarines, because you've heard that discipline is easier in the Trade. Well, in some respects you've heard right. But if you think this means an easy life I can tell you right now that you're in for a very nasty shock. Living together at close quarters in a confined space inevitably leads to a relaxation of formal discipline - there's no spit and polish, no divisions, and no captain's rounds. And, as you've probably already noticed, no regulating petty officers and no cells. But in the Submarine Service there is far more *real* discipline than you will ever experience on a battleship or a cruiser. And, more importantly, there is self-discipline. A submariner must learn that no man's job is more or less important than that of his mates. Each of you will have some special task assigned to you, a task which you may consider of no significance, perhaps a small valve wheel which is to be turned when a certain order is given. But that task will be vital for the safety of the boat and the fives of your shipmates will depend *entirely* on your carrying out your prescribed duty quickly and efficiently when told to do so. A few moments delay in closing a hatch could send *Rapier* to the bottom. A single sound when you have been told to remain quiet could trigger an enemy depth charge attack. It all depends on *you*.'

Hamilton had their rapt attention now and he took the opportunity to ram home his message.

'Absolute and implicit obedience to orders are essential. When a submarine is submerged the only man who knows what is happening on the surface is the officer at the periscope. You must have absolute trust in him because he holds your lives in his hand. And he, in turn, must have complete trust in *you*. When an order is given he must know that he can rely on its being obeyed promptly and efficiently. And that is the essence of submarine discipline - the interdependence of each and every officer and man in the boat. No matter what our ranks may be we are all members of one single team and we can each do our own individual jobs efficiently in the sure and certain knowledge that Joe Bloggs in the next compartment is doing his. It is *that* knowledge which will make you proud to be a submariner.

'As I told you earlier we will all be living together cheek by jowl every minute of the day and night. And that means *I* shall know *you* - and *you* will know *me*. There's an old saying that familiarity breeds contempt. Well, it doesn't apply in a submarine. Familiarity will lead to mutual respect on both sides.' He turned to Blood. 'That's all, Cox'n. Number One will give you the Station Bill later on. There'll be static diving drills during the forenoon watch tomorrow followed by sea trials. Carry on.'

Coxswain Blood saluted, did a smart about-turn that reflected his former days as a gunnery instructor at Whale Island, and faced the assembled sailors.

'Harbour Duty men report to the control room. The rest of you "make and mend" until four bells of the First Watch. Ship's company - fall out!'

Charlie Dobson nudged Hawkins from his slumbers and followed him through the narrow opening of the bulkhead hatchway.

'The skipper don't seem such a bad sort to me,' he

observed as they went aft. 'Do you reckon he can really knock us into shape in a week?'

'Load of bloody shit,' the leading stoker grumbled making his way down the catwalk between the diesel engines. 'Every skipper says the same - I've heard it a dozen times before. And all that crap about discipline?' Hawkins snorted sardonically. 'Just wait till you come up on a charge - he'll throw the bloody book at you just like all the others.'

They entered the mess space immediately aft of the motor room and the stoker lowered himself onto the leather-topped bench facing the table that hung suspended from the deckhead. He took a small cardboard box from the locker above his head and removed the lid.

'You'll soon lose the stars in your eyes after a couple of days exercises, lad,' he warned Dobson. He tipped the contents of the box over the table. 'Come on - I'll teach you how to play checkers. It's the only useful bloody thing you'll ever learn in this floating coffin.'

Mansergh hauled himself up the conning-tower ladder and took a deep breath of the clear night air as he emerged from the hatchway. Jimmy Blake was following closely behind and, standing together, the two young sub lieutenants looked out over the port side at the darkened mass of Mull. Apart from the solitary sentry at the after end of the bridge they were alone. Hamilton, Danton and Ernie Blood had taken over the snugness of the wardroom to prepare the watch bills and discuss the exercises scheduled for the following day. The trainees might have time to rest and relax but the experienced men were in for a busy night.

'I hope you were listening to the CO, Toby,' Blake said quietly. 'Some of that little speech was aimed at you.'

Mansergh nodded. 'Don't worry, I heard him. But Hamilton's the last one to be preaching about discipline and obeying orders. Old Nick's broken just about every rule in the book. That's why he's been sent to this one-eyed dump.'

'Perhaps he has - but he seemed to be talking sense to me,' Blake objected. 'I reckon we could all learn a thing or two.' He stared out across the water at the black shadows of the darkened village of Tobermory. 'I suppose there's no shore leave.'

'Too right there isn't. I put in a request after the muster. He just shook his head and said we'd be too busy to worry about such things for the next month.' Mansergh turned his attention to the north of the village where a small group of nissen huts hung precariously on the side of the hill exposed to the full force of the gales that periodically swept the island. 'That's where the Wrens are billeted,' he told Blake casually. 'Hamilton doesn't know it but one of his old girl-friends is up there waiting to settle an old score with him.'

'You seem to know a good deal about him.'

'I should do - it's my cousin, Caroline Faversham. She had a soft spot for him at one time. And do you know what the rotten bastard did to her?'

Blake could guess but he shook his head. Much as he admired the skipper he was, like most junior officers, not averse to a few tit-bits of gossip.

'He spent the night with her at the Strand Hotel, screwed the arse off her, and then slipped away around dawn and left her to pay the bill. Perhaps that's what he meant by familiarity breeding contempt.'

'Well, it's all water under the bridge now, Toby,' Blake said placatingly. 'And I don't see what she can do about it.'

Mansergh took a gold case from his pocket and offered a cigarette to his companion. 'There's nothing she *can* do about it,' he agreed. 'And there's nothing I can do either. But,' he added ominously as he snapped his lighter and held the flame forward for Blake to take a light, 'I reckon that the two of us together can cook up *something* to scupper the bastard.'

THREE

The first seventy-two hours of the shake-down exercises passed without incident and proved neither better nor worse than Hamilton had anticipated. In fact, on balance, he felt mildly optimistic. The men had made mistakes, which were only to be expected, but they were keen to learn and eager to shoulder their new responsibilities. There were the inevitable shirkers and he was irritated to find that most of them were amongst the leading rates assigned to *Rapier* for the specific purpose of stiffening the crew. While he had no complaints about the way they performed their duties he was uncomfortably aware that they were stirring up trouble in the background and undermining the enthusiasm of the trainees.

'Caliach Point bearing o-9-o, sir.'

Hamilton moved over to the compass. *Rapier* was steering a north-easterly course and the craggy peak of the Beinn na Seilg was clearly visible over the horizon some ten miles ahead of the bows. He glanced at his watch.

'Well done, Number One. Only two minutes late. We'll make a navigator of you yet.' He took a sight on the lighthouse guarding the Cairns of Coll and, tracing his finger across the chart, roughly checked the bearing to confirm Danton's fix. 'Maintain course and speed for thirty minutes and then steer 0-4-5. Recheck your position when you reach Ardmore Point before picking up the buoyed channel.'

'Very good, sir.' Danton scanned the horizon with his glasses and, satisfied the sea ahead was clear of shipping, he glanced sideways at the skipper. 'I thought the men were shaping up quite well today, sir.'

Hamilton shrugged without committing himself. 'It could have been worse. But they had ample warning of the emergency dive. The important question is - how fast will they react without warning? What was the time for the last exercise?'

'One minute sixteen, sir.'

'Well, we've got to get it down to half a minute by the end of the week. If we don't we're likely to get rammed up the arse by one of our own frigates. Stephenson believes in realistic exercises under full combat conditions and no one is going to make allowances if we're slow off the mark.'

Hamilton leaned his elbows on the coaming of the conning-tower screen and watched the rise and fall of the bows as *Rapier* ploughed steadily along the western coast of the Isle of Mull. He realized he was asking a lot from the men but he knew they had it in them. Perhaps in a real emergency, and without the benefit of the cautionary preparatory warning, they might turn in a better time. On the other hand they could easily panic and make that one fatal mistake which could end in disaster.

The new officers, at least, had proved better than expected. Danton, the Number One, had proved to be the type of person it was impossible to ruffle. He was right on top of his job and made intelligent use of his limited combat experience. Spears, too, seemed to have the engine-room staff under firm control. And while he lacked the wild Irish humour of *Rapier's* previous engineer officer, O'Brien, his very dourness inspired confidence.

Both sub lieutenants looked promising despite his earlier misgivings. Jimmy Blake had, as anticipated, proved to be conscientious and quietly determined to learn every detail of the job. But he was a plodder and Hamilton could see that he was having to work hard to acquire his new skills. Mansergh on the other hand had a flair and a brilliance that reflected his distinguished naval background. His brain was sharply alert and he assimilated the routines without effort. Whether the pep talk had done any good was difficult to judge but certainly since *Rapier* had left Tobermory on her first exercise Mansergh had given no cause for concern. He had accepted criticism with grace and obeyed orders without hesitation. Perhaps he was one of those men who responded to the challenge of responsibility.

As the submarine rumbled north-eastwards on her diesels Hamilton turned his mind away from the personalities under his command. Having completed the day's exercises the crew were on patrol routine with only one watch on duty at the main controls. The remainder were off-duty and resting in their messes. If he wasn't to court disaster the key men would have to be at their diving stations.

'Which watch is on duty, Number One?' he asked Danton suddenly.

'Starboard, sir.'

Hamilton nodded. That meant Coxswain Blood would be at the aft hydroplanes and Mansergh was duty officer in the control room. He weighed up the situation and wondered whether it would be too risky.

'Ship fine on port bow, sir! Range ten miles!'

The lookout's warning report swept all other thoughts from Hamilton's mind and he reacted without hesitation.

'Clear the bridge! Diving stations . . . *dive, dive, dive!*'

His thumb stabbed at the klaxon button as he gave the order and the angry squawk of the hooter rasped its urgent message through the narrow confines of the submarine's interior bringing the men to their feet and sending them hurrying to their stations.

AHOOA . . . AHOOA . . . AHOOA.

Hawkins was on duty in the engine room when the alarm klaxon sounded. His customary lethargy fell away in an instant and, reacting without thought or question, he reached forward automatically to shut off the diesels when Stoker Petty Officer Robson gave the executive order.

'Disengage clutches - shut off for diving!'

'Clutches out!'

'Engines off, Chief!'

Hawkins heard his voice acknowledge the order as if it were someone else speaking. The harsh throb of the double-banked diesel units phuttered to silence and there was a sudden pressure on his ear-drums as the engines hungrily sucked the last dregs of air into their valves as the hatches slammed shut. What the hell was all the panic about? he wondered anxiously. It couldn't be another practice drill - the skipper normally gave a preparatory warning to the senior rates so that they could keep a watchful eye on the trainees. Hawkins felt a cold trickle of sweat run down his spine inside his overalls. For all of his vaunted eight years of service in the Trade, not to mention his boasting, the leading stoker had never been on an operational patrol in his life and the horrifying thought that this was for real put him in a muck sweat.

The raucous bellow of the alarm aroused Charlie Dobson from his daydreams with a sudden start and sent him hurrying to his diving station on the starboard side. He stared up at the two valve wheels entrusted to his care and could not decide whether he was frightened or excited. While the submarine was diving and flooding the sea into the ballast tanks through the main vents he had no active role to play in the submerging routine. But if *Rapier* lost trim, or if the electric pumps failed, it was his responsibility to turn the two valve wheels and release the compressed air to the for'ard tanks. Precisely that and no more. Making himself comfortable on the hard steel deck he waited.

Sub Lieutenant Mansergh reacted to the emergency with decisive aplomb. At the first blast of the klaxon he felt his nerves tingle to life and even before the second squawk echoed through the control room he had started to issue the preliminary orders for putting the diving routine in motion. Every split second counted. And if the deck watch failed to respond with equal speed they would find themselves marooned on the bridge as the hatches were slammed shut and the submarine sank beneath the surface. But, in Toby's eyes, that was their problem.

'Diving stations! Clutches out - switches on! Open main vents! Planes hard a-dive!'

Ernie Blood swung the big diving wheel controlling the stern hydroplanes and glanced anxiously to his left to see how Leading Seaman Cooke was coping with the emergency. The young trainee at the for'ard controls was gripping the rim of the wheel tightly and staring up at the depth gauge as he eased the 'planes down. He was pale with tension and beads of sweat glistened on his face.

'Good, lad,' Blood encouraged him quietly. 'Hard down on your helm. Just remember the drill. The bow 'planes control the diving angle.'

The leading seaman nodded and swung the wheel further to the left. He kept his eyes fixed on the flickering needle of the gauge as his lips twisted in a mirthless grin.

'Don't forget to say "when", Chief.'

'Just keep her hard down until the OOW gives you a depth, lad. The skipper knows whether he wants to go deep or level off at periscope depth. *We* don't. Our job is to keep her diving until we're told to stop.'

'Thirty feet!'

Danton snapped the order as he slid down the ladder into the brightly fit control room.

'Level at thirty feet,' Mansergh instructed the two coxswains and Blood sucked his teeth philosophically as the needle edged towards the ten feet calibration.

'Midship your helm when she reaches thirty,' he whispered hoarsely to Cooke. 'That'll take the angle off the dive. I'll bring her level with the aft 'planes.'

'She's listing to starboard, sir,' Mansergh reported as Danton moved to the centre of the control room to take over, pending Hamilton's arrival. The executive officer glanced at the spirit levels in the middle of the depth gauge to confirm the sub lieutenant's warning.

'Blow S-Two!'

Mansergh passed the order back to the Outside ERA at the diving panel to the rear of the two planesmen.

Connor was an old hand in the submarine business. He had to be. He was responsible for the operation of the blowing and venting controls of the main ballast tanks. Reaching forward he pulled a lever and watched the needle of the pressure gauge.

'Pumps on now, sir . . . Starboard Two.'

Danton kept his eyes fixed on the relevant spirit level. *Rapier* was still heeling slightly to starboard. No more than five degrees admittedly but even that was too much. Either the starboard vents had been late in opening for some mechanical reason or the trim had been wrongly calculated. He watched and waited. The pumps would transfer water from the starboard trimming tank and syphon it into the bilges. The movement of ballast would correct the list and restore the submarine's delicately balanced equilibrium. He frowned.

'She's not responding, Wrecker!'

Connor checked the dials and gauges of the diving panel. 'Electrical failure on starboard ballast pump, sir,' he reported calmly. 'Number Two or Number Four by the look of it. Permission to use manual pump, sir?'

'Negative. Release Starboard Two and Four pressure valves.'

Mansergh put the microphone of the Tannoy system close to his mouth. 'Blow starboard Two and Four tanks!' Dobson literally jumped out of his skin as the disembodied voice of the sub lieutenant brayed metallically through the fore-ends loudspeaker. His mind went completely blank for a split second before he realized that the orders related to the two valves which fell within his personal but limited sphere of responsibility. He had no idea why the valves were to be opened - and only a hazy notion of what would happen when they were released.

But the order had been given and he existed only to obey. Raising his arms high above his head he reached upwards, grasped the nearest of the brass-rimmed wheels, and quickly spun it down. Then moving a few inches to the right he repeated the process with Number Four.

'Starboard Two and Four valves open, sir.'

The brief report to the control room completed the routine. Having turned the two insignificant valve wheels and released the high-pressure air Dobson was now only required to remain at his post and await further orders. He wiped his hands mechanically on a piece of cotton waste and, instinctively, stared upwards as if his eyes possessed the power to penetrate the plating of the pressure hull and see what was happening on the surface. He felt suddenly frightened and, for the first time since he had volunteered for the Trade, he comprehended the harsh realities of submarine life. By joining the Branch he had given up that most precious of human rights - the right to determine his own destiny. Admittedly, in theory, every officer and man in the Navy gave up that right in the name of discipline when he signed on. But in a submarine it was somehow different - somehow more terrifying in the enormity of its totality. Sealed inside a cigar-shaped steel tube, cut off from the world and trapped beneath the surface, his continuing existence depended solely on the skill and cunning of his commanding officer and the dedicated efficiency of his shipmates.

Dobson was not an imaginative man but in some small way his limited intellect was able to grasp the concept that the crew of a submarine made up the parts of a single physical body. The Captain was the eyes and brain. The hydrophone operators were the ears. .

Hawkins and his mates in the engine and motor rooms were the heart and lungs that powered the body on its course. And the remainder of them, the planes men, the torpedo men, the lever pullers and valve operators, the switchers and trimmers, were all small muscles in the vast complex of the whole body. Small yet vital. And as if revealed by some mystical vision Dobson suddenly realized the truth of Hamilton's words on their first night at Tobermory.

A foot that slipped on the edge of a kerb could lead to the destruction of the entire body by throwing it into the path of a moving car. An error of judgement that turned the body to the left instead of to the right could lead it blindly over a cliff. And every man aboard *Rapier* controlled some similar nerve or muscle of the total entity. In his own case it was small - almost insignificant. Valves Two and Four were of no more importance to the body than the little finger of the left hand. Cut it off and, apart from momentary pain, the function of the body would continue unimpaired. Yet that same insignificant member could bring instantaneous death by touching an electrical power cable, by activating the fuse of a bomb, or by pulling the trigger of a suicide gun.

Dobson looked up at the pair of innocuous brass-rimmed wheels set high above his head amid the complex maze of pipes, air lines, and electrical conduits that covered the curved plating of the deckhead. And suddenly they became the two most important objects in his life.

Hamilton remained on the bridge as *Rapier* began pushing her bows beneath the surface. Behind him the roar of the diesel exhaust trunks faded away and he heard the heavy thud of the watertight baffles being closed.

Bubbling geysers of water erupted from the vents along each side of the hull as the compressed air was released and he listened to the familiar crash of water battling against the escaping pressure as the sea started flooding into the empty ballast tanks. Having checked that the Deck Watch was safely below, he paused to look at the vessel responsible for the emergency dive. The ship, still little more than a dark smudge against the horizon, had turned towards the submarine and, its curiosity no doubt aroused by the tumbling tumult of water in the distance, was steaming closer to investigate the cause.

Hamilton carefully selected a cartridge and loaded it into the breech of the Very pistol. He realized he was taking a dangerous chance. As soon as the depth gauges indicated fifteen feet Danton was under orders to shut and clip the lower hatch in total disregard for anyone still marooned on deck. Hamilton's mouth twisted sardon-ically. He wondered whether *Rapier*'s executive officer would have the fibre to close the hatch knowing that his skipper was still on the bridge.

The first surge of the sea riding up over the foredeck struck the base of the conning-tower and drenched the bridge with cold stinging spray. It was tempting to test Danton's moral courage to the limit although Hamilton realized he was being irresponsibly foolish. With nerves strung to breaking point by the unexpected emergency the young reservist officer might decide to close the hatch before *Rapier* had reached the correct depth - men often reacted prematurely when under stress. And Hamilton had no desire to find himself swimming for his life as the submarine sank beneath his feet.

Raising his arm he squeezed the trigger and heard the sharp *whoosh* of the incandescent cartridge climbing into the air. It burst with a loud crack and two green flares hung momentarily in space before drifting slowly before the wind and dropping lazily towards the sea. Another wave smashed against the steel ramparts of the conning-tower and, as a wall of solid water descended on the bridge, Hamilton heeded the warning and slid his legs into the hatchway. He climbed down the first few rungs of the ladder and then stopped to close the heavy-steel hatch cover and push the safety bolts home firmly.

'Upper hatch shut and clipped!'

Having fastened the hatch he slipped the flare pistol into his pocket and tumbled swiftly down the ladder into the brightly lit control room.

'Secure lower hatch!'

As Wilson obeyed the skipper's order and reached up to secure the control room hatch Danton stepped forward.

The expression on his face reflected his relief at Hamilton's safe arrival.

'Fifteen feet and diving, sir,' he reported.

Hamilton ignored the information. 'Why wasn't the lower hatch closed?' he demanded.

'The depth gauges were still showing thirteen feet when you came down, sir,' he explained quickly. He looked towards Ernie Blood. 'Isn't that right, Cox'n?'

Blood took care not to look at Hamilton but kept his eyes fixed on the dial of the depth gauge.

'Aye, sir,' he confirmed. 'That's right. Thirteen feet.' Hamilton knew the Coxswain was not telling the truth but he let it pass. Old loyalties die hard and he had little doubt that Blood would have gone well beyond the danger point to save his skipper. He turned his attention back to Danton.

'*Would* you have closed the hatch at fifteen feet if I wasn't down, Number One?'

'Of course, sir,' Danton told him blandly. 'The safety of the boat is the first priority.'

Hamilton nodded. Danton had given the copybook answer even though he had his doubts whether the executive officer meant what he said. He was, however, quite sure of one thing. If Mansergh had been *Rapier's* Number One *he* certainly wouldn't have hesitated. Not just because he disliked the skipper but because he had that streak of ruthlessness in his character that would have made both the decision and the action completely impersonal. Perhaps, in the circumstances, it was fortunate that Mansergh was only the submarine's sub lieutenant.

'I ordered the Cox'n to level off at thirty feet, sir,' Danton reported. 'I thought you'd want to carry out a periscope sweep.'

'You must have been reading my mind, Number One. But in future when I order an emergency dive I want you to take her deep. It's my own fault for not telling you earlier. Fortunately this time it's only a surface ship and it's too far away to be of immediate danger so no harm's done. It would have been a different matter if we'd dived to escape enemy aircraft. It's no use hanging about at periscope depth when the bombs start falling.'

'Sorry - I'll remember next time, sir.'

Hamilton nodded and moved to the venting panel to check the bewildering display of dials, gauges and warning lights that told the initiated every secret of the submarine's trim. 'She seemed to be listing to starboard as we went down, Number One, what happened?'

'Some of the vents were sluggish, sir. When we tried to correct trim the pumps failed and we had to blow the starboard trimming tanks by means of the auxiliary HP lines. Everything's okay now.'

Hamilton nodded and made a mental note to investigate the reason for the trouble. Obviously someone had not done their job properly. On the whole, though, he was not displeased with the performance of the crew. They had got *Rapier* below the surface in just over forty seconds *and* without accidents or mistakes. Both Danton and Mansergh had reacted quickly and correctly to the sudden emergency and there had been a surprising lack of fumbling or overeagerness.

'Thirty feet, sir,' Blood reported from the hydroplane controls. 'Trimmed and level.'

'Up periscope!'

Able Seaman Bishop pulled the lever of the tele-motor controls and the periscope rose obediently from its well in the deck with a soft hiss of hydraulic power. Hamilton pulled down the steering handles, grasped them firmly, and swung the lens through 360° to check the surface horizon. Apart from the ship responsible for the emergency dive the sea was empty and, having completed the sweep, he turned the eye of the 'scope onto a port bow bearing to examine the vessel more closely.

Grimly purposeful in its dark grey war-paint, and with a flurry of white water spuming from beneath its bows, the mysterious stranger was now heading directly towards the spot where *Rapier* had submerged. The vessel was moving fast and as Hamilton watched it approach two signal flares hissed skywards from the port bridge wing. He waited for them to burst and smiled to himself as he saw the two glowing green balls of magnesium float gently down towards the sea. He closed the 'scope handles with a snap.

'Down periscope! Take her deep . . . hundred feet!'
'Group up - full ahead both motors. 'Planes to dive.'
'Twenty degrees starboard helm, Number One.' 'Star-
board twenty!'

'Starboard twenty, sir. Twenty of starboard wheel
on, sir.'

'Midships, Number One.'

'Midships!'

'Helm amidships, sir.'

'Steady as she goes.'

Hamilton had stepped back as the periscope slid into
its well beneath the deck plating and, seemingly unconcerned by the emergency, he leaned against the aft bulkhead and watched the reaction of the men in the control
room. The sharp orders and acknowledgements of the
diving routine had a rhythm and cadence that lilted pleas-
ingly to the trained ear. Despite the quick succession of
tasks to be carried out there was an almost cathedral-like
calm inside the cramped compartment and every action
was performed without fuss or hesitation. To a veteran
submarine commander it was the sure sign of a good crew.

Bearing in mind that the men had only had three days
of practical experience their response to the emergency
was little short of miraculous and Hamilton was forced to
admit that the new training methods at Fort Blockhouse
had taken a lot of the heartache out of shaking down a
new ship's company. Looking back on his own early days
in L- 79 the difference was almost unbelievable.

'Ninety feet, sir,' Blood reported from the aft
hydroplane controls.

Hamilton nodded. 'Move over to the deep gauge,' he
reminded the young leading seaman seated at the for'ard
planes. Cooke acknowledged the instruction, shifted his

eyes to the other dial, and watched the needle swing down.

'One hundred! Take the angle off the bow 'planes! Bring her level, Cox'n.' Danton's eyes seemed to be everywhere as he checked the dials and gauges. 'Close main vents!' He waited for the warning lights to change from green to red and then turned to Hamilton. 'One hundred feet, sir. Vents shut. Trimmed and level.'

'Reduce to half speed, Number One.'

'Half ahead, aye, aye, sir.'

The drumming vibration of the motors faded to a soft hum, and Hamilton pushed his head into the tiny cupboard housing the submarine's Asdic and hydrophone office. 'Any HE, Houseman?'

The operator tuned the knobs of *Rapier's* Type 709 hydrophone and listened intently through the headphone.

'Turbines, sir. Moving fast. I'd reckon a frigate at around eighteen knots. Bearing about four miles off starboard bow. Shall I check on Asdic?'

'Negative. No point in drawing attention to ourselves.' Houseman was only the second operator and he lacked the experience of Murray. Hamilton felt he owed the over- eager rating an explanation. 'They could pick up our probe on their own instruments - the hydrophones are best in these circumstances.'

'But surely it's a friendly vessel, sir,' Danton interrupted. The skipper seemed to be in a hell of a flap about nothing and he'd been dying to ask the question ever since *Rapier* had submerged.

'Did you see any colours or recognition signs?'

'No, sir.'

Hamilton shrugged. 'In that case, Number One, if you can tell the difference between friendly and hostile engine noises you should be working with the Admiralty boffins at Portland. Your talents are obviously wasted in the submarine service.' He regretted the asperity of the rebuke almost before he had finished speaking. Danton was shaping up well and the young reservist didn't deserve to be shot down quite so sharply. But at least it gave him an opportunity to ram an important lesson home to the rest of the men. 'All you can tell from engine noises is the probable type of ship and its estimated range and speed. You can't *identify* a hydrophone effect.'

'I'd disagree with you there, sir,' Mansergh broke in. Hamilton's eyes flashed angrily. Danton, as the submarine's executive officer was entitled to voice his doubts. But Mansergh, a mere acting sub lieutenant, most certainly wasn't.

'You'd do better learning not to disagree with your commanding officer during an emergency dive, Mister Mansergh! This is an operational submarine - not a debating society.' He paused. 'And on what grounds do you disagree?' he added as he presented the rope for Mansergh to make into his own noose.

'Well, sir, most German warships use diesel motors, whereas none of ours do. So if you pick up a diesel HE you can be fairly certain it's hostile.'

'And what would you do - torpedo it?'

'I don't see why not, sir.'

'Then you're a bigger bloody fool than I took you for. Apart from the fact that all submarines have diesel units for surface running you seem to have overlooked that several of our merchant ships use motors these days - *Britannic* for example. And the American Navy has started producing diesel and diesel electric escort destroyers. I suggest you do your homework before making any more damned-fool suggestions!'

Mansergh relapsed into silence. The skipper knew perfectly well what he meant but, characteristically, he'd chosen to humiliate him in front of the entire control room. The target ship would have been glimpsed before diving - and possibly observed through the periscope as well while submerged - the diesel engines were merely another means of identification. No one was likely to confuse a motor-driven passenger liner with a pocket battleship or, for that matter, a submarine.

Sitting morosely at his station alongside *Rapier's* silent engines Hawkins chewed his thumbnail and wondered what the hell was happening. Why didn't bloody Hamilton send some sort of explanation over the Tannoy and put people's minds at rest? The stoker had served in submarines long enough to know that a boat only went deep when there was danger overhead. It was an emergency action that usually heralded a depthcharge attack and the mere thought was enough to turn his bowels to water. And yet commonsense, an attribute Hawkins had in surprising quantity, told him that you didn't find German surface warships cruising on the west coast of Scotland. So what the hell had made Hamilton go deep? He spat the chewed thumbnail onto the deck, acknowledged the rebuke which the chief scowled at him across the top bank of the diesel engines and, like Mansergh, relapsed into brooding silence.

Although Charlie Dobson lacked the leading stoker's experience he knew instinctively that *Rapier's* sudden plunge into the depths betokened danger and he felt like a frightened rabbit being forced further into its burrow to escape from a marauding ferret. He stared up at the two valve wheels and shivered. The silence was the worst. The normal bustling life inside the submarine was stilled and the familiar pulsating hum of the motors was barely discernible. No one spoke a word. There were no orders. And each man remained close to his diving station intent only on the particular piece of machinery entrusted to his care. It was as if *Rapier* had been suddenly transformed into a state of suspended animation manned by a crew of ghostly motionless mutes.

Dobson's heart pounded in panic as the main lights flickered and went out. For a few moments the compartment was plunged into total darkness and Charlie was surprised to find his hands reaching up and groping for the valve wheels like a blind man feeling for the handle of a door. It was an automatic reflex action prompted only by the discipline of his training. Trapped in the blackness the young seaman knew he must locate the controls so that, if an order was given to close the valves, no time would be lost in locating them.

His fingers had just closed over the brass rim of the Starboard Two when the emergency lamps came on and he breathed a heartfelt prayer as the dim glow of the lights filled the compartment. His first unreasoning panic had already subsided and he felt almost lighthearted now that he could see again. He glanced around at the others - Drysdale, Herriot and Lawson, his companions in the foreends space - and noticed that they, too, were more intent on their duties than their fears. And there was no mistaking the fact that they were frightened. Drysdale's face gleamed with sweat and Herriot's hands were clearly trembling as he stood by the switch of the supplementary bilge pump. Even Lawson, a former professional boxer who had volunteered for submarines in preference to the

Commandos for reasons which no one had ever properly established, was swallowing hard to ease the dryness of his mouth.

With their nerves stretched to breaking point, the sharp click of the Tannoy system being switched on sounded like a pistol shot and as a buzz of static crackled through the loudspeaker grille on the starboard bulkhead the four men looked up in anticipation of an order from the control room.

Close all watertight doors! Close all watertight doors!

What little self-control Charlie still possessed evaporated in claustrophobic terror. He looked quickly around the tiny compartment and the mental image of a steel coffin flashed into his mind. A trickle of sweat ran down the inside of his thighs and he felt his legs lose their strength.

The torpedo men in the bow section reacted without hesitation. The for'ard watertight hatch slammed shut and Lawson moved across to pull down and secure the locking lever.

'Steady, lad,' Petty Officer Davies cautioned quietly. 'No need to panic. Close Number Two door.'

Although he knew he was cutting himself off from the only means of escape Dobson obeyed. He did not know why and it was against all his primitive instincts for survival. But discipline prevailed and, seizing the heavy steel door, he pushed it tight up against the rubber seals of the coaming. As the men on the other side of the bulkhead secured the locking lever, Charlie stared at the steel wall that confronted him and felt the tears fill his eyes.

For Christ's sake, what the hell was happening? *Rapier* lurched without warning as her bows rose and she hung in the water at an angle of twenty degrees. Dobson fell forward against the bulkhead and his plimsoled feet scrabbled for a grip on the canted deck plating. Loose pieces of equipment clattered to the floor and he could hear the other men cursing as they lost their balance and were thrown sprawling to the deck. Resting his arms on the bulkhead he buried his face against them and, unobserved, yielded to his fears . . .

'Buck up, lad.' A friendly hand touched his shoulder and he recognized the petty officer's voice. 'I reckon some "sippers" will cheer us all up. You're the youngest, son, you take it first.'

Charlie turned to see the flask in the PO's outstretched hand. Tot bottling, the illegal hoarding of the daily rum ration, was strictly forbidden. But Petty Officer Davies had served in submarines long enough to know the value of a stimulant to quell incipient panic and raise fallen spirits. He had built up his illicit store over a long period against just such an occasion. And with the typical selfless generosity of the submariner he was prepared to share his precious stock with his four companions.

'Thanks.'

Dobson put the flask to his lips and took just enough into his mouth to satisfy his needs. The rum burned as it ran down his throat and a warm glow settled in his stomach. He passed the flask to Lawson and watched the ex-boxer take his sip before handing it on to Drysdale.

'That's better,' he admitted, wiping the back of his hand across his mouth. 'Reckon I ought to save a bit of my ration if we're going to get any more larks like this.'

Petty Officer Davies shook his head. 'Oh no you won't, my lad,' he told him sternly. 'Tot bottling's against the regulations - and you know it is.'

The four men settled themselves on the deck plating

and leaned back against the bulkhead. The rum had steadied their nerves and restored their spirits. Now curiosity replaced their fears.

'What do you reckon's happened?' Charlie asked Davies. The petty officer shrugged. 'Nothing so far,' he said reassuringly. 'We'd have soon known if anything had gone wrong. In any case, if it had, the control room would have been asking for damage reports by now.' He eased himself into a more comfortable position, screwed the cap back on the flask, and slipped it into his hip pocket. 'It's normal routine to close all doors when a sub goes into action. The skipper's just being cautious.'

'Can't say I enjoy it much,' Drysdale grumbled quietly. 'Gives me the bloody creeps.' He looked around the narrow confines of the compartment. 'It's like being trapped in a sodding coffin.'

'It's no good thinking that way, lad,' Davies admonished him gently. 'Look on the bright side. At least we're safe and dry. And even if one of the compartments was flooded the skipper could still get us all back to the surface - a submarine's designed with sufficient surplus buoyancy to cope.' The petty officer paused and cocked his head to one side as the loudspeaker crackled to life.

Attention all hands. Attention all hands. The emergency drill is now completed. Open all watertight doors. Stand by to surface in three minutes.

Hamilton replaced the microphone of the intercom on its hook and turned to Blood. 'You can take the angle off the bows now, Cox'n. And, Number One, tell the switchboard to restore normal lighting. Stand by to surface.'

'Main vents closed, sir,' Connor reported from the diving table.

'Blow all tanks!'

'Pressure on, sir.'

'Uphelm 'planes! Grouper up - full ahead both motors!' Danton watched the needles of the depth gauges move as *Rapier* began its long climb back to the surface. He had suspected all along that the emergency dive had been no more than an unannounced drill but Hamilton had given his executive officer no prior warning of his intention and, like everyone else, he had had to assume that the submarine was in imminent danger.

Only Ernie Blood had guessed what the skipper was up to. When Hamilton had leaned over his shoulder and quietly told him to adjust the aft hydroplanes to create a bow-up angle he knew *Rapier's* captain was trying to put a scare into his new crew. The coxswain grinned to himself. And by hell, judging by what he'd seen and heard, Old Nick had certainly succeeded!

Hamilton waited for the needle of the depth gauge to reach the thirty feet calibration mark and then moved to the centre of the control room.

'Stop blowing! Midships 'planes! Up periscope!'

The mysterious vessel spotted by the lookouts when *Rapier* first dived and which Houseman had tracked on the hydrophones, was lying to on the port beam some three miles distant. Having satisfied himself that the rest of the sea area was clear of shipping Hamilton focused the high- magnification lens onto the other ship and examined it in detail. He identified it as a Castle-class frigate and as he watched her rolling gently in the off-shore swell he suddenly saw a red flare erupt from the bridge to signal that the submarine had been spotted. Hamilton smiled wryly. *Rapier's* periscope had only been showing above the surface for a mere fifteen-to-twenty seconds when the flare went up - the Commodore obviously trained his anti-submarine crews well. It would take a very smart U-boat skipper to escape from that particular frigate captain.

'Down periscope. Take her up Number One . . . Deck Watch stand by.'

Charlie Dobson grinned at his companions in the fore ends mess space as the first rush of fresh air swept through the boat as the hatches opened. It was surprising how brave a man could feel when it was all over. Charlie, however, had no false illusions. He *had* been scared and there was no denying the fact. But at least he'd stood by his post and carried out his orders. Next time it wouldn't be quite so frightening.

A soulful wail of shrill cadences that rose and fell like a banshee's death cry pierced through the loudspeaker and he looked questioningly at the petty officer.

'One a'piece, lads,' Davies translated the bosun's pipe. He grinned at the puzzled expressions on their faces. 'Means you can have a fag,' he explained. 'There's no smoking when we're submerged but all hands are allowed a mid-day cigarette when the pipe sounds. The skipper is just telling us the hatches are open and we can fight up.' He helped himself to a cigarette from Dobson's packet of Players and nodded. 'Thanks very much, mate. Good of you to offer.' He held the flame of the match towards the leading seaman and both men drew the smoke deep into their lungs with obvious satisfaction . . .

Hamilton made his way to the front of the bridge as the submarine broke surface. He glanced around quickly to ensure that everything was secure and called the other men of the deck watch topsides to join him. Moving to the voicepipe, he raised the cover and put his mouth close to the bell-shaped speaking aperture.

'Transfer control to the bridge, Number One. Turn over to the diesels and give me two hundred revolutions. Stand by for helm orders.'

'Switches off! Engage clutches! Stand by to start engines . . . start engines!'

'Clutches in, sir.' There was a slight pause. 'Engines running, sir.'

'Slow ahead both, Chief.'

'Slow ahead both, aye, aye, sir.'

Black oil smoke streamed from the exhaust trunks and quickly died away to a shimmering haze as the trimmers were adjusted. Hamilton listened to the steady throb of the diesel units for a few moments and then called over the Yeoman. Having dictated a brief signal to the waiting frigate he went back to the voicepipe.

'Steer 0-2-7.'

'0-2-7, sir'

With *Castleton* dutifully taking station on the port quarter, *Rapier* swung her bows to starboard and headed towards Tobermory Bay.

FOUR

The plain whitewashed walls and bare concrete floor were hardly the most luxurious surroundings for a party but to Hamilton, fresh from the rigours of watchkeeping on the exposed bridge of a submarine, the fuggy nissen hut offered an opulence fully equal to the Ritz - and it was a damned sight more convenient to get to. He helped himself to a large scotch and joined the crowd.

Most of the guests were WRNS officers and the fact that the drink was flowing in abundance certainly helped to sustain the illusion, even though the scratchy accompaniment from the ancient wind-up gramophone in the corner was scarcely up to the standards of Roy Fox or the Savoy Orpheans. But the atmosphere was bright, noisy, and uninhibited and after seventy-two hours of strenuous training routines it provided just the convivial break he needed to unwind.

A decorative WRN'S first officer detached herself gracefully from one of the groups gathered at the bar and welcomed him aboard with a beaming smile.

'I'm glad to see you took up our invitation, Lieutenant Commander. There are so many ships in and out of Tobermory we're always being accused of leaving people off the list.' Hamilton took a hasty step backwards as she appeared to launch herself towards him. Christ, he thought, they must be bloody man mad up here. His fears, however, were misplaced and as she hurriedly placed the flat of her hand over the glass to prevent it spilling over his uniform he saw that two of the more energetic dancers had bumped into her from behind in their enthusiasm to set up a new lap record for the floor. She smiled mischievously as she read his thoughts. 'Sorry about that - I'm Thomasina Hartman, the wardroom President.'

'Hamilton - Nick Hamilton. To tell the truth I'm a gatecrasher. Someone forgot to include *Rapier* when they were issuing the invitations. One of my Subs told me about it. He always seems to know what's going on. I hope it's okay.' The Wren moved closer. Her black hair was tied back in a severely practical bun but the hardness of the style failed to detract from her classic beauty. Hamilton caught the scent of her perfume and was reminded of an unforgettable evening amongst the hibiscus in Hong Kong in 1941.

'I wonder if I know him?' she asked.

'I think *everyone* knows him from the First Sea Lord down,' Hamilton grinned. 'Even the Commodore made his acquaintance within thirty seconds of our arrival in the bay. Toby Mansergh.'

Thomasina's eyes sparkled. 'Do you mean Toby's in Tobermory?' She giggled at the unintentional pun. 'But why isn't he at the party as well?'

'Because he's under training. And for the first time in

his young life he's getting a taste of discipline.' Hamilton saw the Wren's lip curl in a secret smile but he let it pass. He wanted to enjoy the party - not spend the evening discussing his senior sub lieutenant with one of his obvious admirers.

The sudden arrival of a bearded lieutenant commander holding a pint of beer in one hand and a plate of sandwiches in the other provided a welcome diversion.

'Hope I'm not breaking up the start of a beautiful friendship,' he said apologetically. 'Someone told me you're the skipper of the submarine.'

'That's right - Nick Hamilton.'

The lieutenant commander somehow contrived to hold the plate and the tankard in one hand while he reached forward to shake hands. 'Jack Brody. Good to meet you, Nick. I'm in command of the frigate that was chasing you this afternoon.'

'Well, I'm glad you spotted the recognition signal before we dived. I was afraid you'd take us for a U-boat and start depthcharging.'

Brody grinned. 'With *my* crew? You must be joking. They haven't got their knees wet yet.' He took a deep gulp of beer and cleaned the froth from his beard with the tip of his tongue exhibiting a lack of elegance more appropriate to a dockside public bar than a wardroom party. 'You gave us the slip when you went deep. My damned silly Asdic operator got in a flap and sent me chasing after a shoal of bloody bloaters!'

'It was quite unintentional. I just wanted to give my lads a taste of emergency diving.' Hamilton glanced around to include Thomasina in the conversation but, bored by the prospect of 'shop', she had already joined another group. 'I must admit you spotted us damned quickly when I started surfacing. I don't think my periscope had been up more than fifteen seconds when that flare went off.'

'Just a fluke, old man,' Brody chuckled. 'I didn't even know you'd got your 'scope raised. I'd taken over the Asdic to show the operator how it *should* be done and when I lost the echo I cottoned on to what was happening. I knew you'd surfaced - but I didn't know where. It was no use asking my lookouts, they're as blind as bats. So I told the Yeoman to send up the flare.'

Hamilton grinned. He wasn't sure whether to believe the frigate commander or not. He suspected that Brody was deliberately underplaying his hand. He made a mental note to watch *Castleton* next time they were exercising together. The frigate might have an untrained crew but there was nothing inexperienced about her skipper.

'Your lady-friend seems to have gone, Nick,' Brody observed as he drained his beer and put the empty glass onto the table. 'Come along and meet some of the lads.' He picked up another foaming tankard, removed the froth with the efficiency of a vacuum-cleaner sucking feathers, and steered his new-found friend over to a large group standing by the gramophone. 'Break it up, chaps. This is Nick Hamilton. He's commanding our new clockwork mouse.'

The other officers greeted him with broad grins. All, that is, except one, a slim, dark-haired commander wearing the ribbons of the DSO and DSC, who acknowledged his presence with a cold, unsmiling stare.

'I was hoping to meet you one day, Hamilton,' he said crisply. Hamilton could discern a note of antagonism in his voice. 'I'm Commander Woodward. I was at Dartmouth with Gerry Cavendish.'

Hamilton's mouth tightened. It seemed impossible to escape from the spectre of his former commanding officer. And why the hell was Woodward stirring up old wounds? Although the commander had done no more than make a plain statement of undisputed fact Hamilton had little doubt that something more barbed was to follow.

'I served under him in *Surge*,' he admitted. 'Gerry was a great friend of mine.'

'Really?' Woodward observed with cold sarcasm. 'I suppose that's why you had him courtmartialed?'

The buzz of conversation faded away and Hamilton was conscious of the spotlight focused upon him. Gerry Cavendish had been a popular character in the prewar Navy and the unfortunate incident had been a source of wardroom gossip for years. He'd never met Woodward before and he could not help wondering what his motives were in resurrecting the matter.

'I wasn't responsible for his courtmartial, sir,' he replied quietly. 'I was merely called to give evidence. It's all water under the bridge now. I think it's better forgotten.'

Gerry Cavendish's dummy torpedo attack on the German fleet during the Kiel Regatta in 1938 had been an international sensation at the time. And, as the submarine's executive officer, Hamilton had been an important witness at the subsequent courtmartial which had led to Cavendish's dismissal from the Royal Navy. Or, at least, that was the story foisted on the world's press by the Admiralty.

In fact, as Hamilton had discovered later, the court-

martial had been engineered by British Intelligence and
Cavendish had died a hero's death in 1940 while engaged
as a double agent in the *Kriegsmanne*. The true story,
however, was still a Cabinet-level top-secret and although
Hamilton was privy to the facts he was not authorised to
disclose them. Despite the injustice of Woodward's accu-
sations *Rapier's* captain could do nothing to defend
himself. Officially Gerry Cavendish had died in a motor-
racing accident soon after the outbreak of war. And that
was all most Royal navy officers knew of the affair.

'I prefer *not* to forget,' Woodward said icily. 'And I
hope one day you'll get your just desserts.' He turned
away abruptly and the other officers in the group followed
suit in support of the snub. Only Brody remained and,
with a bellowing laugh, he clapped Hamilton on the back
and guided him back towards the bar.

'Take no notice of that pompous ass, Nick,' he said
cheerfully. 'He hates *all* submariners. When he takes the
training flotilla out on an exercise I often think he really
means to sink the sub he's hunting.'

Hamilton helped himself to another scotch. It was
hardly an encouraging beginning to his period at Tobermory but there was nothing he could do about it. It was
comforting to know that Stephenson, at least, was not
prejudiced.

'Why the hell does Woodward hate submariners so
much?' he asked Brody. 'I thought he was just picking
on me.'

'It's not you personally - although I suppose if you
were involved in the Cavendish affair he's got an added
reason for sniping at you.' Brody sipped his beer. 'It's a
bit sad in a way. Woodward was an outstanding
destroyer captain. Won his DSO at Narvik and a DSC

on Atlantic convoys. Then, a few months ago, he was coming out of Pompey and was torpedoed in error by one of our submarines. It was nobody's fault. His ship was running without lights and it was a pitch-black night. Apparently, he was taking part in a special mission but there was an administrative cock-up somewhere along the line and Northways were not informed that he was going to sea. The Germans had been sewing mines in the area earlier that week and the submarine skipper assumed it was a Boche destroyer laying its eggs. So - torpedoes away and *bang!* Woodward's boat went down in less than a minute and there were only about a dozen survivors.'

Hamilton lit a cigarette thoughtfully. 'Well, at least he's got a damned good reason for hating our submarines,' he admitted. 'I'd probably feel the same in his shoes.'

'Perhaps . . . but that doesn't excuse him for dragging up the Cavendish affair.' Brody started on his beer and grinned cheerfully. 'Come on, Nick, let's forget about Woodward. The world's a big enough place for all of us. And who wants a brass-arsed commander when there's plenty of Wren crumpet available? Let's see who scores first.'

Hamilton smiled his agreement to the suggestion. Although he still had the marks of her fingernails on his back to remind him of their short but fierce encounter, his memories of Wren Jackson were already fading rapidly. Shore trips would probably be few and far between at Tobermory - no doubt Woodward would see to *that* - and this might be his last chance for several weeks. Brody, hot on the scent of a potential conquest, had already disappeared into the throng and, before searching out a likely bedmate, Hamilton decided to fortify himself with another drink. Turning away from the dancers he walked back to the bar to replenish his glass . . .

'Well, well, well. Nick Hamilton. And they say it isn't a small world.'

Rapier's commander felt an inexplicable shiver tingle down his spine as he recognized the husky voice. For some reason he seemed to be walking into a hornet's nest of The Royal Navy's submarine HQ memories tonight. He reached for a glass to give himself time to think before turning to face the owner of the voice.

Caroline Faversham looked as good as ever. The dark blue uniform highlighted the pale blue of her eyes and the crisp white shirt beneath the jacket did nothing to conceal her figure. Despite the unexpected shock of hearing her voice Hamilton could not help reflecting that she wasn't wearing a WRNS regulation issue bra. It seemed a silly thing to think about at that precise moment but that was the effect Caroline had on him. The last time he'd seen her she had been sprawled naked on a hotel bed and crying softly into the pillow while he climbed into his clothes. It was a picture he had never been able to erase from his memory for some reason.

'Good Lord . . . Caroline!' The surprise in his voice was quite genuine. 'What on earth are you doing in Tobermory?'

'Working,' she said equably. 'And by the way, darling, before I forget. You still owe me three pounds.'

Hamilton flushed. She said it with a smile but he knew it was her way of reminding him. It seemed an eternity ago. And yet it was only just over two years. So much had happened in such a short space of time. The scene in the hotel room was as vivid in his mind as if it had only been last week.

'I wish I knew how to apologize,' he began truthfully as he searched for a plausible lie to hide his embarrassment. 'I meant to write and explain but you know how it is. I was sent straight off on an anti U-boat operation and by the time I got back to London you'd been transferred somewhere else. And, as you probably know, I've been out in Hong Kong ever since.'

Caroline nodded but said nothing. She had never understood why he had suddenly put on his clothes and run out of the hotel room that night. He had been the most satisfying lover she had ever experienced. And yet he had dashed off and left her to pay the bill without a word of apology or explanation. No man had ever treated her in such a cavalier fashion before and she was intrigued and curious rather than annoyed.

'I suddenly remembered I was supposed to be at an Admiralty conference,' he lied anxiously, 'and I didn't want to wake you up. I know I shouldn't have left you like that but I was too flustered to think straight.' He carefully omitted to tell her that he had only seduced her out of spite and that, after leaving the hotel, he had gone on to pick up a barmaid. He managed to look suitably contrite. 'Am I forgiven?'

'Well, darling, that rather depends . . .' She left the sentence hanging in mid-air but there was no mistaking the message in her eyes. 'Be a good boy and get me a martini. Then let's find a quiet corner and have a chat.'

Hamilton obeyed the command with a meekness that would have surprised the men who served under him. He did not exactly relish the idea of an intimate tete-a-tete but decided it might not be politic to refuse in view of the circumstances. Not that he was opposed to the idea of a further encounter with her. She was good in bed and it would save him the bother of finding someone else. Hamilton did not believe in looking a gift horse in the mouth, even though Caroline might not have appreciated the simile. Jostling his way to the bar he found a martini and then threaded a dangerous path through the dancers to rejoin her in a discreet corner.

'Thank you, Nicky. Now tell me what you've been doing with yourself,' she said as he sat down. 'The last thing I heard you had some French showgirl in tow - I suppose she was able to teach you a few new tricks.' She sighed. 'I always think we innocent young English girls are at such a disadvantage when it comes to the Continentals.'

Like hell you are, Hamilton thought to himself. For sheer unadulterated lust Caroline was in a class of her own. He smiled secretively knowing that his reticence irritated her.

'Antoinette Bourdon was a matter of duty - not choice,' he told her truthfully and enjoying the knowledge that she wouldn't believe him. He could not help wondering why he was always getting caught up in situations which required him to conceal the truth. Only a small select circle of senior officers at the Admiralty knew that Antoinette had been no more than a pawn in an intricate plot to capture the Vichy French submarine *Gladiateur*.

Caroline smiled. 'I've heard that one before, darling. But just this time I *might* believe you. I can remember there were some very odd stories floating around . . . weren't you in command of her brother's flotilla?'

'As a matter of fact I was,' Hamilton confirmed. 'Now stop probing. You ought to know I'm not going to tell you anything.' He wondered how much she really *did* know.

Working in the cipher office at the Admiralty she must have seen hundreds of top-secret signals.

'And how was Hong Kong?'

'Hot.'

'The place or the girls?'

Hamilton drained his glass without answering. He *had* to find some way of changing the subject.

'Can I get you another drink?' he added hastily. Caroline looked at her glass. 'Why not? But make it something stronger this time. If we're in for a heavy night I'd like to get my strength up.' Her mouth curled in a tiny apologetic smile. 'Sorry, Nicky. I forgot. You don't like girls who make advances, do you?'

Hamilton ignored the provocation, pushed past the potted palm that shielded the corner from the rest of the room, and made his way to the bar. Brody was busily refilling his tankard as he arrived.

'I see you've got yourself a piece, old boy,' the frigate captain grinned.

Hamilton was not amused. A sixth sense warned him to be discreet even though Brody intended no harm. 'I've known First Officer Faversham for a long time,' he replied stiffly. 'We were just having a chat about the old days.' 'No offence, old boy,' Brody said hastily. 'Did you say Faversham? - I must have made a mistake. I thought you were with someone else.' He dug into his pocket and produced a pound note. 'Let me buy you and your lady-friend a drink.'

'Thanks - a large scotch and a double gin.' The whisky was beginning to have its effect and he felt more relaxed. 'Sorry if I was a bit sharp, Jack,' he apologized. 'I've been having a hell of a time with my new crew and I was dead beat when I got here. And now someone's turned up unexpectedly from my murky past. With all that drink you've been pouring into me I'm a bit off balance.'

Brody passed him the two glasses. 'Forget it, Nick. We're all under pressure. That's the reason for having a party.' He winked broadly. 'I've fixed myself up with a little raver for the night . . . how about you? Or don't you like rekindling old flames?'

'I don't mind when there's nothing else around. It's just that this particular old flame always makes me feel like a moth fluttering helplessly in front of a candle.' He took the glasses. 'Thanks for the drinks. And let me know how you get on with your raver. I might like to try her myself.' Caroline was sitting quietly at the table when Hamilton returned. As he put the glasses down he suddenly realized for the first time that she had lost a lot of her old sparkling vivacity and he could detect the fines of stress on her face under the make-up. Something was obviously worrying her and she looked close to tears.

'Can we get out of here when we've finished these drinks?' she asked unexpectedly. 'I don't want too many people to see us together.'

Hamilton stared at her over the rim of his glass and wondered what she meant. Perhaps she was trying to give him the brush-off . . . leading him on and then pulling down the shutters. Well, he couldn't blame her after the way he'd treated her last time.

'Why not?' he asked coldly. 'Do I lower the tone of the place?'

'Stop being difficult.' She chided him sharply and the tone of her voice showed she meant it. 'I can't explain at the moment. But I was thinking of you - not me. I've already lost my reputation in Tobermory.'

Hamilton grinned cynically. 'I see you haven't

changed.' The teasing accusation had a totally unexpected effect. Caroline's face crumpled and he could see her hands shaking as she put down the glass. 'I've been a damned fool, Nick. I shouldn't have let you walk out on me.' Hamilton could see the tears welling in her eyes and he shifted uncomfortably in his chair. He always felt so completely helpless when confronted by a weeping woman and he fiddled awkwardly with his glass.

'It's water under the bridge now,' he said lamely. 'Come on - I'll take you outside and you can have a shoulder to cry on.'

Caroline dabbed her eyes with a minuscule handkerchief as he helped her up from the chair and guided her through the door of the Nissen hut out into the cool evening air. They walked together along the gravel path in silence for several minutes and finally stopped in the shadow of a large cistern containing the camp's water supply. Suddenly, and without any warning, she threw her arms around him and began sobbing. Hamilton stroked her hair gently and nestled her face against his chest as he tried to soothe her.

'Come on, Caroline ... it can't be as bad as all that. What's wrong?'

Her body jerked convulsively as she fought to choke back the sobs and, despite their love-hate relationship, he felt a genuine concern for her. Caroline was usually self-possessed and in full control of her emotions and he could not understand what could have happened to make her so vulnerable.

'Thank God you've turned up, Nick,' she whispered. 'It's taken me a long time to realize . . .' She did not finish the sentence and Hamilton felt her hands clutch at him more tightly. 'Nick . . . don't ask me what happened. Not tonight. I'll tell you one day but I promise you I'm not the girl you used to know and I don't blame you for what you thought of me then. But right now I need you so very much . . .'

Hamilton looked down at her tear-stained face. He did not pretend to understand what she was talking about but he knew instinctively that she was not pretending. The soft pressure of her body against him triggered an inevitable reaction. But it was not the sheer animal lust he used to feel for her and, unable to cope with these new emotions, he tried to lighten the tension.

'Where on earth will we go?' he asked her flippantly. 'I'm getting too old for a roll in the grass - and it's too damn damp anyway.'

'Stop being a bastard. I'm serious. I *want* you.'

'Alright - it's mutual. But where?'

'There's an empty cabin in the Wrens' quarters. It's been cleared out ready for a new intake on Monday. I know the way . . .'

Hamilton allowed himself to be dragged down the path to the wire fence enclosing the unoccupied wooden barrack huts. Something warned him he was heading into danger but he was no longer thinking coherently and it was too late to resist. Caroline found a convenient gap in the fence, guided him through, and stopped outside the door of Encroachment Three while she gingerly tried the handle. It was unlocked and the door creaked on its hinges and she opened it. The interior of the barrack hut was dark but in the dim light of the moon through the windows Hamilton could see a neat row of empty beds. He made a last minute attempt to dissuade her.

'It's too risky,' he warned. 'Some of the other huts are occupied and the Shore Patrols are bound to come round checking at regular intervals. You ought to know the WRNS quarters are out-of-bounds to the men.'

Caroline was already undoing the brass buttons of her uniform jacket. She seemed unconcerned. 'There's nowhere else to go,' she said simply. 'If we take a room at one of the hotels someone is sure to recognize us.' She threw the dark blue jacket onto the nearest bed and her fingers were trembling as she unfastened her shirt and pulled it open. 'For God's sake, Nick. *Help* me ... I can't wait!'

She moaned softly as he reached out in the darkness and helped her to take off the shirt.

'Hurry, Nicky ... please hurry.'

She clasped her arms around his waist and pushed her warm mouth against his lips as he fumbled behind her back to unhook the fastener of her bra. The flimsy lace floated gently to the ground and she shuddered as his hands found her breasts. The nipples were already hard and he felt her hips grinding against him eagerly. Putting his arm behind her waist for support he lowered her slowly down onto the waiting bed ...

PETTY OFFICER DEIGHTON swore to himself and glanced at his watch as he felt the first drops of rain. Only another twenty minutes to go and then he was off-duty. He looked up at the darkening sky and wondered whether it would hold off until midnight.

'Not much going on,' his companion observed moodily as they tramped slowly up the gravel path leading out of the village. He swung his torch towards a fire-point and checked that the sand in the red painted buckets had been topped up. 'This bloody place is like a morgue,' he grumbled. 'We used to get a decent punch-up every night in Pompey.'

'It's always quiet just before pay-day,' Deighton told him. 'And you can't expect Tobermory to be in the same league as Pompey or Chats. The average matelot might like his beer but he don't enjoy the idea of hiking six miles to get it. Still, they'll have some money in their pockets tomorrow night - it might be a bit livelier.'

Briggs nodded his head towards one of the Nissen huts as their heavy boots crunched the gravel. 'I thought they was havin' a party up there tonight?'

'So I heard,' Deighton grinned. 'Perhaps the officers know how to enjoy themselves quietly.' He winked at the leading seaman. 'With all that Wren crumpet on offer I reckon they're too bloody exhausted to make a noise.' A faint sound caught his attention and he peered into the darkness. 'Watch it, mate. Here comes Jimmy the One!' The lieutenant was wearing gaiters and a canvas webbing belt from which hung a holstered revolver. He looked cold and bad-tempered and as he loomed out of the shadows Deighton and Briggs hurriedly came to attention and saluted.

'Anything to report, Petty Officer?'

'No, sir. Not seen a soul about.' He nodded in the direction of the Nissen hut. 'The party in the WRNS wardroom seems to have finished early.'

'That'll be the Commander's influence. Lights out at 23.00 hours. He's a stickler for the rules.' The lieutenant grinned maliciously. He'd had to pass up his own invitation because of shore patrol duty so serve 'em right. 'Two of the men from *Appleton* have missed the last liberty boat,' he told Deighton. 'You'd better check the WRNS barracks just in case. More likely they're lying in a ditch somewhere stoned to the eyeballs. If you find anyone bring 'em in.' Having delivered his instructions and acknowledged the petty officer's salute he turned away and vanished into the gloom.

The rain had settled into a steady persistent drizzle as Deighton and the leading seaman trudged up the hill towards the huddle of huts that made up the WRNS ratings' barracks. Reaching the perimeter fence they turned to the right and slowly circled around the outside.

'So much for bloody Met officers,' the petty officer grumbled as the rain soaked his monkey jacket and trickled down inside his collar. 'I left my sodding oilskin at the SP office when I read the forecast. If I get bloody pneumonia, I'll know who to blame.'

'Cheer up,' Briggs comforted him. 'Jimmy the One's getting wet as well—' He stopped suddenly as he heard a faint rustling sound ahead. 'Hold on a minute. Did you hear that noise?'

Deighton cocked his head and listened. He nodded, winked at Briggs, and grinned in the darkness. 'Let's take it quietly, mate, we might catch 'em at it. I wouldn't mind a free show. It might even be worth getting wet for.' He licked his lips with leering anticipation. 'Christ! They must be bloody randy having it off in this weather.'

He crept forward cautiously but stopped almost immediately as he detected a movement that made the wire of the perimeter fence vibrate. Deighton reached for his torch. 'Shore Patrol! Halt and identify yourself!'

The figure, little more than a formless shadow in the darkness, hesitated as it heard the challenge and turned to run. Then as if having second thoughts it stepped away from the fence and walked towards the two naval policemen. Deighton's lamp stabbed into the drizzling gloom and picked out the gold rings on the uniform sleeve.

'Sorry, sir. Thought you were one of the libertymen who've gone missing.'

'No need to apologize, Petty Officer. I'm glad to see you're on the alert.' The officer started to circle past the SPs to pick up the path leading down to the village.

Deighton's torch, however, kept him firmly in its unwavering beam. The petty officer saw no reason why he should get wet for nothing.

'Just a minute, sir. *If* you please.' The officer halted as Deighton walked towards him. 'The WRNS quarter is out- of-bounds to *all* ranks - and, with respect, sir, that includes officers.'

'Quite correct, Petty Officer. I was just taking one of the ladies back from the party. She was a bit worse for wear, if you know what I mean, and I thought I should keep an eye on her.'

'An officer, sir? I don't think so, sir, beggin' your pardon. The lady officers 'aint billeted 'ere. This 'ere's the ratings quarters.'

'I was taking a short cut,' the officer explained curtly. 'And now, if you don't mind, I'm getting damned wet standing here answering your questions. I'll bid you goodnight.'

Deighton's impressively large form stepped forward and blocked his passage. 'No you won't, sir. Not yet. I've got my orders. I'll have to call up the Duty Officer.'

He placed a whistle between his lips and blew two sharp blasts that echoed shrilly back from the surrounding hills. The lieutenant's answering shout showed he was not far away and moments later they heard the sound of his feet on the gravel as he ran up the hill. He was soaking wet and out of breath by the time he arrived but the prospect of finding a prisoner had dispelled the worst of his temper. 'Well done, Deighton. You've got one of 'em?'

'Not exactly, sir.' He took Gaskill to one side so that he could make his report without being overheard. 'It's not one of the libertymen, sir,' he explained in a hoarse whisper. 'He's an officer. Briggs and me found him coming through the fence from the WRNS barracks. I thought you'd better deal with him.'

Lieutenant Gaskill nodded. 'Quite right, Deighton. It could be a bit ticklish. Do you know who he is?'

'No, sir. But he's a two-and-a-half striper.'

The duty officer rubbed his nose. A lieutenant commander. What the devil was he doing coming out of the Wrens' quarters. Leaving Deighton to rejoin his companion, the lieutenant walked over to the intruder and shone his lamp on the man's face.

'May I have your name and ship, sir?'

'Is it really necessary, Lieutenant? No point in making a mountain out of a molehill.'

'Your name and ship, sir,' Gaskill repeated stolidly. 'Lieutenant Commander Hamilton. HM Submarine *Rapier*.' Hamilton moved closer and dropped his voice so that the two SPs could not overhear. 'I'm sorry about this, Lieutenant. I'm new to Tobermory. I must have lost my way.' He weighed up whether to tell the truth or lie his way out of the situation. Too many people had seen him at the party so an outright lie would soon be exposed. He decided on a half-truth. 'I took one of the officers back to her quarters - she wasn't feeling too well,' he said, repeating the story he had already told Deighton. 'I got lost on my way back to the party and had been walking around in circles until I bumped into your Shore Patrol.' 'I'm sorry, sir. But the WRNS barracks are strictly out of bounds. I'll have to make a report.'

Hamilton thought of Caroline. Although he didn't know the details she seemed to be in enough trouble already without a further scandal. He had left her lying naked and contented on the camp bed and no doubt she was still there. It was imperative that Gaskill and his patrol did not carry out a detailed search of the huts.

'Look, Lieutenant,' he began. 'Can't we forget it. I'd hate to get the poor kid into trouble. I was only seeing her home.'

'So you said, sir. But the WRNS officers are billeted in the village. And there was no point in you coming back to the party - it finished at eleven o'clock.'

'Alright,' Hamilton conceded. He thought quickly as he concocted a plausible story that would divert attention away from Caroline. 'I'll admit it wasn't one of the officers. I was having a bit on the side. No harm done. Just forget you saw me.'

Gaskill stood his ground. 'The Commodore's very strict about these things, sir. I'm supposed to make a report of every incident.' He paused irresolutely as he considered the implications of Hamilton's admission. 'Still, I suppose it *is* a bit embarrassing - wouldn't be good for morale if it leaked out. An officer and a rating . . .'

Hamilton smiled grimly to himself in the darkness. Thank God for bloody snobbery. If he had been caught with another officer he'd find himself on report for being in a forbidden area. But, as he'd adventured below-stairs, etiquette demanded a discreet silence. It wouldn't be good for the Service if it became known that officers went around screwing female ratings. Well, if that was the way they wanted it, so be it. At least Caroline would be kept out of it.

'I suppose it could be a bit nasty,' he admitted. 'I should have thought of that when I picked her up. But I'd had a few drinks at the party and I wasn't thinking straight. Do you think you could keep it quiet in the circumstances?' he added eagerly as if- anxious to conceal the shame of consorting with the lower orders. 'You understand, of course . . .'

Gaskill hesitated and was lost. 'Very well, Lieutenant Commander. I will see that it goes no further. Let's hope my men haven't recognized you - you know the way gossip gets around. Better be on your way.'

'Thank you, Lieutenant. I'm glad you understand. It could have been very embarrassing—' Hamilton put his tongue firmly in his cheek, '—especially if my people found out. Drop into my wardroom next time *Rapier's* berthed and I'll give you a drink.'

Gaskill saluted respectfully. 'I certainly will, sir.' He paused for a moment. 'I hope she was worth it, sir.' Hamilton thought of Caroline's slim white body writhing eagerly beneath him on the creaking camp bed. His smile was lost in the darkness as he returned the lieutenant's salute.

'I think she was,' he said quietly. 'In fact I'd say she *definitely* was.'

THE HARBOUR TENDER pitched wildly as it headed for the submarine's mooring berth in the middle of the anchorage. The rain was now descending in sheets and a cold northeasterly wind whipped the spray back over the bows drenching the occupants. It was pitch-dark but months of experience had endowed the helmsman with cat's eyes and after an uncomfortable ten minutes the black shape of the moored submarine loomed ahead.

Fennels swung the wheel sharply to port, brought the motorboat round in a wide sweep, and reversed engines at exactly the right moment to bring the tender safely under the lee of *Rapier's* hull. An unseen deckhand on the fore casing threw down a rope and Parker, the other half of the motorboat's crew, held it firmly as the lieutenant commander grasped the upturned fin of the port bow hydroplane and hauled himself up to the deck.

'Good party, sir?'

Hamilton scowled as he swung his leg over the side of the conning-tower screen and saw Mansergh leaning nonchalantly against the periscope standard, apparently oblivious to the teeming rain.

'What the devil are you doing on the bridge in this weather?' he demanded brusquely. 'If you're on Duty Watch you should be down in the control room.'

'I just felt like a breath of fresh air, sir,' the sub lieutenant explained cheerfully. There was a hint of insolence in his grin. 'And I wanted to make sure you were safely aboard before I turned in.'

Hamilton grunted. There was only one reason why Mansergh had waited up. Curiosity. And he had no intention of satisfying it. Moving to the after section of the bridge he ordered the lonely seaman keeping watch to go below and get into some dry clothes. Then, having dismissed the lookout, he turned to follow him down the ladder into the control room.

'Did you see Caroline, sir?'

Mansergh's unexpected question stopped him in his tracks. Damn the man! How the hell did he seem to know about everything that happened? To his annoyance Hamilton found his own curiosity aroused and, pausing at the hatchway, he looked at the sub lieutenant.

'Caroline Faversham? Why - do you know her?'

'Of course, sir. We're sort of cousins,' Mansergh said easily. Although it was too dark to see clearly Hamilton could just discern the insolently condescending smile on his lips. A sixth sense warned him that Mansergh knew a great deal more about the evening's events than seemed possible. 'But you're a bit behind the times, sir. Her name's not Faversham any longer.'

Hamilton made no reply but he could hear the note of complacent triumph in Mansergh's voice. So *that* was why Caroline was upset. She was married. And, by the sound of it, not very happily either.

'Perhaps she introduced you to her husband, sir,' Mansergh continued blandly as if savouring the biting chill of the knife as he slowly inserted it.

'No,' Hamilton snapped shortly.

'What a pity . . . I'm sure you'd have liked him. He's a commander on the staff at Tobermory. Used to be in destroyers I believe.'

Hamilton clenched his hands in the darkness as he felt an icy hand close around his heart. Somehow or another he knew Mansergh was mixed up in all this. In fact, in all probability, he was the instigator. He thought it had been too much of a coincidence when Caroline had turned up at the party. He suddenly remembered his encounter with the shore patrol and shuddered. Good God - what a bloody awful mess.

'We may have been introduced,' he told Mansergh casually. No matter what happened he had to maintain appearances. 'There were a lot of people there. If I knew the name . . .?'

'Oh, you wouldn't forget him if you met him, sir. His name's Woodward - Commander Woodward.' Mansergh paused to allow the name to register and then, leaning forward, lowered his voice. 'I gather he has some peculiar reason for hating submariners. I rather imagine you'll have given him another one tonight.'

FIVE

'Two points to starboard. Half ahead both. Diving in five minutes - stand by diving stations.'

Hamilton closed the cover of the voicepipe, rested his elbows on the lip of the bridge screen in his favourite posture, and stared ahead over the bows. It was good to be at sea again after the traumas of the previous week and the cold clean air helped to put matters into perspective. He had heard nothing from Caroline since the night of the party and Mansergh had not mentioned the incident again. Perhaps there was no basis for his suspicions after all. Hamilton had a facility for concentrating on the events of the moment and forgetting the past. It was an ability that had served him well on many previous occasions and he regarded the forthcoming training exercise - aptly codenamed Mousetrap - as an ideal opportunity to put first things first.

Yet, lurking at the back of his mind, was the ever-present fear that something would go wrong. He had little doubt that all hell would be let loose if Woodward discovered the truth. And, if the worst came to the worst, he knew he could expect little support from Commodore Stephenson - a noted stickler for good old-fashioned morality. Hamilton watched a fine curtain of spray whisper back from the bows and saw the tiny droplets of silvered water sparkling like a diamond rainbow in the late-afternoon sun. He reflected on the peaceful tranquility of the Scottish coast and the almost perfect summer weather. It was difficult to imagine that the world beyond the horizon was at war.

And where did Mansergh fit into the jigsaw? Hamilton was annoyed with himself for allowing his thoughts to return to the Caroline affair. Command of a submarine demanded hundred per cent concentration and anything that distracted attention was a dangerous irritant. But why the devil hadn't Mansergh warned him that she was now married - and to Woodward of all people? He must have known they would meet at the party; in fact, Hamilton was beginning to have a strong suspicion that the sub lieutenant had engineered it. But for what purpose?

'The time is 16.57, Danton reminded him. Hamilton nodded and tried to drag his mind away from his personal problems. According to instructions *Rapier* was to submerge at five o'clock and steer a westerly course into the Atlantic. Fifteen minutes later two Coastal Command flying-boats would leave their base on the mainland and, having located the submarine's position, they were to call up a hunting group from Tobermory. It was the graduation exercise of the latest training intake and, on the Commodore's orders, it was to be as realistic as possible. 'Stand by to take over lower steering. Course 2-7-0.'

'On lower steering, sir. Course 2-7-0. Half speed. Standing by for diving, sir.'

'Two minutes.' He turned to Ernie Blood. 'Stand down, Cox'n. Diving stations in two minutes.'

As Blood swung himself down into the hatchway, Hamilton picked up his glasses to check the horizon. The sea and sky were empty and as the Ross of Mull faded into the haze astern *Rapier* seemed no more than a lonely pinpoint in the vast wastes of the ocean.

'Take over the diving watch, Number One. Level off at thirty feet.'

'Aye, aye, sir.'

'All hands clear the bridge. Secure for diving.'

The two lookouts and the duty signalman followed Danton into the hatch and shinned quickly down the ladder, leaving the skipper alone on the narrow bridge in the sunshine. Hamilton looked over the screen to ensure that the fore and aft decks were clear and put his mouth to the voicepipe.

'Take her down, Number One. Periscope depth.'

As the roar of the diesel exhausts suddenly cut and *Rapier* nosed gently into the sea Hamilton swung himself down into the conning-tower hatch, closed the lid firmly, and pulled the catches.

'Upper hatch shut and clipped,' he reported to the men below and then, with unhurried ease, he climbed down the ladder into the control room.

'Maintain course and speed, Number One. You'll find me in the radio room if you need me.'

Hamilton's ideas of realism would have hardly met with approval by the planning staff at Tobermory. He grinned to himself. The brass-hats thought they knew the lot - and perhaps they did when it came to hunting U-boats. But for all their experience not one of them had ever commanded a combat submarine. And they had no idea just how cunning a submarine skipper could be. He pulled the curtains of the wireless compartment and inserted himself into the tiny box alongside the radio operator.

'Any traffic, Nicholson?'

Leading Telegraphist Nicholson was an experienced operator but *Rapier* was his first taste of submarine work. He wasn't sure whether he liked it or not but when he was busy there was little time left for worrying about it. He found it difficult, however, to adjust to the long periods of inactivity while the submarine was submerged and the ensuing boredom only served to trigger his fears.

Outward transmissions were, of necessity, strictly limited. And once beneath the surface all transmitting and receiving ceased although, providing the submarine remained at periscope depth, sending signals and listening to replies was still possible. But there were dangers. With modern techniques a signal of only thirty seconds' duration was sufficient for radio direction finders to locate the source of transmissions and obtain cross-bearings. It was a secret U-boat commanders were yet to discover although, ultimately, Admiral Doenitz would realize the reason why Allied surface units were able to locate his sea-wolves with such apparent ease. And, suspecting that the *Knegsmarine* had developed similar means of direction-finding, British submarines made the minimum use of their wireless to avoid falling into the self-same trap. It was better to be safe than sorry.

'No traffic yet, sir,' Nicholson reported.

'You've checked the Coastal Command wavelengths?'

'Yes, sir. Nothing heard.'

Hamilton nodded and settled back to wait. It wasn't cricket but he was not unduly concerned. His task was to

give the trainee hunters on the surface a run for their
money and if it meant taking an unfair advantage by
listening in to their radio transmissions he saw no reason
for not doing so. An intelligent U-boat skipper would do
exactly the same thing given the chance. And if the staff
in control of the exercise were stupid enough to reveal
their secrets over the air that was their affair. It was an
error the convoy control officers of Western Approaches
Command would never make.

It was worth waiting for. Once the air search pattern
had been established he could steer *Rapier* in the opposite
direction and fox them. Admittedly he could not maintain
his evasive tactics for too long but even a few hours of
futile tracking would be sufficient to blunt the enthusiasm
of the hunters. It was a pity, he thought malevolently, that
the weather was good. But you couldn't expect to have it
all ways.

Sooner or later he would have to make for the dummy
convoy and then, if he made a mess of things, the escorts
would find him, make a simulated attack, and claim a
victory. They had failed to make a 'kill' on the previous
exercise and Hamilton had every intention of maintaining
his record of success. It was not a matter of pride. Nor
even an attempt at one-upmanship. Hamilton's reasons
lay much deeper than mere self-glorification.

If the aircraft and escort ships failed to locate the
submarine, and if *Rapier* made a successful attack on the
convoy, the exercise would reflect little credit on the staff
responsible. The men under training may have learned
something but their failure to register a 'kill' was neither
good for morale nor the reputations of their instructors.
There was no satisfaction in baiting a mousetrap if the
mouse took the cheese and escaped with maddening regu-

larity. And with characteristic Machiavellian cunning Hamilton reasoned that if *Rapier* proved to be *too* successful the powers-that-be would take him off target duties and revert him to operations again.

'Aircraft have taken off, sir,' Nicholson reported. 'They're flying a westerly course with a two-hundred-mile search pattern running north from Stornaway.'

Hamilton nodded. 'Any traffic from the convoy yet?'

'Not a sound, sir. They're probably maintaining radio silence and relying on lamp signals.'

Rapier's skipper focused a mental picture of the chart in his mind. The convoy would be on its way south before reversing course past the Outer Hebrides and then swinging south again through the Little Minches to Tobermory - that was why the RAF was searching the northern sector. And that meant he'd have to double back to the east of Lewis and strike the convoy as it came down the Minches on the last leg of its journey home. The delay would add to his difficulties because every passing hour narrowed the probable time of attack and would make the escort that much more alert. But it was the only tactic he could adopt if he was to avoid the patrol aircraft. He yawned. The exercise was timed to last forty-eight hours. Plenty of time yet to perfect his plans.

'Try Northways,' he told the operator. 'Let's see what's going on in the real world. It'll make a change from all this bloody make-believe.'

Nicholson turned the knobs of the Type 55 receiver to the correct waveband, listened intently for a few moments, and then began jotting down the cipher blocks of a meaningless code message. Hamilton made no effort to interrupt him and, as he waited, he could not help reflecting that this was another aspect of realism neglected by the staff when planning the exercise. Coding and decoding took valuable minutes of precious time, and errors in deciphering could have disastrous consequences. Yet all the signals connected with exercise Mousetrap were being transmitted *en claire* and that, of course, was the reason he was able to eavesdrop with impunity. In Hamilton's view it only served to give a false picture of the U- boat war. Messages could be acted upon immediately they were received whereas in practice the commander on the bridge could waste ten minutes having the signal decoded and a further ten minutes enciphering the reply. He shrugged. Who cared - it was their problem, not his.

The telegraphist tore the top sheet from the pad and passed Hamilton the completed signal without comment. It was, in any case, all double-Dutch to the operator and the blocks of coded letters meant precisely nothing. But Hamilton's lethargy vanished as he recognized the priority prefix and, taking the flimsy, he vanished through the curtain in the direction of the wardroom.

Opening the safe he removed the relevant code book and sat down at the table. Then, after locating the correct page, he began decoding. The first few groups were sufficient to indicate the importance of the message and he found himself hurrying to reach the end. Having completed the task he smoothed the paper out on the table.

MOST SECRET IMMEDIATE
    From: Admiralty,
    To: AIG 47, HQCC, FO S/M
    Raider Z reported area Denmark Straits proceeding

east. Sighted 15.00 8 July. Convoy HX 546 to be routed
south immediately. All available ships to proceed to
search areas. Further information to follow.

11-20B/10.

HAMILTON CURSED QUIETLY to himself as he read
the signal through for the second time. If the raider
followed the usual route *Rapier* could be within striking
distance inside forty-eight hours. And yet here he was
playing bloody clockwork mouse on a convoy training
exercise. Walking to his desk he pulled out the relevant
chart and spread it across the table so that he could study
the situation.

Despite the good weather they were enjoying off the
West coast the latest Met reports had indicated heavy fog
to the north. That would rule out an effective air search
and no doubt the raider's captain would try to break for
home under cover of the bad visibility. Admittedly a
number of Home Fleet ships were fitted with radio location devices but the range was still too short for a major
search operation. Hamilton, like most naval officers, was
still unfamiliar with the mysteries of radar and he had
only the haziest notion of the principles and capabilities
of the invention. He looked up sharply as he heard
someone cough. Ordinary Seaman Henneky was
standing just inside the wardroom curtains.

'Message from the radio room, sir.'

Hamilton turned the decoded signal face down on the
desk to conceal its contents from prying eyes and took the
slip from the runner.

'Thank you, Henneky. Tell Nicholson to remain

tuned to Northways and to forward all signals to me as soon as they are received.'

'Aye, aye, sir.'

He waited until Henneky had disappeared through the curtains before opening the code book again. This time he made short work of deciphering.

SECRET IMMEDIATE
From: FO S/M

TO.: **All submarines north of latitude 56°N. Repeated Admiralty, AIG 47.**

ESTIMATED **position of Raider Z at noon today 64°32'N 25°i3'W. Course ESE. Speed 10 knots. Surface forces unlikely to intercept. Proceed at all speed and attack.**

12-05B/10

HAMILTON LEANED over the chart to check *Rapier's* position. According to his DR calculations the submarine was north of latitude 56°N. Only by a few minutes admittedly but that was unimportant. The only snag lay in the fact that *Rapier* was no longer under the direct control of FO S/M. But did that debar him from obeying the flag officer's operational orders in a crisis situation? He considered the problem for a few moments and then, getting up from the table, he walked to the internal telephone and spoke to Danton.

'Something's cropped up, Number One. Hand over the watch to the senior Sub and come down to the wardroom.' Replacing the telephone he returned to the table and was still deeply engrossed in the chart when Danton came through the curtains.

'You wanted to see me, sir?'

Hamilton picked up the decoded signals and passed them to the First Officer. 'Read these, Number One. Then tell me what you think.'

Danton scanned the signals quickly, glanced down at the chart to check *Rapier's* position relative to the information from FO S/M, and shook his head.

'What damned bad luck, sir. We're probably better placed than anyone to attack. And we can't.'

'You consider the second signal does not apply to *Rapier?*'

'I don't see how it can, sir. We're under the orders of Flag Officer (Training) while we're at Tobermory. Northways is transmitting to operational submarines.'

Hamilton had realized that Danton would go by the book and no doubt he was right to do so. He rubbed his chin thoughtfully.

'It seems a pity,' he said slowly. 'I reckon we could be within the target area within forty-eight hours if we push ahead on the surface.'

Danton shook his head again. 'No way, sir. There'd be hell to pay if we went off and left the convoy swanning around on its own. These exercises cost money. I don't think you'd be very popular.'

Hamilton sighed. 'I suppose you're right, Number

One. But keep these signals buttoned. I'd prefer no one to know about them.' He stared at the chart again as an idea began forming in his mind. Perhaps there *was* a way. 'We're expected to attack the convoy tomorrow. Right?' Danton nodded his agreement. 'Well, suppose we locate it and make contact today,' *Rapier's* skipper continued. 'That would give us ample time to move north and join in the hunt for the raider. *And* no one could accuse us of disobeying orders.'

'But it's customary to attack the convoy on the second day, sir,' Danton pointed out. 'Most of the first day and night is taken up with station-keeping exercises and communications practice.'

'I fully appreciate that, Number One. But the only reason for delaying the attack until the second day is to narrow the search area for the submarine. The convoy *must* pass through the Minches between certain hours and it's almost impossible to miss. There's nothing in our instructions to prevent an attack being made at *any time* we choose.' He moved to the chart again and traced the convoy's course with his finger. 'According to the staff instructions they should come south to the Ross of Mull and then proceed due west into the Atlantic before swinging north to skirt the Outer Hebrides. By taking the ocean route the escort commander can be almost certain of avoiding contact with the submarine - it would be like looking for a needle in a haystack if they maintain radio silence. That's the reason why I waited in the Minches last time. It was the only area I could be sure of catching them. And most of my predecessors seem to have had the same idea to judge by some old reports I was reading last week.' 'But how are we going to locate the convoy on its outward passage?' Danton asked doubtfully. 'There's over a thousand square miles of open sea they can use.'

Hamilton nodded. 'Quite so, Number One. But if I've judged Woodward correctly he'll alter course westwards at a precise and predetermined point. Remember, some of his units are still working up and if they hit fog or thick weather anything could happen. By selecting a positive mark for the turn he knows the stragglers will be able to catch up without relying too much on their own navigation.' Hamilton put his finger down on the chart halfway between the islands of Coll and Islay. 'In my opinion he'll turn here, Number One. At Dubh Artach light. And *that's* where I intend to wait.'

Danton could see the logic behind Hamilton's reasoning although he found it difficult to share his skipper's confidence. There was also now little doubt in his mind that, by bringing forward the time of the attack on the convoy, Hamilton intended to flout the rules and go after the German ship once he had completed his part in the exercise. And while killing two birds with one stone might be an admirable ambition in certain circumstances Danton was afraid that, in the present situation, the lieutenant commander was over-reaching himself. *Rapier* was an old boat and she was in no condition to hunt a well-equipped raider. And with her present inexperienced crew it was inviting disaster. He could not help wondering what his own decision would have been in the face of a similar dilemma.

'You'd better get back to the control room and resume your watch, Number One. Reverse course and make for Dubh Artach light. Remain at periscope depth.'

'Aye, aye, sir.'

The evening clouds were already gathering on the

horizon when *Rapier* arrived off Dubh Artech and Hamilton prudently remained at periscope depth to avoid the possibility of being spotted by a passing aircraft. He was used to playing a waiting game and, as the submarine restlessly quartered the patrol area like a hungry tiger pacing the edge of a water-hole in anticipation of an incautious antelope, he put the finishing touches to his carefully prepared scheme.

According to the almanac the moon was not due to rise until midnight and, so far as Hamilton was concerned, the blacker the night the better. He smiled to himself as he mentally reviewed his tactics. By the time the exercise was over Woodward's pride was going to be painfully dented and the Commander was going to have yet one more reason for hating submariners . . .

'Up periscope!'

Gripping the steering handles as the column rose from the deck he pushed his face against the rubber eye-shield and searched the stygian gloom of the horizon. There was nothing in sight and, staring into the blackness, he began idly speculating whether Woodward knew about his escapade with Caroline yet and what the hell he would do about it when he did. Although he had made sure that Mansergh was too busy to go ashore he was probably being over cautious and had locked the prover-bial stable door after the horse had bolted. The submarine's mooring buoy was connected to a shore telephone line and Toby had doubtlessly made good use of the facil-ity. But nothing had happened so far and, hopefully, the affair would blow over without the Commander ever discovering the truth.

A dark shadow moving in the middle distance suddenly attracted his attention and he swore quietly at himself for letting his mind wander. Flicking the switch of the high- magnification lens he examined the elusive shadow more closely.

'North-west bearing - what HE are you getting?'

There was a brief pause while Houseman checked the bearing on his headphones. 'Small petrol motor, sir. Probably an outboard. Sounds like an inshore fishing boat.' He listened again. 'Bearing red-four-zero. Moving at five knots.'

Hamilton nodded. The HE report merely served to confirm his own observation. One swallow didn't make a summer - and one fishing boat didn't make a convoy. He closed the steering handles and stepped back.

'Down periscope!'

Returning to the rear of the control room he stared at the chart and cursed Stephenson, Woodward, and the whole bloody exercise. Why the hell was he messing about chasing a dummy convoy when an enemy ship was within striking distance of his torpedoes? Even more irritating was his conviction that Stephenson, had he known of the situation, would have immediately cancelled the exercise and sent all available ships north to join the search. But unfortunately, the Commodore was away in Rosyth at a planning conference and Woodward, a stickler for routine and procedure, would insist on carrying out the ordained exercise in total disregard of the events taking place outside his immediate sphere of responsibility.

'HE due north, sir! A number of ships. I'm getting sounds from reciprocating engines.'

'Stand by diving stations! Give me the course and speed, Houseman.'

'Course approximately south, sir. Estimated speed seven knots.'

'Half ahead both motors! Up periscope!'

Although there was no moon and the world above the surface was pitch-black, conditions were far from ideal. The sea was as smooth as glass and Hamilton knew that, despite the darkness, the whisper of spray from the tip of the periscope would be clearly visible to the eyes of an experienced lookout. But it was a chance he had to take and he could only pray that his luck held. Turning the upper lens a few degrees to starboard he detected the fleeting shadows of the oncoming ships and, as they approached closer, he was able to make out the details of their formation - a frigate leading, a corvette and a trawler on the port wing, and behind them the shapes of the two freighters representing the escorted merchant ships. The faint flash of a signal lamp from the bridge of a vessel beyond the main group indicated there were more escorts, probably another corvette and trawler, with one, or perhaps two, frigates bringing up the rear. It was a formidable display of strength but, if he played his cards skillfully, the ring of escort ships would be powerless to save the two merchantmen they were protecting.

Woodward, as SNO, would almost certainly be on the bridge of the leading frigate and, Hamilton thought gleefully, he'd have a grandstand view of the convoy's destruction. He peered through the periscope again in an effort to find out whether *Castleton* was present amongst the escorts. If anyone could spoil his plan it would be Brody. Two years' experience on North Atlantic convoys must have taught him most of the tricks. Most, but hopefully, not all.

He wondered whether Brody had ever sailed in a

convoy which had come under attack by the U-boat ace Otto Kretschmer. If so, the chances of his plan succeeding were minimal. But it was worth a gamble if only to irritate Woodward.

'Down periscope. Full ahead both motors. Steer two-five-zero.'

Rapier gathered speed and Danton automatically glanced at the chart to confirm Hamilton's attack course. He frowned in surprise. The skipper seemed to be taking the submarine to the west *away* from the convoy's antici-pated course. And what was the point of that?

'HE turning, sir,' Houseman reported. There was a brief pause as he checked his hydroplanes. 'Target now moving west.'

'Relative position?'

'Two miles to starboard and slightly astern, sir.'

Ping . . . ping . . . ping . . . ping . . .

'Escorts have made Asdic contact, sir,' Danton informed him quietly as he heard the hollow echo of the sonic pulses striking *Rapier's* hull plating.

Hamilton nodded. So, despite outward appearances, Woodward's men were on the alert. He smiled to himself. Well, good luck to them!

'Up periscope!'

'Nearest escort is increasing speed, sir. Moving away from background HE. Sounds as if it's coming this way.'

Hamilton nudged his eyes against the lens. Despite his inexperience Houseman's reading of the surface noises was unexpectedly accurate. The leading frigate was steaming along the bearing of the Asdic contact with a froth of white water growing from its bows as it gathered speed, and he could picture Woodward leaning anxiously over the bridge screen and peering into the darkness in search of his quarry. Moving the tip of the 'scope to starboard he watched the remainder of the convoy ploughing stolidly westwards in accordance with instructions. A signal lamp flashed from the frigate and the two ships of the port wing screen obediently broke away from the main body to join the hunt.

. 'Down periscope! Steer three-six-zero. Stand by to surface!'

Danton looked up sharply at the totally unexpected order. Every instinct urged him to question the command but discipline prevailed and, reminding himself that the skipper must have good reasons for his strange decision, he passed the preliminary routine instructions over the submarine's Tannoy system.

His confidence, however was not shared by everyone and, in the motor room, Hawkins looked across at his opposite number as the order was relayed over the loudspeaker.

'What the hell's the Old Man going to do, Taffy? Bloody surrender?'

The Welshman shrugged. Unlike Hawkins, he rarely bothered about such things. He merely did as he was told, obeyed orders, and made for the nearest bar whenever he went ashore. Life for Taffy Evans was gloriously simple.

'Uphelm 'planes!'

'Reduce to slow ahead both, Number One.'

'Group down - slow ahead both motors.'

'Fifteen feet, sir,' Blood reported from the aft hydroplane controls.

'Open lower hatch. Bridge party stand by.'

Danton watched the flickering needles of the dials on the diving panel. The surfacing routine was ticking over with the smooth precision of an expensive watch and it was difficult to realize that only two weeks earlier most of *Rapier's* crew had been raw recruits fresh out of basic training. Hamilton had certainly done a superb job in raising morale and achieving a high standard of efficiency in such a short space of time. Turning away from the instruments he suddenly realized that the sinister high-pitched pulse of the Asdic probe was no longer echoing against the hull plating.

'We've given them the slip, sir. They've lost contact.'

Hamilton shrugged casually. 'No need to get excited, Number One. It's not a bloody miracle. Asdic is an under-water detection device. Once a submarine comes to the surface the apparatus is useless. I suppose it should be very obvious when you think about it but, unfortunately, nobody *did* - until a smart U-boat commander exploited the weakness.' He grinned at the executive officer. 'Well, I intend to take a leaf out of Kretschmer's book. I'm going to show Commander bloody Woodward what a *real* U-boat attack is like!' He turned to the seaman waiting attentively in the background. 'Open the lower hatch, Wilson!'

He started up the conning-tower ladder followed by the two lookouts and Barrington, the Yeoman of Signals. Reaching the top he unclipped the upper hatch, threw it open, and scrambled out onto the bridge. The frigate was steaming hard astern as it tried to regain Asdic contact and he smiled to himself at the thought of an impatient Woodward cursing the unfortunate skipper for losing the submarine. He could afford to be amused,. The alteration of course and increase in speed had placed *Rapier* between the escorts and the convoy in a perfect attacking position and, resting his elbows comfortably on the coaming, Hamilton watched the confusion astern as signal lamps flashed angrily and tempers shortened.

'Objects dead ahead, sir. Range 1600 yards . . . two merchantmen.'

Hamilton turned quickly in response to the lookout's report, found the two dark shadows moving slowly against the blackness of the horizon, and bent over the torpedo sight.

'Stand by with the flare, Yeoman!'

The first shadow edged into the cross-wires of the open sight and Hamilton pushed the button of the camera-gun to verify the accuracy of his aim at the post-mortem after the exercise.

'Fire!'

The cartridge streaked into the sky to explode with a sharp double crack. Hamilton watched the two red balls of glowing fire drifting gently in the wind and leaned over the voicepipe.

'One point to starboard.'

Rapier's bows swung obediently to the right and he waited for the sights to align with the second freighter.

'Fire!'

Another signal spluttered upwards into the blackness to proclaim the submarine's success but before it had burst into colour Hamilton was at the voicepipe again. 'Full ahead both! Two points to starboard!'

Rapier leaped forward like an unleashed greyhound as Hamilton swept astern of the freighters and headed towards the unsuspecting starboard wing escorts on the disengaged side of the convoy. He could just picture the expression on Woodward's face when he discovered that he'd 'lost' a corvette as well as his two precious merchant-men. No doubt it wasn't cricket to shoot the gamekeeper.

But perhaps it was time for the commander to learn that the Germans didn't play cricket!

'Frigate approaching from astern, sir!'

Christ, that was bloody quick! Hamilton reflected as the lookout made his report. There was only one man likely to react so fast - Brody! Immediately the first flare appeared in the sky the frigate commander must have swung *Castleton* back towards the convoy. It wasn't easy to catch Jack Brody with his pants down and he had obviously realized that *Rapier* was adopting Kretschmer's brilliant tactical ploy of attacking on the surface inside the defensive screen.

A star-shell climbed high into the night sky as *Castleton* fired its bow 4 in gun and, seconds later, the comforting blackness was transformed into glaring brightness which starkly exposed every detail of the surface to the naked eye. Hamilton felt like a woman caught in front of an open window without her clothes by the beam of a voyeur's torch. And equally embarrassed.

'Dive, dive, dive! Clear the bridge!'

As the diving klaxon rasped its urgent warning the men tumbled down the ladder into the control room and, bringing up the rear, Hamilton slammed the upper hatch shut with a bang.

'Take her to eighty, Number One,' he shouted down the shaft as he rammed the clips home. 'Reverse course!'

He slid down the ladder, heard the lower hatch secured behind him, and joined Danton.

'I intend to run directly underneath the frigate's keel,' he explained quickly. 'It's the only sure way to break Asdic contact. After that we'll run like hell for inshore waters. If I dodge through the islands I may be able to give 'em the slip.' Hamilton turned to watch the needles of the depth indicators swinging down. Brody's instant response had been unexpected and he was beginning to regret his decision to bait Woodward deliberately by going after a hundred per cent success. The Commander would never forgive him for being made to look a fool and in his efforts to even the score he was likely to turn rough. It also crossed Hamilton's mind that Woodward might use the opportunity to settle accounts with him over Caroline. He glanced at Toby Mansergh and wondered whether the sub lieutenant realized what he had started when he had engineered their meeting at the party ...

WOODWARD WAS in the blackest of tempers as *Castleton* suddenly reversed course away from the convoy and slowed to ten knots. He had elected to sail in Brody's frigate because he had marked him down as the most experienced escort captain on the exercise. But he was already beginning to entertain dark doubts about his choice. Brody was too damned independent for his liking.

'What the devil are you playing at, Lieutenant Commander?' he snapped irritably. 'We had the submarine ahead of the bows until you lost contact. What are you doing now - running away?'

Brody took no notice of the senior officer's rudeness. He knew precisely what he was doing and was, in fact, deriving a good deal of personal amusement over the Commander's annoyance. Hamilton's bulldozing tactics had certainly upset the silly bastard. And a bloody good job too!

'We lost contact because the submarine passed below us, sir,' he explained quietly. 'It's a favourite trick of the U- boats. They know we can't pick up echoes from a submerged object directly beneath the hull. That's why I've reversed course. And that's why we're going to stop.' Before Woodward could object he turned to the Quartermaster. 'Stop both engines, Mister Hoskins.'

'Stop both engines, sir.'

Woodward glared at Brody as the repeater of the bridge telegraph tinkled in the engine room below and *Castleton* began losing speed. 'You're not going to catch him by standing still,' he observed sarcastically. 'Or is that the idea - to let Hamilton escape and to make me look a fool?' You couldn't look a bigger one than you are, thought Brody. He kept the irritation out of his voice. 'The maximum speed of a submerged submarine is around eight knots, sir,' he explained patiently. 'If we had maintained our previous speed we would have overrun it and the captain could then have doubled back and given us the slip. By stopping unexpectedly I'm playing him at his own game. Before he has had time to realize what's happening he'll have run ahead of our bows again and we'll have positive contact.'

A shouted report from the Asdic operator confirmed Brody's conjecture with surprising promptness. 'Contact made, sir! Bearing five degrees off starboard bow. Speed seven knots.'

'Hold him, Robertson. Slow ahead both, Quartermaster. Stand by depthcharges'. Brody was not, of course, preparing a full-scale depthcharge attack. But, for the purposes of the exercise, *Castleton* was equipped with dummy canisters fitted with low-power explosive charges which could be heard inside the target submarine if they detonated within lethal range. It was a simple and effective way to simulate a depthcharge attack without danger to the submarine.

'Do you still have him, Robertson?'

'Yes, sir. Still bearing five degrees off starboard bow.'
'Good! Put the echoes through to the bridge.'

Robertson pushed a switch and the characteristic *ping- ping* echo of a positive contact bleeped through the bridge loudspeaker.

'A pity you don't have some full-size depthcharges to drop on him,' Woodward commented sourly. 'That young man could do with a good shaking up - he thinks he's too clever by half.' He leaned against the charthouse listening to the pulses.

Ping-ping . . . ping-ping . . . ping-ping . . . ping . . ping . . . ping . . .

The Commander was suddenly alert. 'You damned fool, Brody! You've lost him again!'

Castleton's captain was tempted to order Woodward off the bridge and leave him to fight his own battles. Had he been hunting an enemy U-boat he would have certainly done so without hesitation, or fear for the consequences. But, he reminded himself, it *was* only an exercise so what the hell did it matter.

'Nothing unusual, sir,' he said cheerfully. '*Rapier's* probably altered course and gone deep. Hamilton obviously intends us to work for our money.'

Woodward accepted the explanation with bad grace. Moving to the starboard side of the bridge he simmered angrily as *Castleton* turned to the south in an effort to renew contact. The frigate blundered forward in the darkness like a blind man searching for the edge of the pavement in the middle of a desert. After a few minutes Brody reversed course and probed hopefully northwards. But success continued to elude him and he wracked his brain for an explanation of Hamilton's sudden vanishing trick.

'Are you sure you're still hunting *Rapier*?' Woodward asked sharply. He joined the frigate captain in the centre of the bridge. 'Don't you find it all rather odd?'

'Odd, sir? I don't understand.'

'It's quite simple, Lieutenant Commander. Hamilton is probably still on the far side of the convoy and steaming out of the area as fast has he can go. I think that, by complete chance, you had made Asdic contact *with a U- boat*'

'That's absolutely impossible, sir.'

'Is it?' Woodward asked coldly. 'Perhaps I'm behind the times and our Asdic sets can distinguish between friendly and enemy submarines.' He glared at Brody. 'In my opinion we are hunting a U-boat and you will act accordingly.'

'But supposing you're wrong, sir,' Brody protested. 'Supposing it *is* Hamilton ... I can't attack one of our own boats.'

'You *can* and you *will*! And that's an order! If, and I very much doubt it, my opinion proves to be wrong the responsibility will be mine entirely. It won't need to lie on your conscience.'

'But we've no depthcharges,' Brody pointed out wildly. 'We can't make an attack without weapons.'

'In that case,' Woodward told him imperturbably, 'it will be your job to flush the enemy to the surface and ram him! Chase him inshore and he'll be forced to surface to avoid running aground in the shallows.'

Brody gripped the rails in frozen horror. Woodward must have flipped his lid completely. The Commander's hatred of submarines was notorious, but this was sheer bloody murder. Well, there was only one thing to do in the circumstances - humour him. Provided *Castleton* conveniently failed to re-establish Asdic contact, *Rapier* would be safe. And Brody knew it was up to him to ensure that contact was *not* made. His plans, however, were doomed to instant failure by a shout from the starboard wing lookout.

'Disturbance on the surface - ten cables fine on starboard bow, sir!'

He hurried to the right-hand side of the bridge and raised his glasses as Woodward joined him at the rails. It was the commander who located the tell-tale signs first.

'A large air bubble, Brody. It's the U-boat! We've got him!' He turned to the quartermaster before Brody could intervene. 'Two degrees starboard helm, Mister Hoskins! *Stand by to ram!*'

SIX

Hamilton stepped away from the periscope column and cocked his head to one side as he listened to the steady pulse of the Asdic probe bouncing off the hull plates. In his mind's eye he could picture the frigate coming up fast from astern and he mentally measured off the distance . . . hundred yards . . . fifty yards . . .

'Asdic contact lost, sir,' Danton reported as the sonar pulses stopped.

'Hard a'starboard! Full ahead both motors!'

Hamilton had once seen a U-boat escape its hunters in exactly similar circumstances and he had little doubt that the sudden change of course and speed would outwit Woodward. As the frigate passed directly overhead it would lose contact for upwards of a minute and, by the time the escort had run clear and could use its detection apparatus again, the submarine would be out of danger. He grinned to himself at the thought of Woodward's annoyance. It would be the crowning insult for the submarine to slip through his fingers after 'losing' two ships in the convoy he had been entrusted to protect.

'Engine noises have stopped, sir,' Houseman reported anxiously from the hydrophones.

Hamilton frowned. Why the devil had the frigate stopped? Had the engines failed or, as seemed more probable, was it part of a subtle plan to counter his attempt to escape Asdic detection? The intelligent reaction of the frigate's captain, however, finally convinced him that he was pitting his wits against Brody - and he had a profound respect for his antagonist's skill and cunning as a hunter.

'What's happened, sir?' Danton asked as he joined him beside the periscope column.

'Brody's playing us at our own game,' Hamilton explained quietly. 'He's shut off his engines so that *Castleton* won't over-run us completely. Then, whichever way I move, he'll be able to locate us again on his Asdic and renew the hunt. I've turned ninety degrees to starboard and increased speed in an effort to run out of range before he can restart his engines.'

Ping . . . ping . . . ping . . . ping . . .

'He seems to be reading your mind, sir,' Danton observed as the sonar pulses began reflecting against the hull again.

Hamilton was too busy deciding his counter tactics to worry about Danton's well-intentioned commiserations. Survival in a submarine depended upon instantaneous action, not philosophical appraisals.

'Port helm - course zero-nine-zero! Stop all fans and motors. Rig for silent running. Take her down to 150, Cox'n!'

Rapier nosed on to her new course as the motors were switched off and, still moving forward under the impetus of her own momentum like a pedal cyclist freewheeling down a steep hill, she slid slowly and silently towards the bottom as the hydroplanes tilted. Once again the sudden alteration of course confused the frigate's Asdic operator and contact was momentarily lost as the submarine angled steeply into the depths . . .

Years of experience in the subtleties of underwater warfare brought a swift reaction from Petty Officer Davies as Hamilton's order was relayed through the loud-speaker system.

'Shut down the fans, lads. And I don't want to hear another sound until the skipper gives us the okay.' He glanced at Dobson. 'And take off them bloody great boots, Charlie. The hydrophones up top will be able to hear every step you take.'

Dobson nodded and, sitting on the deck, quickly unlaced his boots and slipped them off. It seemed impossible for anyone on the surface to hear him moving about inside the fore compartment but if the PO said they could he was quite happy to believe him.

'What now?' he asked in a whisper.

'Just sit on your todd, mate, and shut up,' Davies instructed him hoarsely. 'Find yourself a book to read. We could be running silent for a couple of hours.'

Dobson shivered. The tomblike hush inside the submarine was almost more unnerving than the sudden changes of course and speed they had experienced earlier. And with the fans turned off, the air was already beginning to grow stuffy. Making himself comfortable against a bulkhead he picked up an old copy of *Picture Post* and started to look at it. It took the experienced eye of a veteran like Davies to spot that the young leading seaman was holding the magazine upside down . . .

Hamilton allowed a full ten minutes to elapse before venturing on his next move in the cat-and-mouse game.

The frigate had so far failed to re-establish Asdic contact and while *Rapier* remained drifting silently in the depths its hydrophones were useless. Walking across the control room in his stockinged feet he leaned over Houseman's shoulder.

'What's the HE?'

'The frigate's lying to port, sir. About a mile away and moving at five knots. It sounds as though the other two escorts are moving closer.'

That will be the corvette and trawler from the convoy's port wing, Hamilton decided. If he didn't do something soon *Rapier* would be effectively trapped with no chance of escape in any direction. He moved back to the control room and picked up the phone to the motor room.

'Give me two knots ahead, Chief.'

'Motor room, aye, aye, sir. Two knots.'

The lazy thrust of *Rapier's* propellers was aided by the three-knot tide running inshore and the submarine moved slowly eastwards towards the mainland while Hamilton bent over the chart-table to study the map. Until he could use the periscope he was completely blind and, as a result of the initial convoy attack and the subsequent chase by the escorts, he could no longer be sure of their exact position. The submarine was heading vaguely towards Colonsay but there was always the possibility that the currents had taken her further to the north in the direction of the Firth of Lorn or the group of small islands guarding the entrance to Loch Melfort. Whichever course *Rapier* was following she was heading into danger - the rock- strewn west coast with its riptides and swirling currents was a notorious graveyard for ships.

'I reckon we're past Dubh Artach light,' he whispered

to Danton as he called him over to join him at the navigation table. 'Probably about here.' He made a small cross on
the chart to the south of the light and in line with Colonsay. 'I'll continue to drift with the current for another ten
minutes and then, if we can still hear engine noises, I'll
have to risk increasing speed and try to run north.'

Danton nodded. He was even more lost than the
skipper and, in his inexperience, he was beginning to tire
of the relentless hunt. Woodward had proved his point by
putting *Rapier* down out of harm's way. So why not call
the exercise off? If they were forced any further to the east
into the treacherous inshore waters of the Argyllshire
coast things could start getting damned dangerous. He
made the unwelcome but obvious suggestion.

'I suppose we could surface and give the Commander
best, sir. This cat-and-mouse game seems a bit pointless.'

'I don't intend to risk it, Number One. Apart from the
fact that I have no intention of giving up unless I have to, I
reckon we could be in even worse trouble if we surface.
Woodward's in a damnable mood - he'd as likely ram us as
look at us.'

The whispered conversation in the control room
circulated slowly down the length of the submarine,
passing from mouth to mouth and, like all rumours, gathered even more alarming embroidery the further it
progressed from its source. By the time it reached the
motor room, Hamilton's sober judgement of the facts had
been transformed into an imminent warning of destruction and Hawkins felt his guts churning in nervous anticipation as his companion relayed the gory details of the
message. He glanced up at the deckhead as if expecting to
see the sharp bows of an avenging destroyer cutting
through the steel pressure hull at any moment and beads

of perspiration trickled down his face. The fact that *Rapier* was safely submerged to 150 feet made no impression on his overactive imagination and he felt the muscles of his rectum tighten as he tried to restrain the urgent need to empty his bowels.

'You look awful, mate,' his companion whispered. 'What's the matter?'

Another griping spasm seized Hawkins's guts but he tried to keep up appearances. 'It's them bloody sausages we had for breakfast, Bill,' he explained hoarsely. 'I'll swing for that bloody cook one day!'

He glanced towards the main switchboard and saw that the chief ERA and the stoker petty officer were deeply engrossed in a crossword puzzle. Holding a finger to his lips to warn Harris to keep quiet he rose to his feet and padded silently down the far side of the softly humming motors towards the midship's section, fervently praying that he'd get to his destination before he did it in his pants.

Hamilton looked up sharply as he heard the noise. Despite a certain familiarity about the sound he could not identify its origin and Chief ERA Connor supplied the answer from the instruments on the diving panel.

'Someone's just used the flushing valve in the seamen's heads, sir,' he reported in a low voice.

Of all the idiotic and damnfool things to do!

If enemy ships had been hunting them, *Rapier* would have been bracketed by a lethal pattern of depthcharges within seconds. And Hamilton needed little imagination to know what would follow. A series of terrifying and ear-splitting explosions, the pressure hull torn open by the shock of the detonations, and by now every man in the crew would have spent the last few frantic moments of his life struggling for survival in a roaring tumult of black water as the hungry sea engulfed the stricken submarine. He shivered.

Fortunately this time the man's stupidity would not bring destruction raining down upon them. But it meant that all his carefully calculated efforts to escape the escorts had been brought to naught. Hell and damnation!

'Full ahead both motors! Mansergh - get down to the heads and arrest that man. I'll deal with him later. Hanging's too good.'

Mansergh ducked through the rear bulkhead hatchway and made his way towards the stern in search of the culprit. He could appreciate the reason for Hamilton's annoyance although, personally, it appealed to his sense of humour. Fancy being told to arrest a man because he needed a shit!

Ping . . . ping . . . ping . . .

'It didn't take 'em long, sir,' Danton observed grimly as the Asdic probes pulsed against the hull casing. 'We're not going to get away with it *this* time.'

'I haven't given up yet, Number one,' Hamilton snapped. He turned to Houseman. 'How do you read the HE?'

'One large ship abaft the stern on the port side, sir. Two others coming up on the starboard beam.'

Hamilton checked the gyro repeater. Zero-four-seven. Almost due east. If this estimate of *Rapier's* position was accurate they were getting dangerously close to Colonsay. But boxed in to the north and south there was no room to manoeuvre.

'Five degrees port helm.'

Fison turned the wheel and kept his eyes on the gyro repeater. He shifted the chewing gum from the left side of his jaw to the right and continued chewing phlegmatically. 'Five degrees port helm on, sir.'

'Midships.'

'Wheel amidships, sir. Steering zero-four-two.' Hamilton returned to the chart. In their present situation it was about as much help as a street map of London in the middle of the Sahara desert. Until he could fix the submarine's exact position it was impossible to know what lay ahead. And, risk or no risk, it would mean using the periscope.

'Bring her up to thirty feet, Cox'n.'

The two planesmen put the big diving wheels to 'rise' and *Rapier* climbed steadily towards the surface like a pike swimming lazily upwards in search of a small fly hovering above the water . . .

Commander Woodward gripped the bridge rails and sniffed at the air like a hunter scenting his prey as *Castleton* forced her quarry relentlessly eastwards. Scarba Island was already visible over the frigate's bows and the tumbling waters at the base of the reefs edging the northern tip of Jura glimmered whitely in the darkness as the sea beat against the rocks.

'Only three miles now, sir,' Brody reminded the Commander anxiously. He was concerned at the thought of Hamilton running blindly pell mell towards the shore but he was, by now, equally worried about his own responsibilities. Woodward might be in charge of the exercise but as *Castleton's* captain his overwhelming duty was to avoid hazarding his ship - even if it meant disobeying the orders of a senior officer. It was an uncomfortable dilemma.

'I am quite aware of the distance,' Woodward said coldly.

'And no doubt so is that U-boat commander. I'll wager he loses his nerve before *I* do.'

Brody raised his night glasses and peered into the darkness ahead. The boom of the breakers against the rocks was now clearly audible above the throb of the engines and the darker shadow of the land beyond the reefs was just discernible through the spray.

'He probably doesn't appreciate how close he is to the shore. You seem to have forgotten that a submarine captain is as blind as a bat unless he raises his periscope.'

Woodward shrugged. 'That's his problem. But if he *does* - we've *got* him. He'll have the choice of running on to the rocks or being rammed.'

'But supposing it's *Rapier*,' Brody protested desperately. 'We can't run one of our own boats ashore.'

'If it *is Rapier,* which I very much doubt, Hamilton will have enough sense to surface before it's too late. In my opinion the mere fact that the submarine has remained submerged *proves* it isn't Hamilton. If it is then he's a bigger fool than I took him for.'

It was useless to argue with Woodward in his present mood and in an effort to keep his temper Brody concentrated on searching the darkness through his glasses. He stiffened suddenly as he focused on an area of broken water from which the spume rose like a swirling fog.

'What the hell's that?' he asked *Castleton*'s coxswain. Hamish Campbell had been born in the Western Isles. His father was a fisherman - and his father before that. There was scarcely an inch of the rugged Argyllshire coast he didn't know.

'Aye, sir. I see it. It's the Grey Hag of Corryvreckham,' he pronounced dourly. 'When the Grey Hag's on the water it's a warning to keep clear. Many a mon's paid wi' his life for not heeding the sign.'

'What damned rubbish are you talking?' Woodward interrupted.

Campbell's weather-worn face registered shocked disapproval as he turned to the commander. Wi' respect, sir, it's noo rubbish. If ye dinna believe me take a look in yon Pilot Book.' He paused dramatically. 'And by the time ye ken what I'm telling ye it'll be too late.'

Castleton was closer to the shore now and Brody stared at the flying spume thrown up by the raging cross-currents. The primeval fury of the sea bubbling and roaring in a lather of foam was enough to convince him that Campbell's warning had a firm basis in fact.

'Full starboard helm!'

Woodward whipped round angrily as he heard the order. 'What the hell do you think you're doing, Brody? Cancel that order and maintain course!'

The countermanding instruction fell on deaf ears. Brody was by now too concerned with the safety of his ship to worry about the wildcat schemes of his senior officer. The frigate was turning slowly - painfully slowly- and she gave the impression that she was being drawn bodily into the maelstrom raging under the lee of Scarba Island.

'Stop port engine!'

The telegraph tinkled obediently and the thrashing power of the starboard propeller added its weight to the rudder to bring the frigate round in a tight circle. Brody kept his eyes fixed on the Grey Hag as *Castleton* reversed course and he waited until Corryvreckham was safely astern before giving the order to midship the helm and restart the port engine. He felt drained and exhausted as if he had pulled the ship away from the very gates of hell by his own physical effort. The wrath of Commander Woodward was of little account by comparison.

'HE MOVING ASTERN, SIR,' Houseman reported from the hydrophones. 'They've called off the chase.'

'Are you sure?'

'As sure as I can be, sir. The frigate has made a high speed turn and reversed course and the other two ships are steering north-west.'

Hamilton wondered whether Woodward was setting an elaborate trap. Or perhaps he had prudently turned tail to avoid the dangers of a lee shore.

'Reduce to half speed!' He needed time to think. If the hunters had retreated it could only mean one thing. They were getting too damned close to the coast. 'How far ahead are we now, Houseman?'

'Near enough two miles, sir.'

Hamilton glanced at the control-room clock. It was almost midnight and the moon was not due to rise for another thirty minutes. It would still be pitchblack darkness on the surface and it would take a good lookout to spot the questing tip of a periscope at a range of two miles especially in the confused waters close inshore. Leaving all other considerations aside he knew it was a risk he would have to take unless he wanted to find himself hauled up in front of a courtmartial and charged with hazarding one of His Majesty's ships.

'Up periscope!'

The order had barely left his lips when he felt *Rapier's* bows twist viciously to the left. And, moments later, they dipped suddenly down as the submarine lost trim.

'Full starboard helm!' He turned angrily to the

coxwains controlling the big diving wheels. 'Concentrate on your duties! Keep her level!'

Blood's face glistened with sweat as he juggled the stern hydroplanes. 'She's not responding to the 'planes, sir. I'm doing the best I can but I've never seen anything like it before. We're out of control.'

'She's not obeying the helm either, sir,' Fison added anxiously.

Rapier twisted like an eel as a mysterious force caught the submarine in its grasp and hurled it sideways. The expressions on the faces of the men in the control room reflected their alarm at the boat's inexplicable behaviour.

Danton hurried to the diving panel to find out what was wrong while Mansergh, acting on his own initiative, joined Blood at the hydroplane controls. The sub lieutenant looked at the depth gauges and quickly checked that both coxswains were operating the hydroplanes correctly.

'We're going down, sir.' Despite the horror of the situation Mansergh's voice sounded calm and controlled. 'Forty feet and diving.'

'Full ahead both motors! Hydroplanes up angle . . . maintain full starboard helm, Fison.'

'Aye, aye, sir. Wheel on hard a'starboard. But we're still swinging to port . . .'

'Fifty feet and diving, sir,' Mansergh reported quietly. 'Everything's in order on the panel, sir,' Danton confirmed. 'All hatches secure. Main vents shut. Torpedo doors shut. Exhaust valve closed. No leaks or damage indicated.'

Rapier shuddered as if a giant hand had gripped the hull and was dragging the submarine bodily into the depths. A million-and-one possibilities flashed through

Hamilton's brain but commonsense dismissed each and everyone out of hand. But what the hell was causing *Rapier* to run out of control? And how the devil was he going to stop it? 'What course are we steering?' he asked the helmsman. Fison shook his head. 'I only wish I knew, sir. The gyro's swung through 360° twice already.'

'They must be trying out some new secret weapon,' an unidentified voice observed cheerfully from the rear of the control room. 'Spinning us round like a bloody great gramophone record so that we disappear up our own arsehole!'

The very coarseness of the joke triggered a thought in Hamilton's mind. Perhaps that was the reason Woodward had turned tail and run off so quickly. Delving back into the distant recesses of his memory he recalled the German U-boat ace, Otto Hersing, experiencing a similar phenomenon in the Dardanelles during the 1914-18 war.

'Full astern both motors! Blow all tanks, Number One!' He dismissed the fear from his mind as he rapped out the orders to surface. The very idea was ludicrous. If he went on like this he'd start to imagine *Rapier* being crushed in the powerful tentacles of a giant octopus. Such things were beloved by Victorian fiction writers and no doubt they made good reading around the fireside on a winter's evening. But they just didn't happen in real life. Or *did* they? Otto Hersing's horrific experiences in *U-21* had certainly been fully authenticated in official records.

Lurching across the canted deck of the control room he reached the plotting table and clung to a convenient support with one hand while he examined the chart. He kept his suspicions to himself for fear of exposing himself as an imaginative fool. Or, even worse, of appearing to have lost his nerve. At first sight the chart did nothing to confirm his fears and he was about to shrug off his doubts when it occurred to him that perhaps *Rapier* was both further to the south and much closer inshore than he had calculated. His finger traced down the western coast of Scarba and into the Gulf of Corryvreckham. As he read the starkly worded Admiralty warning to shipping printed on the chart his blood froze. His instinct had been right. *Rapier was trapped in a gigantic whirlpool!*

'Ten feet, sir.'

'How's the helm, Fison?'

'Still swinging to starboard, sir. Bows pointing one-nine- zero.' The young helmsman looked worried - not without good reason. The pressure on the tiller felt as though someone had tied a tow-line to *Rapier's* bows and was dragging her round in circles like a child trying to capsize a toy yacht in a pond.

'Stand by engines ... up periscope!'

The spume rising from the raging maelstrom of the whirlpool hung over the sea like a grey impenetrable fog and, even with the periscope on full magnification, it was impossible to see more than a few yards. Somewhere in that awesome spray-scattered gloom were the rocky reefs of Scarba and the slightest miscalculation would throw *Rapier* onto their sharp voracious teeth. Hamilton knew that his 1900 bhp diesel engines would provide more than enough power to haul the submarine out of danger *but* if they were to avoid the hazards of Scarba Island he had to ensure that *Rapier's* bows were pointing in the right direction when the power came on. And there were other equally immediate problems. The stomach-churning corkscrew motion of the submarine was creating its own havoc inside the boat and a number of the control-room hands were being violently sick in consequence although Hamilton noted, with almost Olympian detachment, that not a single man had left his station.

He moved to the gyro repeater and stared down at it in silence. 280. That meant the helpless submarine would have-to swing through another full circle before he could attempt to escape from the clutches of the relentless vortex. Concentrating his attention on the gyro he tried to shut out the wild imaginings of his mind. He sensed Danton standing at his side.

'We're caught up in a whirlpool, Number One,' he explained in an undertone. 'Take a look at the chart - bottom of Scarba Island. I've come to the surface so I can use the power of the main engines. If *they* don't do the trick we've had it.'

'Zero feet, sir,' Blood reported from the stern hydroplane control. 'But we're bumping badly.'

'Start engines!'

Clinging to the supports at the side of the main switchboard, Chief ERA Morgan reached towards the switches and warned the clutch operator to stand by. Like the rest of the men trapped inside the submarine he had no idea what was happening. *Rapier* was bucking and pitching like an unbroken horse and the motion was beginning to react even on *his* hardened stomach. He'd once experienced a typhoon when he was serving on the China Station in the submarine *Otway* but it had been little more than a stiff breeze by comparison with the buffeting *Rapier* was taking in Corryvreckham. In a typhoon a submarine could at least dive deep and escape the worst of the surface storm. But in their present circumstances the forces acting on the submarine's hull seemed even more powerful at depth than on the surface -

although, admittedly, the rotating motion was less hard on the stomach than the present wild jolting.

'Switches off! Clutches in!'

Grasping the double-poled handle firmly Morgan closed the switches and, clinging to the panel, he retched agonizingly over the bucket at his feet. The paroxysm passed and, wiping his hand across his mouth, he leaned over the intercom.

'Switches off, sir. Clutches in. Motor room standing by.'

'Start main engines!' '

'Engine room, aye, aye, sir.'

Hamilton felt the pressure inside the control room suddenly rise as the diesels sucked air into their inlet ports and he swallowed a couple of times to clear the sensation in his ears. Looking down he saw the gyro moving steadily around the compass . . . 080 . . . 090 . . . 100 . . .

'Get up into the conning-tower and open the top hatch, Sub,' he told Mansergh. 'But stay on the ladder until I give you fresh instructions.' He turned to Wilson standing at the bottom of the ladder. 'Close the lower hatch as soon as he's inside. I don't want the control room flooded.'

Wilson opened the lower hatch and Mansergh grinned as he started to climb into the darkness of the conning-tower. 'Perhaps I should take an umbrella, sir,' he shouted down.

'Just get on with it, Sub,' Hamilton told him curtly. There was no time to engage in light-hearted banter. If *Rapier* ran through the vital bearing before her engines had reached full power he would have to let the submarine swing through a full circle before trying again with all the agony such a delay would entail, he turned his attention back to the gyro. 230 ... 235 ... 240.

'Full ahead both!'

The explosive roar of the diesels echoed through the hull and, crouched at his station in the fore-ends, Charlie Dobson fought back his panic. His left arm was badly bruised where he had been thrown bodily against the steel plating of the pressure hull and his ears were still ringing from the shrill scream of the compressed air hissing through the pipes slung beneath the deckhead when the ballast tanks were blown clear in readiness for surfacing. Not for the first time since he had joined *Rapier* he concluded that the extra three shillings per day he hoped to receive when he qualified just wasn't worth it. He was engaged to be married later in the year and he wanted to live long enough to enjoy it. He decided firmly that once they were safely back at their moorings in Tobermory - *if* they got back - he would apply to the skipper for a transfer back to surface ships ...

There was an inevitable time-lag as the engines built up to full power. The bronze propellers raced to maximum revolutions, churned at the water wildly for a few seconds, and then began to grip. Hamilton saw the gyro steady itself and, as it settled at 265, the dizzy rotating motion faded away.

'Responding to helm, sir.'

'Midships!'

'Midships, aye, aye, sir.'

Rapier gave a convulsive heave as she pulled clear from the drag of the vortex and the gyro steadied on 268. The worst of the pitching motion died away almost immediately, and the deck plating moved rhythmically under their feet as the submarine resumed its familiar rolling gait.

'Two degrees starboard helm. Steer 270.' He called Danton across from the chart table. 'Take over down here, Number One. I'm going topsides to find out where the hell we are.'

Hamilton swung himself onto the narrow steel ladder, vanished through the circular opening in the deckhead, and climbed up through the darkness towards the shadowy substance of Mansergh who was still clinging valiantly to the ladder just below the opened upper hatch.

'On the bridge, Sub! Let's see where we are.'

Mansergh obediently hoisted himself through the hatchway onto the bridge and turned to give Hamilton a helping hand as his head appeared through the opening. The sub lieutenant was soaking wet from head to toe and his feet squelched inside the flooded sea-boots. But despite the discomfort he was still grinning cheerfully as he followed Hamilton to the after end of the bridge. Holding on to the rails they stared astern at the mist-like spume drifting like a sinister cloud over the tumbling black waters.

'The Grey Hag of Corryvreckham, sir,' he observed quietly. 'Never thought I'd ever see it this close - or get caught in its clutches and escape to tell the tale.'

Rapier's skipper watched the wraith-like mist fading into the darkness and shivered at the memory. 'Why didn't you warn me? You seem to know all about it.'

Mansergh turned away from the rails and looked Hamilton in the eyes. 'You don't think I'd deliberately let you sail into the Grey Hag?'

Hamilton shrugged. 'I don't know what to think.' He

paused. 'And how do you know about it - you're not from this part of the world?'

'Heaven forbid, sir,' the sub lieutenant laughed easily. 'Me wearing a kilt - you must be joking! I used to come up here for a bit of the old shooting and fishing. Lord Davidson's a relation on my mother's side, you know. His estate is just over the water at Tarbet. I came down to Scarba one day when I was doing a spot of sea fishing and I remember the boatman telling me about it.'

'I suppose Woodward knew about it as well?'

'He may have done. On the other hand he may not. I doubt if he ever had any need to go close inshore along this section of the coast so he probably never checked the charts.' Mansergh paused as the thought struck him.

'You're not suggesting that the Commander deliberately chased you into the Grey Hag? He may not like submariners but he's not stark raving mad.'

'I must admit it *had* crossed my mind,' Hamilton said thoughtfully. 'If he found out about my escapade with—'

'You can take it from me, sir, he knows nothing. Caroline told me he doesn't even suspect that anything happened. She certainly won't say anything - and neither will I.' Hamilton made no comment. He turned away, walked to the voicepipe, and whistled up the control room.

'The clouds are clearing, Number One. Send someone up with my sextant and I'll take a couple of star sights to fix our position.'

He closed the lid of the speaking tube and, walking slowly to the after section of the bridge, stared thoughtfully astern. *Rapier's* wash spread like a frothing white wedding gown against the black satin of the sea and the simile provoked a further question.

'Why the devil didn't you warn me she was married?'

Mansergh's expression was blankly innocent. 'I thought that, as Caroline had asked to see you, she'd tell you herself. A woman's prerogative and all that rubbish they keep on talking about. And to be perfectly honest,' he added blandly, 'I was hoping you'd walk into a bundle of trouble.'

'I don't know what I've done to you, Mansergh, but you seem to have it in for me one way or another. Weil, so be it. But just remember that I am still your commanding officer and I can make things very unpleasant for you. I could make your life on *Rapier* such a misery you'd be begging for a transfer inside a fortnight. I'm not making any threats but I suggest you think on it.'

Mansergh's riposte was cut short by the arrival of Able Seaman Lloyd with Hamilton's sextant and Mansergh moved away discreetly as Lloyd handed the instrument to the captain. He waited until Hamilton had taken his sights and passed the data to the control room where Jimmy Blake was sitting with the Admiralty Star Tables ready to calculate the submarine's position.

'I overheard you talking to Number One about a raider, sir,' Mansergh said casually and in the hope of changing the subject. 'What's it all about - or aren't you sharing your secrets?'

'There's no mystery. I picked up an Admiralty signal reporting Raider Z heading north about Scotland on its way back home. Northways ordered all submarines to intercept - but we weren't included.'

Hamilton saw the sub lieutenant's mouth turn down sardonically. He had little doubt what Mansergh was thinking.

'That's a pity, sir. But it's probably a wise decision.

This old tub's hardly operational. We'd be asking for trouble if the weather turned nasty.'

'My sentiments exactly, Mister Mansergh. I'm glad we agree for once.' Hamilton paused as he enjoyed the irony of the situation. 'But as I seem to have a reputation for disobeying orders I don't see why I shouldn't live up to it.' Mansergh's face suddenly brightened. 'You mean we're going to intercept, sir?'

'Yes, Sub Lieutenant. That's *exactly* what I mean. I hope you approve. Or are you just hoping I'll run into a bundle of trouble again as you so charmingly put it a few minutes ago.'

Mansergh grinned. The crafty old bastard! At long last he was beginning to understand why Caroline found Lieutenant Commander Nicholas Hamilton so irresistible.

SEVEN

'*Western Isles* is calling again, sir.' There was a note of anxiety in Nicholson's voice as he came to the curtained partition of the wireless compartment to report the latest message. 'They're requesting our position.'

Hamilton straightened up from the chart table. He could well imagine the panic behind the scenes in Tobermory. 'Ignore it, Nicholson,' he said calmly. 'Maintain radio silence.'

The telegraphist hesitated. 'There was a general signal from Northways a few minutes before, sir. *Subsunk* alert. Coastal Command are carrying out an air search in the area south of Mull and surface ships are being sent out from Greenock.'

'If they're looking for *Rapier* they're about four hundred miles adrift. I only hope they charge the fuel they're wasting to Woodward's account.' His cryptic comment meant little to the men in the control room - or to Nicholson. They were naturally unaware of Hamilton's suspicions and, aside from the fact that the submarine was steaming north on the surface at maximum speed, they had no idea where they were going, or why. 'Just keep listening, Sparks. And make sure I'm informed of all signals.'

Nicholson vanished behind the curtain to continue his lonely vigil of the airways, sat down in front of the Type 55 W/T set, and slipped the earphones over his head. As soon as the telegraphist had gone, Mansergh put down his book and walked across the control room to join Hamilton at the chart table. He kept his voice low so that no one could overhear.

'We've been maintaining radio silence for thirty-six hours now, sir,' he reminded Hamilton politely. 'Don't you think you ought to put them out of their misery at Tobermory? You heard what Nicholson said - if they've started an air search we must have been posted missing.' Hamilton measured carefully up the line of 8°W and pencilled a small cross to the north-east of MuCkle Flugga in the Shetlands to represent *Rapier's* DR position at noon. He showed no inclination to comment on the sub lieutenant's statement and picked up a pair of dividers.

'I realize this is your way of getting even with Woodward. And serve him right,' Mansergh continued when he saw that Hamilton was not responding. 'But if we don't call in soon they'll be sending off the next-of-kin telegrams. And that's not fair on the men or their families.'

Hamilton swung the pointers in a wide arc and jotted some figures on the slip of paper alongside the chart. Then, putting his pencil down on the table, he straightened up and faced the junior officer.

'Surely you don't think I'd allow the men's families to suffer just to satisfy an egotistical urge to take my revenge on Woodward?' He paused and glanced down at the chart. Satisfied with his plans he returned his attention to Mansergh and fixed him with his steely blue eyes. 'I'm going after that raider. And I don't intend to give myself away by using the radio. It's as simple as that.'

'Despite the next-of-kin telegrams?'

'Yes, Sub. But with luck it won't come to that. FO(S) won't authorize the telegrams for at least seventy-two hours and by that time I should be able to break wireless silence and make my report. You're new to this game but believe me, this is what war is all about. Other people's feelings cannot be allowed to interfere with operational considerations. Our first priority is to attack the enemy. Everything and anything else must take second place to that object.' Mansergh could see Hamilton's point but he remained slightly puzzled. 'What about the other submarines in the search, sir? Northways hasn't been calling *them*.'

'That's natural enough. The other boats have been specifically assigned to hunt down the raider. Their approximate positions are known and they would be expected to remain silent. In our case we're not under the operational orders of FO(S). In fact we're not even supposed to be in the area. The last time we were seen we were heading for Corryvreckham - and that was thirty-six hours ago. So far as Tobermory is concerned we're still somewhere in the Firth of Lorn and as we haven't reported they've got to assume we're in difficulties. So they inform Northways of the situation and that triggers off the standard search routine for locating a missing boat.'

Mansergh's lips twisted sardonically. 'You're going to be bloody popular when they find out what's happened, sir.' 'That's the gamble I've got to take. But if *Rapier* brings that raider to book no doubt all will be forgiven and forgotten. It's a funny thing about the Navy. You can get away with breaking every damn rule in the book - providing you're successful.' Hamilton grinned suddenly. 'And *I* ought to know.'

He broke off as the bridge voicepipe whistled and reached across to pick up the tube. 'Captain here.'

'The weather's closing in, sir,' Danton reported. 'The wind's falling off and visibility is down to a mile or so.'

'Thank you, Number One. I'll be up shortly.'

Hamilton looked thoughtful as he returned to the chart. Although it added to his difficulties the possibility of fog suited his plans admirably. He motioned Mansergh to the plotting table and, leaning over the chart, he scrawled a vague circle with his pencil centred on the Faroes.

'Let's hear what you make of the situation, Sub. It's good practice for you. All we know at the moment is that Raider Z was last seen in the Denmark Strait. It's the *Kriegsmanne's* favourite route through our blockade fines and it's well covered by surface and air patrols. And no doubt they're fully aware of the fact. If you were in command of the raider, and bearing in mind that the fog is closing down, what route would you take?'

Mansergh examined the chart carefully. So far as he could see the German captain had little choice. 'I'd push north of the Arctic Circle and head for the Norwegian coast somewhere in the vicinity of the Lofotens.'

'Not very original, Sub. They've used that route so often I reckon they've ploughed a furrow in the sea. Any other ideas?'

The sub lieutenant rubbed his chin and stared down at the chart again. Every avenue of escape seemed to be blocked either by surface units from the Home Fleet or by standing submarine patrols. He shrugged. 'I don't know, sir. The Navy seems to be waiting whichever way I decide to go. I suppose I'd stick to my original idea and keep well north of the Arctic Circle to make use of the poor visibility.'

'Why not run south-east via the Faroes and Shetlands?'

'You must be joking, sir. I'm supposed to be getting back to the Fatherland - not walking into the arms of the enemy!'

'I'd agree with you if visibility were good,' Hamilton conceded. 'The raider would never get past our air patrols. But if the fog shuts down, Coastal Command will have to call off its air searches.' He paused for a moment. 'You know, Sub, it often pays to do the obvious. Remember the way *Scharnhorst* and *Gneisenau* sailed straight up the Channel and got away with it? And the way the U-boats attacked our convoys on the surface? They succeeded because it was so obvious no one thought it likely. And, take it from me, the German Navy is prepared to gamble on chances we'd never risk ourselves.'

He leaned over the chart and drew a faint pencil line to mark his own theoretical course of the raider. 'My guess is that our friend will come much further south than expected on the assumption he can avoid our routine patrols. Originally I thought he'd run north of the Shetlands, which is why I put *Rapier* here - south and east of the Faroes. But now we've got thick weather I reckon he'll go for the really *big* gamble.' Hamilton circled the Orkneys and Shetlands. 'If I was commanding that raider I'd go plumb through the middle of the Fair Island channel because that's the *one* place the enemy won't be expecting.'

'But what about our radar stations, sir? Surely they'd pick up any unidentified intruder.'

'From what I can gather - and everyone's so damned secretive about these things - our latest radar sets have an extreme surface range of about twenty miles. If we assume we have scanners right on the coast that will still leave a radar-free avenue about ten miles wide. And *that's* where *Rapier* will be waiting!'

KORVETTENKAPITAN SCHULTZ PULLED the flap of the leather greatcoat across his throat and shivered in the clammy cold. Rolling banks of fog were building up to both port and starboard and in the last hour visibility had closed to less than a mile. It was not the sort of weather cautious seamen enjoyed but, in the circumstances, it suited his book admirably. Turning away from the rails he paced slowly up and down the bridge, lost in private thoughts as *Oldenburg* nosed her way through the swirling mist at a steady eight knots.

He paused at the starboard telegraph to listen to the regular throb of the freighter's MAN diesel engines and made a mental note to recommend Chief Engineer Halstadt for a decoration when he made his report to the Director of Operations. The raider had been at sea continuously for over six months and never once, in a voyage of almost 100,000 miles, had the engines given so much as a hiccough, thanks to Halstadt's tender and unremitting care. He moved on to the wheelhouse and put his head inside.

'Any echoes from your box of tricks, Hans?'

Klept looked up from the *FuMB I* radar detector and shook his head. 'Not a thing, *Herr Kapiton*,' he reported.

He stared at the swirling fog through the opened port. 'Do you want me to turn on the *Seetakt?*'

'Too risky,' Schultz told him. 'I don't want the enemy picking up our beams. Just keep your eyes on the *Metox* and let me know when it shows anything.'

The raider's captain ducked out of the hatchway and returned to his favourite position in the centre of the bridge. Leaning his forearms on the rails he watched the crews of the port and starboard 5-9 in guns standing by their weapons, poised in readiness for instant action. With visibility down to a mile, quick reaction to an emergency was imperative. If the enemy found them there would be no warning. A shadow would suddenly emerge from the fog and *Oldenburg*'s survival would depend on the immediate and accurate response of her guns.

Schultz, however, viewed the situation with a certain optimism. By brazenly entering enemy controlled waters the odds were necessarily in his favour. Any ship he encountered *must* be hostile. The English, on the other hand, could make no similar split-second assumption. Recognition signals would have to be flashed - and in that fatal hiatus of indecision *Oldenburg*'s guns would have time to find their range and blow the intercepting ship out of the water. It had happened during the crucial night action that marked the climax of the battle of Horn's Reef. Schultz had been a lowly midshipman in those days. But he could still remember the British cruiser turning towards *Westfalen* urgently flashing the night challenge on its searchlights - and the deafening blast of the battleship's 11 in guns that replied. His memories were rudely interrupted as the raider's executive officer joined him at the bridge rails.

'Looks like your gamble is going to pay off, sir,' he said cheerfully.

'I would hardly call it a gamble, *Oberleutnant*. OKM's situation report fixed the English big ships as being well to the north. The enemy will hardly be expecting me to take a short cut through their home waters.'

Neidermeyer picked up his night glasses and scanned the grey wall of fog stretching ahead of *Oldenburg's* bows. Somewhere off the starboard beam he could hear the raucous bellow of a ship's siren but it sounded too far away to be of immediate concern.

'It beats me how our High Command always seem to know the exact location of enemy ships,' he complained as he lowered his binoculars. He glanced sideways at the *Korvettenkapiian* and grinned. 'Perhaps Raedar employs a couple of the Fiihrer's personal astrologers in the Operations Room of OKM. I wonder if they have to requisition the Supply Department for crystal balls?'

'I doubt it,' Schultz said heavily. *Oldenburg's* captain was not noted for his sense of humour. 'And I'd be careful about making jokes like that when we get ashore. The wrong people might be listening.'

Neidermeyer ignored the reproof. 'I have heard a rumour that our cryptanalyst in the *B Dienst* can read the English naval codes.'

'It's always possible,' Schultz agreed. 'It would certainly explain why OKM was able to divert us away from that enemy cruiser squadron off Dakar.'

Neidermeyer shrugged. Even supposing the Old Man knew he was unlikely to confide in a junior officer. And he suspected, correctly, that only a handful of very senior officers knew the secrets of the *B Dienst*. An ability to read the enemy's signals was the dream of every admiral and there was no reason why Germany should not have broken the British codes. After all, the enemy had exploited their knowledge of the *Kriegsmarine's* wireless messages in the Kaiser war so it was only fair if the tables had been turned this time.

He raised his glasses again and stared out into the fog. The clammy dampness made him shiver and he thought enviously of the code-breakers safely tucked away in their comfortable bunkers in Berlin. The backroom boys had the right idea. It was only fools like Schultz and himself who braved the weather and the enemy in search of glory. Wars were won by the faceless men who worked in places like the *B Dienst* - not by the men who did the *real* fighting.

'I suppose you're looking forward to seeing your new son,' Schultz said suddenly as he lowered his binoculars.

Neidermeyer nodded. Little Klaus had been born two months after *Oldenburg* had sailed from Kiel and although OKM had radioed full details of the happy event he was longing to see Greta and the baby. He decided that Schultz was a strange old cuss. He'd obviously taken the short cut through the Fair Island channel so that his executive officer could arrive home a few precious days earlier.

'My daughter's getting married on Friday,' Schultz continued, unaware that he had shattered the *Oberleutnant's* illusions. 'I promised to be back in time to give her away but that little game of hide-and-seek in the Denmark Straits has put me behind schedule. That's why I decided to take the Fair Island route. I'll need to allow at least two days to get from Kiel to Bavaria.'

'Periscope! 1,000 metres starboard bow!'

Any further discussion was brought to an abrupt stop

by the lookout's warning and the two officers hurried to the starboard wing of the bridge.

'Must be a U-boat, sir,' Neidermeyer suggested optimistically as he raised his binoculars and searched the surface. 'No sign of a periscope now. Perhaps the lookout was seeing things.'

'I hope he was, *Oberleutnant,*' Schultz observed grimly.

'If we've been spotted by a U-boat I don't give much for our chances.' He nodded over his shoulder at the jackstaff on the poop. 'Not when we're flying the Red Ensign.'

'Torpedo tracks! Starboard beam - amidships!'

Schultz peered over the side in time to see a line of air bubbles streaking towards the raider. With detached objectivity he concluded that the periscope must have belonged to a British submarine after all - German U-boat torpedoes, the electrically powered *Type G-ye*, left no telltale tracks on the surface. He had hardly completed his thoughts when the RNTF Mk IX struck the hull plating and a sheet of yellow flame rose mast-high as it detonated. The force of the explosion hurled him bodily across the bridge and in the fleeting second it took him to scramble back onto his feet he knew *Oldenburg* was doomed.

'Out port lifeboats! Abandon ship! Every man for himself!'

A second torpedo nudged the stern, the striking pin of the contact pistol stabbed back into the priming charge, and the 750 pound warhead tore the starboard propeller shaft from its mountings as it exploded. *Oldenburg,* already listing sharply to starboard as the sea surged through the gaping hole amidships, bucked violently with the concussion of the second explosion, and began to settle by the stern. There was a disciplined rush to swing out the port side sea-boats and, while the men were struggling to release the davits, a petty officer ran up the companionway from the for'ard end of the ship to report a large fire raging in the narrow passages of the lower deck space. But his warning was too late. Sweeping aside everything in its path the fire seared through the bulkhead of the for'ard magazine before the flood valves could be opened. There was a terrifying roar and a pillar of flame soared a hundred feet into the air as the 59 in ammunition exploded.

By the time the mushrooming cloud of smoke had cleared, not a trace of the raider remained on the surface. The grey sea lapped unconcernedly over *Oldenburg's* final resting place and only tiny fragments of splintered wood, a broken crate, and a solitary lifebelt remained bobbing on the surface to mark its grave.

When Lotte Schultz went to the altar in the tiny whitewashed Lutherean church at Eidelheim the *Korvettenkapitan's* pew would be empty. And, three hundred miles away to the north, in a quiet residential suburb of Berlin, little Klaus Neidermeyer would now face life without a father and with only the small framed photograph of a young man wearing *Kriegsmarine* uniform to remind him of the tragedy.

THE MOTORBOAT from *Western Isles* was already standing by as *Rapier* glided into the bay to pick up her mooring buoys and, watching the evolution from the top of the conning- tower, Hamilton found it difficult to believe that the seamen drawn up in a smartly immaculate line on the bow casing were the same indisciplined shower responsible for the chaotic shambles on the night of their first arrival at Tobermory. He glanced up at the home-made skull-and- crossbones flag fluttering triumphantly from the periscope standards and shared their pride. They'd worked bloody hard to achieve their newfound efficiency and *Oldenburg* was a just reward for their efforts.

'All fines secured fore and aft, sir,' Danton reported as the petty officer on the fantail held up his arm. 'Finished with motors, sir?'

Hamilton nodded absently. Leaning his elbows on the starboard coaming he stared at the tender and wondered what his reception would be. He had little doubt that the motorboat was waiting to take him off to *Western Isles* and he was in equally little doubt that The Terror would give him a roasting when he arrived on board.

'Lieutenant Commander Hamilton, sir! The Commodore's compliments and will you please report to him immediately. Permission to come alongside?'

The shouted invitation from the tender's coxswain did no more than confirm what he had already assumed. He turned to Danton. 'Take over, Number One. Usual routine. And make sure no one is allowed aboard until I get back. I want to see which way the wind's blowing before the lads start giving their version of the story.'

He returned Danton's salute, swung his leg over the side of the conning-tower and climbed down the external rungs to the deck. The tender was standing by the bow mooring buoy and Hamilton acknowledged the salute of the fo'c'sle petty officer as he made his way along the fore casing. He jumped down into the sternsheets of the motorboat, nodded to the coxswain and, moments later, the commodore's barge was heading across the smooth waters of the anchorage in a flurry of spray towards the HQ ship . . .

Stephenson was sitting at a battered oak desk in his day cabin and he looked up as Hamilton was ushered through the door by the duty midshipman.

'Come in, my boy, come in. Sit yourself down.' He smiled benignly. 'This really is the return of the prodigal. I must admit I didn't expect to see either you or *Rapier* again.'

Hamilton said nothing and kept his own counsel. If the Commodore intended to roast him for disobeying orders it seemed an odd way to begin. He decided to wait and see what happened.

'Damned bad luck - a compass failure coming right on top of your wireless breaking down,' Stephenson observed equably. 'Still, it's an ill wind as they say.'

Hamilton was about to point out that *Rapier* had suffered neither mechanical misfortunes but the expression in the Commodore's eyes warned him not to be too hasty.

'I'm sure you're right, sir,' he agreed noncommittally.

'I realized you were having problems when you didn't reply to my signals and I guessed your radio was on the blink. Mind you, it caused us quite a bit of worry at the time - especially with a U-boat in the area.'

Hamilton looked up sharply. 'A U-boat, sir?'

'I'm sorry, I keep forgetting you don't know what's been happening,' Stephenson apologized. 'It seems the escorts picked up a U-boat on their Asdic soon after you made your dummy attack on the convoy. Woodward's ships chased it towards the coast but lost contact at Corryvreckham. Brody reckons it may have got caught up in the whirlpool. If he's correct I doubt whether it survived. From what the locals tell me it's been a grave-yard for ships for centuries.'

So *that* was Woodward's excuse, Hamilton thought grimly. The Commander certainly knew how to cover his tracks. If *Rapier* had been lost in the whirlpool Woodward would have undoubtedly claimed it to be an unfortunate accident. And in all probability he would have got away with it.

'The compass fault was equally obvious,' Stephenson continued. 'As soon as I heard you'd been located north of the Orkneys I realized what had happened.' His bland blue eyes gazed innocently at the Lieutenant Commander. 'There could be no other possible explanation for you to have been so far off course.'

Hamilton had difficulty in repressing a smile. So *that* was how the Commodore intended to explain away *Rapier's* unexpected and totally unauthorized appearance in the Fair Island channel. Stephenson was well-known as a fire- eater. He *must* have realized the truth. But because Hamilton's actions had resulted in the destruction of the enemy raider he was quite prepared to close the Nelsonic blind eye to invent this preposterous cover story.

Hamilton's instinct for self-preservation grasped thankfully at the straw the Commodore was offering. He smiled. 'As you say, sir. It's an ill wind . . .'

Stephenson pushed his chair back to indicate that the interview was concluded, stood up, and held out his hand.

'Well done, my boy. I'm glad it was one of my Tobermory ships. It's about time the Admiralty woke up to the fact that we're fighting seamen up here and not just damned schoolmasters.'

Hamilton grasped his hand. He was still feeling a

trifle dazed by The Terror's unexpected meekness. 'Thank you, sir.'

The Commodore cleared his throat ominously and the bland eyes hardened. 'Just one thing before you go, Lieutenant Commander.' Hamilton felt sure he could detect the faint flicker of a malevolent smile on Stephenson's face. 'I suggest you get that wireless fixed and have the compass overhauled. If *Rapier* goes awandering again I shall hold you personally responsible.'

Hamilton hurried up the stone steps of the jetty to greet Brody as the Commodore's barge brought him smartly alongside the landing stage of the Admiralty pier.

'I hope I'm the second to congratulate you and not the first,' the frigate captain grinned with a nod in the direction of *Western Isles*. 'How did you get on?'

'I'm not too sure,' Hamilton admitted. 'I'm damned certain he knows I deliberately disobeyed orders to go after that raider. But he's dreamed up some cock-and-bull story about a compass failure to make it look like an accident.' He stopped to show his pass to the sentry guarding the end of the pier and then followed Brody onto the quay. 'What the hell do you make of a bloke like that?'

'Be thankful for small mercies, Nick,' Brody consoled him. 'Stephenson's taken quite a shine to you. In any case his bark's a lot worse than his bite. Underneath that armour-plated exterior there beats a heart of solid steel. And I'm quite sure he's cock-a-hoop that one of his ships has engaged and sunk an enemy vessel.'

'I suppose you're right. But what the hell do I do about Woodward? I'd intended to lodge an official complaint as soon as I got back but the Commodore was so full of the raider I didn't get the chance.'

Brody stopped at the door of the Sutherland Hotel,

pushed the blackout curtain to one side, and ushered Hamilton into the private bar. It was fortunately almost empty - most of the officers were already back on board their ships preparing for a dawn exercise the following morning - and, ordering two large whiskies, he steered the submarine commander to a small table in the corner.

'Did he tell you about Woodward?' he asked as they sat down.

Hamilton shook his head. 'No - mind you he did say something about a U-boat that sounded rather odd. But I didn't get an opportunity to ask him what he meant.' He raised his glass to the frigate captain and felt the spirit bite the back of his throat as he swallowed it down. He decided to keep his suspicions to himself. It would be interesting to see if Brody confirmed them.

'Woodward's gone completely round the twist. They've taken him off to the psychiatric wing of the Naval Hospital at Rosyth. Nutty as a fruitcake.' Brody's mouth twisted in a humourless grin. 'He insisted we were chasing a U-boat but I knew damn well it was *Rapier*. I tried arguing with him but he wouldn't listen. In the end I told him to go to hell and reversed course.' He swallowed his whisky and leaned forward. 'I'm sure the bastard was deliberately trying to kill you - although God knows why!'

Hamilton could think of at least one very good reason why but he said nothing and drank his whisky thought-fully. Woodward *had* cold-bloodedly chased *Rapier* into the whirlpool. And, to cover his tracks, he'd pretended to have mistaken the submarine for a U-boat. It sounded almost too logical for the action of a madman.

'Another one, Jack?' he asked as he picked up the empty glasses.

'Why not? I've finished my stint here. *Castleton*'s off

to Liverpool tomorrow to join the 19th Escort Support Group. Goodbye Tobermory!'

Hamilton walked across to the bar, ordered two large scotches, and returned to the table with a glass in each hand.

'Cheers, mate!' Brody raised his drink in mock salute. 'Here's to your DSC. I heard a buzz that Stephenson's recommending you. It'll go well with the other one.' Hamilton shrugged. He was not particularly interested in medals and citations. If any decorations were going begging there were several members of *Rapier's* crew who ought to get them. He put his glass back on the table and returned to their original conversation.

'I don't quite understand it. If Stephenson swallowed the U-boat story why the devil has Woodward been whipped off to a mental home? He was quite within his rights to attack a U-boat even if, as it turned out, he'd made a mistake as to its identity. It wouldn't be the first time a friendly submarine has been sunk in error.'

'True - but the attack on *Rapier* was only the beginning,' Brody explained. 'Once he was sure he'd run you into the whirlpool he got hold of a rifle from somewhere and began shooting at the sea and insisting he was firing at a U-boat periscope. It seemed harmless enough so I left him to it - I'd got more than enough on my hands getting *Castleton* back to Tobermory safe and sound. Well, about fifteen minutes later, I was in the chartroom working out our course when the bo's'n comes rushing in and says Woodward is out on the bridge telling the Quartermaster to steer at a half-submerged rock which he claimed was the conning tower of a submarine coming to the surface.'

Brody swallowed another mouthful of scotch before continuing. 'Any damned fool could see it wasn't a U-boat. But when I got on the bridge Woodward was yelling to the helmsman, *"Ram the bastard before he submerges! Ram the bastard!"* He was leaping up and down like a bloody madman and it took three of us to get him into my sea cabin. Then, when we'd got him safely inside, he started crying like a baby.'

Hamilton said nothing. He sipped his drink slowly as he pictured the bizarre scene on the frigate's bridge.

'I kept him locked in the cabin,' Brody went on, 'and as soon as we berthed I called the Surgeon Commander aboard to look at him. Thirty minutes later an ambulance launch was alongside and they were carrying him off strapped to a stretcher. The Doc told me they'd take him to Rosyth.'

'Did he give any indication what might have caused it?' Hamilton asked.

'Nothing beyond a lot of medical mumbo jumbo,' Brody shrugged as he drained his glass. 'It boiled down to combat fatigue and delayed shock after losing his boat in the Channel. Mind you, the Doc was very encouraging. He said it could happen to any of us.' He put the empty tumbler on the table. 'Pink elephants are bad enough but to hell with pink submarines . . . let's have another drink.' Hamilton nodded and pushed his glass across. Why not? They were supposed to be celebrating. And if Brody was off to the 19th Escort Support Group in the morning it would be their last evening together for a long time. Leaning back in his chair he stared blankly at a somber print of a dead stag which was hanging on the wall over the table.

Woodward's breakdown had completely altered the situation. If the man was mentally sick it was pointless to make a complaint about the Corryvreckham incident although Hamilton could not help wondering how much had been due to the Commander's instability and how much to a personal grudge. Perhaps on balance he should be charitable. Mansergh had not been ashore since the night of the party and it was highly unlikely that Caroline would have said anything. Looking at the situation objectively he decided there was no way in which Woodward could have found out about his wife's infidelity, and the attempt to sink *Rapier* must have been no more than an outward manifestation of the Commander's paranoid hatred of submarines.

'Mind if I join you?'

Hamilton looked up and saw a young RNR lieutenant standing beside the table with a large tankard of beer grasped firmly in his hand. There was something vaguely familiar about his face but Hamilton could not place it. He nodded and pushed an empty chair towards him with his foot.

'Why not? No point in getting drunk on your own.' He nodded in the direction of the bar where Brody was giving his order to a dour-faced barmaid who looked as if she more properly belonged to the front pews of the local kirk than the private bar of a licensed hotel. 'Jack's off to an operational unit tomorrow - we're just celebrating his escape from Tobermory.'

'I'll drink to that any time,' Gaskill grinned cheerfully. 'But at least you chaps get away to sea on exercises every now and again. Just think what it's like being stuck here day in and day out on shore patrol duties.'

Hamilton sat up sharply. No wonder the lieutenant had looked familiar. Tobermory seemed a hell of a place for coincidences and accidental meetings. The arrival of

Brody with two more large glasses of whisky put a stop to any further reflections.

'I see we've got someone else to join the party,' the frigate commander grinned as he sat down. 'Drink up, old boy, and get onto the hard stuff. It's the quickest way to oblivion I know even if it isn't the cheapest.'

'Just try stopping me, sir.' The lieutenant introduced himself. 'My name's Gaskill - Martin Gaskill.'

'Nice to meet you, Martin. I'm Jack Brody from *Castleton* - and this is Nick Hamilton.' He winked broadly. 'You'll be seeing his ugly mug in all the newspapers soon. He's something of a local hero since he sank that raider.' 'Congratulations, sir.' Gaskill paused as he recognized *Rapier's* skipper. 'Of course - we've met before. I was in charge of the Shore Patrol that stopped you after the party at the WRNS wardroom a few weeks ago.'

Hamilton smiled sheepishly. 'I was hoping you'd forgotten that particular incident.' He grinned across at Brody. 'Martin found me wandering down the road. He thought I was Jack the Ripper looking for some innocent young Wren to rape. I'm afraid I rather disappointed him.' He turned back to Gaskill and cloaked his question carefully behind a disarming smile. 'I hope you kept your promise not to mention it in your report?'

'Of course, sir. And Commander Woodward fully agreed.'

'Woodward'.' Hamilton's blood ran cold. 'How the hell does he come into it?'

'Well, sir, it's a bit of a rum story.' Gaskill leaned forward and lowered his voice. 'Apparently someone found the Commander's wife asleep in an empty hut in Encroachment Seven in the WRNS barracks.' He licked his lips as he reached the juicy part of his story. 'I wish I'd have been the one to find her - they say she was stretched out on a camp bed stark bloody naked!'

Brody grinned over the top of his glass. 'Now that's something I'd give a month's pay to see. Caroline Woodward's a real cracker. Did you meet her at the party, Nick?' Hamilton shook his head. 'Only vaguely. I believe we were introduced but that was all.' It was a lucky coincidence he'd told Brody he was talking to Caroline Faversham when they'd met at the bar. He took a deep swig at the whisky to fortify his nerves before turning back to Gaskill. He hoped his interest wasn't too obvious. 'But what's all this got to do with me and Woodward?'

'Well, sir, next day the Commander came down to the office and asked whether the patrols had reported anything suspicious. He seemed to have the idea that someone had been having it off with his wife. He didn't say so directly, of course, but it was fairly obvious. I mentioned we'd met you on the road near the WRNS barracks and that you'd reported seeing nothing unusual.' Gaskill winked at *Rapier's* skipper confidentially. 'Naturally I didn't say anything about that Wren you picked up, sir.'

Hamilton drained his glass. Woodward was quite capable of putting two and two together and there was now little doubt that he knew all about the party - and what happened afterwards. And if he didn't know he could guess. Perhaps his nervous breakdown was a good thing in the circumstances. At least he would be unable to satisfy his paranoiac thirst for revenge while he was securely locked up in a mental hospital.

Gaskill gathered up the empty glasses. 'My shout, I think. Same again?'

The two Lieutenant Commanders sat in silence at the table while Gaskill went to the bar. Brody was thinking of nothing in particular. The effect of three doubles after the binge in *Castleton*'s wardroom was making his head spin and he was having difficulty in focusing his thoughts coherently. He picked up his tumbler with an unsteady hand and raised it in a toast. 'To hell with Tobermory! Here's to the gallant gentleman who stuffed the Commander's wife.' His voice slurred as he completed the toast. 'God bless her and all who sail in her!'

Gaskill lifted his glass in response. Having recently completed his commissioning course at Greenwich he could still vaguely remember odd phrases from the lectures on naval history. The executive order given by the captains of the early steamships seemed particularly appropriate in the context - the more so as he muddled the words with unintentional aptness.

'Mrs Woodward! Down funnel ... up screw!' He turned to Hamilton with his glass still raised. 'How about you, sir?'

Hamilton stared down at his tumbler. A picture of Caroline, naked and smiling as she reached eagerly forward to draw him onto the bed, shimmered up from the pale golden surface of the whisky. A slight unsteadiness in his hand rippled the whisky inside the glass and the picture broke into a million pieces and suddenly vanished. He raised the tumbler to his companions and the three glasses chinked together.

'To Caroline,' he said simply.

EIGHT

Hamilton was a little disappointed to find Wren Jackson no longer sitting behind the reception desk at Flotilla HQ but consoled himself with the thought that perhaps enough was enough. And he still hadn't forgotten her long fingernails clawing his back. At least Caroline took her pleasures in a slightly more ladylike manner.

'Your pass, Lieutenant Commander!'

He came to an abrupt halt as the female dragon who now occupied the desk snapped out the request. She was the wrong side of forty, with iron-grey hair pinned back into a severely practical bun, and a figure which could be euphemistically described as generous. As he handed over his identity pass he noticed the hairs on her chin and was tempted to enquire whether she had asked her commanding officer for 'permission to grow'. He decided she was not the type to appreciate frivolity and he waited in silence as she pressed the buzzer on her desk and reported his arrival to Captain (S).

'Captain Rogers will see you now, Lieutenant

Commander.' She bared her teeth in what she fondly imagined was a ravishing smile. 'Please go through.'

Hamilton entered the familiar office, saluted the flotilla captain and then, having complied with the formalities, threw his cap down on the chair and grinned.

'What happened to the little dolly bird you used to have outside, sir?'

'Pregnant,' Captain (S) explained briefly. 'Same thing happened to the girl I had before. You damned sea-going commanders have only got to look at a Wren to put her in the family way.'

'I never touched her with a barge pole, sir,' Hamilton told him as he shook his head and protested the lie with convincing innocence.

'It wasn't a barge pole that put her in the club,' Rogers pointed out with a grin. 'It might have been long and hard but that's where the resemblance ends.'

'No chance of a similar accident with this new one, sir. Is that why you picked her?'

'I won't deny that that was certainly one reason. But apart from that particular recommendation she also has the ability to control impertinent young submarine commanders when they come up to see me. And that's more than I usually succeed in doing.' Rogers pulled open a desk drawer and brought out his pipe and tobacco pouch. 'By the way - congratulations on your DSC. It's not everyone who can win a gong while they're attached to a training squadron. But you always were different to everyone else.'

'Thank you, sir. To be honest I didn't deserve it. I broke every rule in the book.'

'And don't think I hadn't noticed,' Rogers said drily as he applied the flame of the match to the bowl of his pipe.

He sucked hard to get the tobacco going. 'Well, now you've finished your six months' stint at Tobermory I suppose you'd like to know what's in store for you next?'

Hamilton glanced out of the window at two brand new T-class submarines fresh from Vicker's yard at Barrow tied up to the quayside and waiting their final commissioning trials. Much as he loved *Rapier* she was now getting to be an old boat and her years of hard service from the Arctic to the South China Sea had taken an inevitable toll. A change of command and a spanking new T-boat was the summit of his current ambition.

'As long as it's not in another backwater like Tobermory, sir,' he told Rogers firmly. 'I think you already know I want to get back to an operational flotilla again.'

'Well, to begin with, you can take your covetous eyes off those two new boats in the basin. They're already spoken for. In fact, your old Number One, Collis, is getting one of them.'

Hamilton shrugged to hide his disappointment. Collis was a good chap. But he was an RNVR officer and a mere greenhorn by comparison with his own experience in submarine command. Why the hell did they keep passing him over?

'What about me, sir?'

Rogers put down his pipe, clasped his hands together, and leaned forward across the desk. 'I'll be perfectly honest with you, Hamilton. I don't know. You've apparently been selected for some special job but it's so hush-hush I've no idea whether it's in Tomsk or Timbuctoo. All I can tell you is that you're to take seven days' leave and then report to the Admiralty for a preliminary planning conference next Thursday. Meanwhile *Rapier* is to be paid off and taken down to Barrow for a refit. Sorry I can't be more helpful but that's all I know myself.'

'I understand, sir. It's not the first time I've been assigned for special duties. By the time you're told what it involves it's usually too late to change your mind.'

Rogers pushed back his chair and stood up. 'Well, that's it. All I've got to do now is wish you luck.' He came around the side of the desk to shake hands. 'By the way - how's Caroline?'

Hamilton's eyes narrowed as he released the Captain's hand. That damned young idiot Toby must have been gossiping again.

'She's okay so far as I know, sir,' he said slowly. 'Why?'

'I heard a buzz that she and her husband agreed to separate after he was discharged from hospital last month.'

'So I believe,' Hamilton confirmed cautiously. He wondered how much Rogers knew about the affair. They'd been very discreet and in fact, since Woodward's discharge, their contacts had been limited to briefly snatched telephone calls. If Toby had been blabbing his mouth off he'd wring his bloody neck. 'I didn't realize you knew her, sir.'

'Not that well, unfortunately. But we're distantly related and I heard about it on the family grapevine. You know how it is.'

Hamilton wondered just how many more people were related to Caroline. It seemed as if half the Royal Navy had some family connection with her. But of course, as he had discovered during his long haul up from the lower deck to the wardroom, inter-marrying within the Service was the rule rather than the exception. Family influence could play an important part in an officer's career and those with relations or friends in powerful positions could anticipate preferment for both promotion and plum appointments. The old concept of 'interest' had never really died out despite the platitudes of the politicians.

Strangely enough his last telephone conversation with Caroline had been concerned with an almost identical issue. Ever since her formal separation from her husband, Hamilton had been trying to persuade her to start divorce proceedings so that she would be free to remarry. But Caroline, aware of the old-fashioned prejudices of the Quarter Deck, had pointed out that marriage, in these particular circumstances, could easily bring his career to a sudden halt. And as the stepdaughter of a vice admiral she knew what she was talking about.

A man could have a mistress, even several mistresses - a wife in every port as the old saying went - and good luck to him. But to marry a divorced woman, especially the former wife of a fellow officer, could bring social ostracism and professional disaster in its wake. Hamilton had tried to dissuade her but deep down in his heart of hearts he knew she was right. If he wanted to remain in the Navy after the war, marriage to Caroline was completely out of the question.

'I suppose you must be related to my Fourth Hand, Toby Mansergh, sir,' he parried in an attempt to change the subject.

'That's right. We're second cousins or something. I never could work these things out.' Rogers hesitated as he opened the door. 'Sorry if I asked an embarrassing question but I thought you two had something going between you.'

Hamilton's face was completely expressionless as he stood in the doorway. 'Nothing like that, sir. She's just an old friend from before the war - I met her at one of Gerry Cavendish's yachting weekends. By the way,' he added innocently as if it was only of passing concern, 'how is Commander Woodward now? I gather he's been discharged from hospital.'

'I understand he's made a splendid recovery. The doctors say it was a bad case of delayed shock compounded by battle fatigue. A few months rest and the right treatment have got it out of his system and he's a hundred per cent now. No doubt his promotion to Captain helped. Mind you, when we heard about his wife leaving him most of us were afraid he'd crack up again. But he seems to have taken it very well. I suppose he'd been half expecting it. I gather a separation was on the cards before he had the breakdown. However he's fine now and the last I heard the Medical Board had passed him fit for sea service and a command appointment.'

As Hamilton replaced his cap and saluted he could not help wondering whether Woodward really *was* cured. He seemed to have made a miraculously rapid recovery.

'I'm very glad to hear it, sir.'

Walking slowly down the corridor away from Captain (S)'s office he hated himself for being such a bloody hypocrite. But he'd learned one very important lesson since he'd attained wardroom rank. Never reveal your personal feelings to a senior officer. And, no matter what happens, always keep up appearances.

OPERATION TENFOLD WAS Hamilton's first experience of a top-level Admiralty planning conference and he had to admit that he was not very impressed. Certainly very little planning seemed to have gone into organizing it. No one in the main reception lobby knew anything about the meeting and Hamilton felt a little like a wooden counter in a game of snakes and ladders as he was shuffled from one room to another. An anonymous Admiralty clerk on the ground floor sent him upstairs where a red-faced Paymaster Commander promptly ordered him back down again. And an exploratory sortie to the east wing only served to confuse everyone concerned. Giving up his quest he sat down on an uncomfortable bench just inside the sandbagged entrance and watched the bustling throng with idle curiosity.

It was also his first encounter with Admiralty bureaucracy in all its glory and he concluded, a trifle uncharitably, that it must require at least ten civil servants and deskbound brass hats to keep one single sailor at sea. No wonder he had so many forms to complete as part of his duties as a commanding officer - it was probably the only way the Admiralty could keep pace with the demand for staff toilet paper!

'Lieutenant Commander Hamilton, sir?'

He looked up to find a freshly' scrubbed able seaman looking anxiously hopeful that his search had ended in success. Hamilton stood up, nodded, and tucked the brief-case under his arm.

'The Operation Tenfold conference is downstairs, sir. If you will come this way please.'

Hamilton followed him along a maze of narrow corridors opening off into tiny cupboards that served as offices for the overflowing staff and then down a wide stone stair-case leading to the basements and vaults beneath the main building. He noticed the thick concrete blast walls which had been erected to reinforce the roof and, passing through a gas-proofed door, he felt a blast of cold air on his face. The sub lieutenant who had taken over the role of escort from the able seaman guided him even deeper into the underground labyrinth and grinned as he saw Hamilton shiver.

'Air-conditioning, sir,' he explained. 'The pressure is kept slightly above normal to prevent poison gas entering. I suppose you have much the same sort of arrangement in a submarine.'

Hamilton was about to point out that the air inside *Rapier* after a long dive was neither cold nor sweet-smelling but decided to leave the sub lieutenant to his blissful ignorance. They stopped at a large steel door guarded by an armed marine sentry. Covell-Bliss pushed the red button on the left hand side of the entrance and with a soft hiss of hydraulics the massive door swung open to reveal a bare concrete-walled cellar filled with rows of chairs and desks. Hamilton walked through and found his place marked by a small card on which his name and rank had been printed in laborious block letters. Glancing quickly around the crowded room he concluded he was one of the most junior officers present and his mind went back to the conference with Rear Admiral Mabberly in 1939 which had led to his first special mission. He hoped that Operation Tenfold would not result in a similar tragedy.

At the far end of the cellar was a raised dais on which stood a long trestle table piled high with files, intelligence reports, departmental briefs, and folded charts. Above and behind the table was an enormous large-scale map of the Belgian coast.

The senior officers gathered together on the platform

were busily chatting between themselves and, in the main body of the room, surprised shouts and noisy laughter echoed against the low concrete ceiling as old friends and former shipmates recognized each other. Hamilton, however, could see no one he knew and he fiddled idly with the pad of Scrap paper on the desk in front of him as he waited for the conference to begin.

'Looks as if they're planning something big,' he observed to an RAF Squadron Leader on his left. 'Any idea what it's about?'

'Not a clue, old boy. This is a Navy show. I'm only here to give my AOC some help if someone starts firing awkward questions at him. How about you?'

Hamilton shrugged. 'You're better off than I am. I don't even *know* why I'm here. I only wish they'd get on with it so I can find out.'

The large clock above the dais ticked steadily beyond eleven o'clock and one of the staff officers touched the Vice Admiral's arm to remind him of the time. He nodded and as the senior officers took their places behind the trestle table he stepped to the edge of the platform. The murmur of conversation faded away and the small ramrod figure in the dark blue, gold-laced uniform was suddenly the focus point of all eyes.

'Is everyone present, Sub Lieutenant?' he asked Covell- Bliss in a voice more suited to the quarter-deck in an Atlantic gale than the echoing confines of the concrete bunker in which the conference was taking place. He waited arms akimbo for the sub lieutenant's confirmation. 'Yes, sir.'

He nodded and glowered pugnaciously at the men seated before him. 'Good morning, gentlemen. And welcome to Operation Tenfold. I am Vice Admiral

Winter. Take a good look at me. Some of you will be seeing a lot of me in the next few months and I don't intend to waste time on introductions when we meet again. You have been called here for what is optimistically known as a preliminary planning conference. This means that someone very high- up has selected a project and told us to get on with it. It also means that most of the plans have already been worked out and you are only here to be told your individual roles in the scheme of things.' He nodded to Covell-Bliss who obediently switched off the main lights and turned on two small spot-lamps to illuminate the wall map.

'This is one of the trickiest operations the Navy has ever been called upon to carry out. By comparison Zeebrugge in 1918 and St Nazaire last year were pieces of cake. And I mention these two raids specifically because Operation Tenfold is based on the lessons learned from each.' He paused and smiled. 'It may surprise some of you to know that the Admiralty does, on occasions, learn from its mistakes.' There was a dutiful ripple of laughter from the men assembled in front of the platform. Taking a pointer from the table and half turning, he held the tip against the map at a point on the Belgian coast roughly halfway between Ostend and Zeebrugge.

'The Germans are building a new base here at Zeehoven. According to intelligence reports it consists of a large reinforced concrete pen to house their E-boat flotillas and when the Allies finally decide to invade Europe it will place an important defended base on our left flank from which the German Navy will be able to launch surface torpedo attacks on our invasion fleet.

'Generally speaking it is the opinion of the High

Command that any naval bases close to the landing areas can be taken out by air attack at the relevant time. And I have no doubt that this appreciation is correct. However, as you probably all know, the U-boat pens at L'Orient and various other bases have proved to be impervious to everything we've thrown at them.' He nodded to the Air Commodore sitting on his left. 'Perhaps you'll explain the technicalities, Sir Malcolm.'

The Air Commodore stood up heavily and waited while a Flight Lieutenant hung up a large diagram showing the respective penetration depths and blast patterns of various RAF bombs in current use. Then, without preliminaries, he launched into a boring technical lecture on the ballistics and problems of air bombardment.

'The old fool doesn't know the first thing about it,' the Squadron Leader whispered to Hamilton. 'The last bomb he dropped was a fifty-pounder on some Kurdish tribes in Iraq from a Westland Wapiti in 1933. The boffins have given him a brief and he's reading it blind.'

Hamilton grinned and nodded. The Air Commodore was making heavy weather of the subject and he felt his eyelids drooping as the fruity voice droned on monotonously. He gathered that the RAF had no bomb capable of even denting the U-boat pens. Skip bombing was apparently impossible for reasons which the Air Commodore failed to make entirely clear and even the latest one-ton blockbusters had insufficient penetration to be effective. The RAF spokesman completed his lecture, mopped his perspiring face with a spotless handkerchief, and sat down with the air of a man expecting to receive a round of polite applause.

The room, however, greeted the completion of the

lecture more with a sense of relief than approval and
Hamilton felt sure he could detect a rasping snore from
one of the seats behind him. The Air Commodore was
followed by a spritely army Colonel wearing the green
flashes of the Commandos on his shoulders.

'Well, chaps, you've heard what the RAF can't do. So
now it's the Army's turn.' He bounced off into a racy
explanation of how a Commando unit would tackle the
task only to explain, finally, that for logistical reasons it
would be impossible to land sufficient explosives to
complete the job. 'Mind you,' he wound up, 'we could
certainly get the chaps into the pens. But the experts at
Woolwich said we'd need a thousand tons of explosives to
achieve anything worthwhile. And that would entail a
force of at least five thousand men just to carry the stuff
ashore. Frankly, and I hate to say it, but it just isn't on!'

Hamilton yawned. He failed to see the point of
having a conference so that everyone could give their
excuses for not undertaking the task themselves. He
began doodling on the scrap pad as Vice Admiral Winter
took the stage again.

'So you see, gentlemen, Operation Tenfold is impossible. And that's where *we* come in. I need hardly remind
you of the old adage that there is nothing the Royal Navy
cannot do.' He glanced over his shoulder at the Army and
RAF representatives on the platform. 'No offence
intended, gentlemen.' There was a rumble of subdued
laughter from the naval officers and Hamilton winked at
the Squadron Leader. 'But,' Winter continued, 'the question is - *how* do we do the impossible?'

He paused dramatically and stared round the faces
sitting at the desks in front of him. 'Well, I'll tell you.
We're going to use underwater explosives. And if any of

you stayed awake during your lectures at Greenwich you'll be aware that the blast power of an underwater explosion is ten times greater than the same amount of explosives detonated on or above the surface. So the problem of sheer bulk, which Colonel Mallory mentioned, is immediately solved. To obtain a destructive power equal to a thousand tons of high-explosives we need only transport a hundred tons to the pens. And by naval standards this is a very small amount of deadweight cargo.'

Hamilton's drowsiness vanished as he listened to Winter's explanations. It was still going to be a damned difficult operation but, by making use of underwater explosives, it was certainly no longer impossible. He wondered where he fitted into the plan.

'In many ways the task of getting the explosives into the pens is easier than might be expected. As I said at the beginning, the base is still under construction and although the pens themselves are virtually completed the Germans have not yet finished building the gun emplacements for the shore defences. They have, however, erected a large stone mole across the entrance to act as a breakwater and to prevent silting. And this mole, like that at Zeebrugge in 1918, will be our main problem. It already carries a number of shore batteries and machinegun positions and if we are to succeed in our primary task these will have to be taken out. A Royal Marine Commando unit has been assigned for this particular operation and I will deal with the details later.

'So far as land operations are concerned the Army are supplying the services of one airborne company which will parachute down behind the base to prevent the arrival of reinforcements. Units of the Resistance, suitably armed, will take out the pill boxes and emplacements within the perimeter and they will be supported by a second Commando unit if this proves necessary!' The Vice Admiral refreshed himself with a large gin and tonic, put the empty glass back on the table with obvious satisfaction, and continued his briefing.

'The attack on the mole will be similar in detail to the Zeebrugge raid although, in this instance, we will not be using blockships to seal off the pens. You will remember that the destroyer *Campbelltown* was an outstanding success at St Nazaire and we obviously considered this possibility very carefully. However, either by chance or design, the geographical position of the mole and its distance from the shore makes it impossible to run a surface ship bows-on into the pens - there is simply not enough sea-room to turn a destroyer once it is inside the mole. Having considered the problem from all angles it was finally decided that the only vessel large enough to carry the necessary amount of explosive charges and yet small enough to turn inside the mole would be a submarine. And, of course, there was the added bonus that a submarine could be submerged in the target area so that the explosion could be triggered *underwater!'*

Hamilton's lethargy vanished as he realized what the Vice Admiral was saying. So *that* was the reason he'd been told to attend the conference. What the hell did they think he was - a *kamakazi!* The ensuing ripple of subdued excitement from the assembled officers suggested that he was not the only one to be surprised by the idea and the Admiral had to hold up his hand for silence.

'I can well understand your alarm, gentlemen. But I can assure you that our experts have been through the plan in the greatest detail. We are satisfied it is practical. .

There will, of course, be an element of risk. But any operation of this nature carries its own peculiar hazards. Now, before I pass on to the details, are there any questions?'

A post-Captain wearing a full set of campaign ribbons from the Kaiser war stood up. 'Can you indicate the approximate strength of the support force, sir?'

'It is our intention to keep supporting units to a minimum. Bear in mind that this is not a defended base in the normally accepted sense of the word. It is still under construction. There will naturally be substantial air support but so far as the seaward assault is concerned the smaller the numbers involved, the better.'

The Captain rose to his feet again. 'Can you not be more precise, sir?'

Winter threw him an irritated glance. 'Operation Tenfold is envisaged as a short sharp attack with a limited objective. Provided the submarine is adequately covered the number of ships involved can be kept to a minimum.'

But Captain Kershaw was not so easily satisfied. He had remained on his feet while the Vice Admiral replied to his supplementary question and he returned to the fray as soon as Winter had finished.

'*How* many ships, sir?'

The Vice Admiral sat down and nodded to Commodore Walters. It was *his* damned scheme. It was up to *him* to satisfy the questioner. Walters rose from his seat and peered at Kershaw over the top of his half-moon glasses.

'The Operation is divided into three sections,' he explained. 'Assault landings to neutralize the mole defences. An attack phase to destroy the E-boat pens. And the re-embarkation and withdrawal movement to recover the commandos and submarine crew. There will be a second force to take off the airborne troops further to the north—' he pointed to an area on the wall map, '—here at Z Beach. The assault phase will be carried out by landing craft supported by four destroyers. The attack on the pens will have four motor launches in support to provide smoke screens and close-range weapon cover. The submarine crew will withdraw in rubber boats and will be picked up by two designated MLs.'

'What's the matter, sir?' an unidentified voice observed from the darkened rear of the room. 'Are we running short of ships?'

Vice Admiral Winter glowered angrily as he stood up. 'I am under strict orders to use the minimum number of units. However I can assure you that, in the opinion of my experts, the vessels allocated in support are quite adequate. We do not face the same problems we encountered at St Nazaire. And,' he glared at Captain Kershaw, 'I would remind you that the crew of the submarine C-j made their escape quite successfully in similar circumstances at Zeebrugge.'

'I was *at* Zeebrugge, sir,' Kershaw reminded the senior officer. 'The crew of *C-j* suffered severe casualties during their withdrawal - the Boche gunners cut them to pieces. I am also aware that, at Zeebrugge, the submarine crew members were not the centre of the action. Their task was to ram and destroy the viaduct linking the mole to the mainland. Having done so they withdrew to seaward while the attention of the German defences was concentrated on stopping the block-ships. In the plan you have outlined this morning the submarine will be the *centre-piece* of the attack and its crew will have to withdraw through waters enclosed by the mole with every available gun bearing on them. In my opinion four motor launches are a totally inadequate force to support such an operation.'

Hamilton felt like patting the old Captain on the back. Thank God *someone* had some sense. He saw Commodore Walters whisper to Winters and the Vice Admiral nodded.

'I fully appreciate your concern, Captain Kershaw,' he said placatingly. 'I should have explained that the MLs are only the *close* support. There will also be a destroyer standing off the mole to cover inshore operations as required.'

'I understand I am to be given command of the destroyed concerned, sir,' someone interrupted from the back row. Hamilton stiffened as he recognized the familiar voice and he turned his head quickly to see the speaker. Christ Almighty! Of all people - *Woodward!* What was this - a bloody murder conspiracy? Hamilton pinched himself to make sure it was not all just a terrifying nightmare.

'That is correct, Captain Woodward,' Winter confirmed.

'In that case, sir, I think I am entitled to express an opinion. On the basis of the facts given so far I can only take the view that the men in the submarine are being asked to commit suicide. There is absolutely no chance of getting them off safely.'

Good for you, Hamilton thought to himself although he could not help wondering whether Woodward would revise his opinion when he knew who was to command the submarine.

Winter nodded sagely. He was encountering rather more opposition than he had anticipated. But he didn't blame them. In private he shared their reservations. The

chances of survival *were* minimal. But that was not sufficient reason in itself for calling off the operation. The
men involved were not aware of the pressures being
exerted on the Admiralty by the PM and the War Cabinet. Neither were they aware that all available shipping
resources were being concentrated for the forthcoming,
and very top-secret, Operation Torch.

'I am not sure that I follow your objection, Captain,'
he countered. 'I gather your opinion is based on the
numbers of men to be recovered after the submarine has
reached its objective.'

Woodward had not intended to be tied down to
specifics. There were many other cogent reasons why he
thought the whole concept suicidal but, certainly, the
number of men involved was relevant. He nodded.

'Yes, sir.'

Vice Admiral Winter beamed at the confirmation.
Having skillfully produced his red herring and seen it
swallowed he was quick to exploit his advantage. He
looked out over the rows of faces. 'I think this is a matter
for the experts, gentlemen. I have therefore arranged for a
representative from the Submarine Branch to attend the
meeting to give you his views.' He peered into the darkness beyond the dais. 'Will you please stand up, Lieutenant Commander?' Hamilton rose to his feet. Perhaps
he'd been a trifle premature in his conclusions. Perhaps he
had only been ordered to attend the conference in the
capacity of an expert.

'Sir!'

The Vice Admiral studied him in silence for a few
moments. So this was this fellow Hamilton he'd heard so
much about. Well, let's see if *he* takes the bait too.

'Lieutenant Commander Hamilton has had considerable experience of special missions, gentlemen. And I daresay most of you are familiar with his successes in *Rapier*.' Having introduced his victim with suitable flattery Winter put the question to him without warning. 'Assuming that the regular crew is taken off before the submarine reaches the mole, Lieutenant Commander, how many men would be required for the final stage of the operation?'

'It's difficult to be precise at short notice, sir. But if the submarine was required to dive at the end of the approach run I'd say two officers, both coxswains, a helmsman, and between two and four specialist ratings.'

The vice admiral nodded approvingly. 'I see - let's say eight men. Ten at the maximum.' He turned to Woodward. 'Would you say that ten men could be lifted safely given the resources at your disposal?'

Woodward suddenly realized he had walked into a self-made trap by allowing Winter to tie him down to only one aspect of his initial objection. Picking up ten men would still be difficult but it was not impossible.

'Yes, sir. We should be able to handle that number.'

The Vice Admiral looked pleased with himself as he returned to Hamilton. His manipulation of the objectors had been little short of masterly and he wondered whether he had missed his vocation in life. Perhaps he should have read for the Bar instead of joining the Navy.

'And what do you say, Lieutenant Commander?' he asked quietly. 'Is Operation Tenfold feasible?'

Hamilton thought quickly. Until the conference had got under way he had had no inkling of the objective or the plan and he had certainly not had time to consider the scheme in detail. But he'd faced equally difficult situations successfully in the past and, in theory, it *was* possible.

'I'd like more time to go through the details, sir,' he said cautiously. 'But I would say the proposals you have outlined are viable.'

'Let me put it another way, Lieutenant Commander. Would *you* be prepared to take *your* submarine on such an operation?'

There was an expectant hush in the conference room as Hamilton hesitated before giving his answer. *Rapier's* commander knew he'd pulled off equally hazardous tasks in the past although this particular operation was undoubtedly the most dangerous he had ever faced. Looking around the sea of silent faces his normal caution was swept away by a rush of bravado. And, over-riding everything, was a determination to demonstrate that courage was not the sole monopoly of the traditional officer class.

'Yes, sir. I would be quite willing to command the submarine. And,' he added recklessly, 'I'm damned sure I could pull it off!'

Vice Admiral Winter tried to hide his elation. With the stumbling block of the submarine removed the other officers involved would withdraw their objections. Operation Tenfold was on! He smiled to himself as he sat down. *Pity I served you an ace, Lieutenant Commander. Game, set, and match to me, I think.*

HAMILTON WEDGED himself behind the tiny desk in his cramped and crowded cabin and stared down at the list of names on the sheet of paper in front of him. When he had called for volunteers every single member of the crew had stepped forward without hesitation and, while he had anticipated an eager response, he could not help feeling a certain personal pride in their loyalty.

Selecting the half-crew necessary to get *Rapier* to the entrance to the mole presented no great problem. They would be safely lifted off by the escorting destroyer before the submarine made its final dash towards the E-boat pen. But the ten men who would remain with her until the final seconds of her ultimate destruction was a different matter. For, despite his brash confidence at the planning conference, Hamilton knew he was virtually signing the death warrant of each and every man he took with him.

In some cases the choice was simple. Ernie Blood, *Rapier's* senior petty officer and first coxswain, was impossible to omit from the list. He had served with Hamilton from the day of the submarine's acceptance trials and had been in the control room and on the bridge during the attack on the *Nordsee* off Norway in 1940 right up to the battle for Hong Kong almost two years later. And it went without saying that the veteran coxswain was equally anxious to sail with *Rapier* on her final mission. Hamilton placed a tick against Blood's name and moved on.

The choice of the second officer was more tricky. His Number One, Peter Danton, was no longer available, following his selection for the next 'perisher' course due to start in a month's time. Hamilton considered it to be a splendid piece of good fortune although Danton had not seen it in the same fight. Bitterly disappointed at losing his chance of taking part in the raid he had even offered to withdraw from the Command Course in order to sail with *Rapier* but, despite repeated applications to Flag Officer

(Submarines), all his attempts to volunteer had been refused.

Hamilton looked down the list. There would be no need to have an engineering officer aboard during those final few minutes and he deleted Spears from the list with a quick stroke of the pen. He was now left with only two names - Toby Mansergh and Jimmy Blake - either of whom would have sold their souls for the opportunity. He stared at the sheet of paper as he weighed up their potential. Both had turned out to be good reliable officers and it was a difficult decision to make. No doubt the unlucky loser would blame him until his dying day for missing his fleeting chance of glory. But it had to be done. He picked up the telephone.

'Send in Sub Lieutenant Blake, Number One.'

There was scarcely room for two inside the tiny cabin but Blake somehow contrived to squeeze in and Hamilton announced his decision without preliminaries.

'I'm sorry, James. I've decided to take Mansergh with me. I'm afraid you'll have to wait for another opportunity.' He smiled wryly. 'And the way this damned war's going I doubt if you'll have to wait very long.'

'But it's not fair, sir,' Blake burst out angrily. 'I'm senior to Mansergh in the list. If anyone's selected it ought to be me.'

Hamilton could understand the sub lieutenant's disappointment. But he had his own private reasons for his choice. 'As I've said - I'm sorry. But that's the way it has to be. There'll be plenty more opportunities.'

Blake's mouth twisted bitterly. 'I suppose I should have remembered, sir. If you want to get anywhere in this Navy you have to be born with a silver spoon in your mouth or know the right people. It seems Toby has more pull than I have.'

Hamilton could feel his temper rising but he held himself in check. He knew what it was like to have a chip on your shoulder and, coming from the same lower deck background as Blake, he could sympathize with the reasons for the sub lieutenant's ill-founded resentments.

'Take it easy, James. Remember where you are,' he reprimanded him quietly. 'Mansergh's background has nothing to do with it. In fact my decision was taken for precisely opposite reasons. Both of you will make good officers in your own different ways. But there are a thousand Toby Manserghs in the Service and one less won't make much difference either way. On the other hand there are, unfortunately, very few people like us who have been through the lower deck. And if the Royal Navy is to survive after the war the upperyardmen will have to play an increasingly important part both in administration and the senior sea-going commands.

'You can take it from me that Operation Tenfold is a one-way ticket and the chances of survival are virtually nil. I doubt if I will come back but, if I don't, I think I can claim with due modesty to have done enough already in the course of my combat career to stand as a precedent in favour of promotion from the ranks. I know you'd like to share the honours and glory with me - and I don't blame you for that. But the Navy needs young men like you if it is to have any sort of future. And I have no intention of seeing you killed unnecessarily. You'll be a damned sight more use to the Navy as a fine officer than as a dead hero. It's people like you who will have to carry on when my generation has gone. And don't you ever forget it. Dismiss!'

The sub lieutenant saluted, pulled the dividing curtain to one side, and stepped out into *Rapier's* wardroom. His mind was a seething confusion of disappointment, resentment, and envy for Mansergh's luck. But, above all, was the bitter realization that the one officer in the Navy he thought he could trust had let him down. Hamilton, of all people, had surrendered to nepotism.

He decided to go on deck for a breath of fresh air but, with his thoughts on other things, he failed to notice Charlie Dobson waiting outside in the narrow passageway that ran from the fore-end's mess space to the for'ard bulkhead of the control room. He grunted an apology as he nearly fell over the young leading seaman and was about to continue aft when Dobson stopped him.

'Excuse me, sir. Is the Captain free?'

Blake nodded. 'There's no one with him at the moment - but he's busy selecting the names of the volunteers. I suppose it's about your marriage leave?'

'Yes, sir. Well, in a way it is.'

'Okay. Hang on and I'll ask him if he can see you.' Blake went back into the wardroom and found Hamilton still working his way through the list. 'Dobson's outside, sir. He wants to see you about his leave.'

'Send him in, Sub. He probably wants to ask me where he ought to go for his honeymoon.' He screwed the cap back onto his pen, glanced at the photograph of Caroline on his desk, and folded his hands together as he waited. The task of picking volunteers was worse than selecting hostages for execution and any opportunity to escape from further decisions for even a few moments was welcome.

Dobson bustled in, removed his cap, and came to

attention. 'Dobson, Charles. MJ 7546. Permission to make a request, sir?'

'At ease, Dobson. By the way, I was watching your mooring party this morning. Very well handled. Keep it up and you'll get your PO rating.' Hamilton smiled. 'Now what is it you want to see me about - something to do with this forthcoming wedding, I suppose.'

'Yes, sir.' Like many ratings Dobson stood in awe of his skipper and now that it had come to the point he lost his tongue.

'Don't worry, Dobson, everything's organized. Seven days commencing at midnight on the 23rd. I've had formal approval from the Flag Officer. You realize, of course, that this is part of your normal leave entitlement? Unfortunately they don't give you anything extra for getting spliced.' Dobson nodded. 'Yes, sir. I realize that.' He hesitated again. 'Sir, I would like to withdraw my application.'

'I hope there's nothing wrong, Dobson. She looks a nice girl judging by the photo you've got stuck in your locker. Is there anything I can do to help?'

Dobson shifted his feet awkwardly. 'It's nothing like that, sir. Thelma's a good sort - she wouldn't let me down. It's just that I don't want to miss the show when it comes off and I heard a rumour it's fixed for the same week.'

'You shouldn't listen to rumours like that,' Hamilton said mildly, neither confirming nor denying the date for Operation Tenfold. 'There'll be no difficulty in you joining the passage crew. Mind you it means you'd have to postpone your wedding indefinitely. We can't go arranging dates that might give away any trade secrets.' He chose his words carefully. Although *Rapier's* crew were aware that the submarine was to take part in a major operation they had been given no indication what it involved and even the men who had volunteered and been selected would have no idea what lay ahead until they started on the final phase of their operational train- ing. 'Would you like me to put your name down for the passage crew?'

'No, sir. Begging your pardon, sir. I want to volunteer for the second stage. I want Thelma to feel real proud of me when we go up the aisle.'

Hamilton was suddenly silent. He needed two more leading rates and Dobson was one of the brightest seamen on the boat. But he was little more than a boy. And he certainly had no idea what would be involved.

'The final stage of the operation will be damned dangerous, Dobson. More than that I can't tell you. But if you volunteer you're more likely to be buying a ticket for a funeral than a wedding. Do I make myself clear?'

Dobson swallowed and nodded. 'Yes, sir. But I'd still like to go with you. And I know Thelma would understand.'

Hamilton pulled the list towards him and stared down at it. For a few brief moments he could not trust himself to speak. But he knew Dobson was right. Better to remain single until it was over. There were more than enough widows in the world already. Picking up his pen he made a mark against the leading seaman's name.

'Very well, Dobson. You're on the list. Training begins on Monday.' He looked up at the young sailor. 'And mind you don't say anything to anybody about the operation - not even your precious Thelma.'

Dobson replaced his cap and, smiling broadly, saluted. With a smart about-turn that threatened to dislodge the pile of files balanced precariously on the desk, he ducked through the curtain.

Hamilton watched him vanish. Then, swinging around in his chair, he stared down at the list. He could not help wondering why he had allowed young Dobson his chance of glory while refusing the sub lieutenant a similar opportunity. Was it simply because Blake was an officer with a career ahead of him and who could be of value to the Navy in the difficult years after the war. Or because, having lighted the torch for the lower deck, he needed someone to pass it on to? And, looking at Caroline's photograph, he began to wonder whether he himself had only volunteered merely to prove that he was equally as good as the officer- class he professed to despise.

NINE

Gernheim swore as he put the phone back on its hook. The korporal was an idiot. But what else could you expect from a Wuttenburger? He listened to the rain beating against the side of the hut and shivered as he started getting into his greatcoat. It was a pity the *Wehrmacht* didn't encourage its NCOs to use their initiative. As an afterthought he picked up the telephone again and dialed a two-digit number. He lit a cigarette while he waited.

'Is that you Otto? Kurt speaking. Tell me, is your radar still on the blink? That fool Schmidt says he can see ships off-shore and wants me to take a look. I ask you - on a night like this! It's pissing down!'

Otto Schneider chuckled. That was the advantage of being a technician. You didn't have to get wet and, if you were lucky, you didn't get shot at either. 'Sorry, Kurt. No use relying on the *Seetakt* for the next few hours. We've found the trouble. It wasn't an instrument malfunction - the bloody Maquis have wrecked the scanner. It'll take at least twelve hours to get a replacement from Gruppe West.' 'Why the hell don't you guard the damned thing?'

Gernheim grumbled. 'The Fuehrer won't have much faith in the Atlantic Wall when he finds out we have to rely on Schmidt's eyesight.' He sighed heavily. 'I'd better go and see what he's bleating about. And if you don't want me to catch pneumonia you'll get that bloody radar contraption of yours fixed before I go on duty tomorrow night.'

'You've got a hope. Just think yourself lucky you're not on the Eastern Front.' He chuckled to himself and put down the phone before Kurt could answer back.

Gernheim scowled blackly as the connection went dead. It was little consolation but he knew Schneider was right. A brisk walk along the mole in the pouring rain was infinitely preferable to cowering in a frozen slit trench with a Russian T-34 tank rolling ponderously towards you. He fastened the top button of his greatcoat and glanced at the clock. Five minutes to sunrise. Perhaps when the tide turned just after dawn it would bring better weather. He opened the door of the hut, braced himself in anticipation, and stepped out onto the rainswept emptiness of the mole.

The lonely pill-box was situated at the far end of the great concrete harbour-work. Exposed to the elements and swept by the sea whenever storms hurled the waves against the lower piers, it was not the most comfortable of havens but Korporal Schmidt, like Gernheim, had no wish to exchange it for a fox hole on the Eastern Front. And standing at the observation slit he kept a careful watch through his Navy-issue binoculars as he waited the officer's arrival. The long night vigil was nearly over and, despite the scudding black rain clouds, the rosy fingers of the rising sun were already beginning to lighten the eastern sky although, irritatingly from Schmidt's point of view, the horizon to seaward remained as murky and impenetrable as ever.

Gernheim shook the worst of the water from his coat as he entered the pill-box. His temper had not been improved by the long slog through the rain to the observation post and he was eager to vent his annoyance on someone.

'What's all this bloody nonsense about seeing ships, korporal?'

Schmidt turned away from the observation slit and lowered his glasses. 'Ask Koenig, sir - he was the one who saw them. I haven't seen a bloody thing.'

Koenig was a recent recruit to the 109th Regiment. A former member of the Hitler Youth, he had volunteered for service two months before his Class of 1925 was due for conscription and, with misplaced adolescent enthusiasm, he felt he was betraying the Fuehrer's trust by sitting around on his arse keeping watch on the Atlantic Wall when he could have been fighting with a combat unit in Russia.

'I definitely saw ships, sir,' he told Gernheim. 'They looked like enemy coastal craft - Vospers, I'd say. They seemed to be approaching the coast but then they turned away.'

The officer was unimpressed. If Schmidt had called him out in the middle of the night just because this stupid little wet-nosed kid thought he'd seen something he'd—

'How the hell can you see in the dark?' he growled. 'You don't even look old enough to be let out at night without your bloody nursemaid.'

'I passed the *Luftwaffe* night vision tests, sir,' Koenig said smugly.

'Well, you're not in the damned *Luftwaffe,* boy!

You're in the bloody army. And if you want to see some more night visions, including a few stars, just try calling me up here again on a wild-goose chase.'

'He might be right, sir,' Schmidt intervened. He was peering through the observation slit again. 'I can see *something* - bearing north west.'

Gernheim pulled his Zeiss glasses from the case slung around his neck and stared out to sea. His eyes had adjusted to the darkness during the long walk along the mole but the driving rain beating in from the sea made it almost impossible to see anything clearly. He sensed rather than saw a shadow move on the horizon and, a moment later, he thought he could detect the curving bow wave and *kielwasser* of a fast-moving coastal patrol boat. Perhaps Koenig's sighting hadn't been imagination after all. He lowered his glasses and glanced across at the young soldier. 'What was it you said - *vorspiel* A prelude to what?' 'No, sir. Not *vorspiel* - Vosper. It's an English motor torpedo boat.'

Gernheim nodded and resumed his observation of the horizon. An English motor boat. Probably an enemy coastal flotilla returning to base after an all-night anti E-boat patrol. What else *could* it be? The English would not waste their energies attacking a base that was still under construction. It was a pity the surface warning radar was out of action. Schneider's probing electron beam would have quickly revealed whether further ships lay hidden in the darkness beyond the range of the human eye.

'I think I can see some more boats - north-west by west,' Schmidt reported excitedly. 'They're moving this way, sir, with all lights extinguished.'

The officer swung his glasses to the left. He was a soldier not a sailor and he couldn't distinguish one ship from another. But Schmidt was right. A group of darkened ships was definitely moving towards the entrance and instinct warned him they were up to no good.

'Koenig - call *Oberst* Boehme immediately and tell him we have two groups of unidentified vessels approaching. Ask him for permission to sound the alarm. And, korporal, you take the rest of the men to the battery and stand by the guns.'

Schmidt called his crew to action stations and, dragging open the steel door of the pill-box, followed them out into the rain to the twin 40 mm weapon nestling snugly dry under its glisteningly wet tarpaulin.

'Bekker! Where the hell's Bekker?'

'Here, sir.'

'Get your lamp and flash the night recognition signal. You know what it is, I hope?'

'Yes, sir. H-E-A.'

'Right, then, get on with it!'

Gernheim followed the signaller onto the narrow stone parapet. The rain had eased to a fine drizzle but the chill wind blowing in off the sea made conditions highly unpleasant and he shivered. The sky to the east was lighter now and, glancing back over the harbour, he could just make out the ugly slab of reinforced concrete forming the roof of the E-boat pen sprawled like an enormous overturned tombstone and lying on a green sward of dew-soaked turf. The murmuring rumble of the congregation leaving the churchyard deepened into a sullen roar and he turned his attention seawards in time to see the first wave of ground-attack Mustang aircraft screaming across the wavetops at zero feet. Bright tongues of flames flickered from behind the wings and smoke erupted along the leading edges as a salvo of rockets hurtled towards the flak batteries.

A pandemonium of noise assailed his ears as the gun defences opened fire and, amidst the crash of bursting rockets, the thundering roar of aircraft engines and the sullen thud of heavy naval guns and shore batteries, the banshee wail of the alarm sirens added a grotesque and terrifying descant to the main theme of the battle hymn. A shell crashed against the parapet, exploded in a sheet of bright yellow flame, and Gernheim dived for cover as splinters of red-hot steel and sharp concrete scythed across the exposed mole.

'Open fire, Schmidt!' he yelled from behind the solid safety of a concrete blast wall. 'Open fire!'

But the korporal was beyond reach of human orders. Two rockets from the first wave of fighters had burst inside the gun emplacement and the smoking remains of the weapon tilted skywards like the blackened impotent bones of a skeletal hand gesturing mutely at the sun. Schmidt himself lay huddled in the corner with half his face blown away. Maas and Schubert were both dead. And Paul Koenig, the young recruit, was leaning against the side of the gun pit clutching his stomach with both hands. Gernheim could see the blue-grey mass of the boy's intestines, protruding between the scrabbling bright red fingers and, turning his head away, he was violently sick as the second wave of Mustangs swooped towards the mole.

'FIVE MINUTES TO ZERO, SIR!'

Hamilton was hunched silently over the for'ard bridge screen lost in his private thoughts and Mansergh had to repeat the reminder before he emerged from his brooding reverie.

'Thanks, Toby.' He cast the memories aside and concentrated on the task ahead. In a few more minutes there would be no time left for thinking.

'Is everything alright, sir?'

'Yes, fine. I was just remembering some of the other scraps I've taken *Rapier* into. I reckon that Hong Kong was the worst. But it'll seem like a picnic compared to this.'

Mansergh knew he was lying. Hamilton wasn't a man to dwell on past battles. And it wasn't difficult to guess what his thoughts had been.

'How was Caroline when you saw her, sir?' he asked casually. 'Hasn't changed her mind yet, I suppose.'

'She was okay.' Hamilton recalled the memory of the final moments at the station when he returned to his ship two days previously. Both of them had known that they might never meet again but, typically, neither had shown any great emotion. 'I haven't managed to persuade her - and, by God, I've tried hard enough.'

Mansergh checked the darkened ships ahead and then swung his glasses to port. Everything seemed quiet enough. Obviously the Boche hadn't rumbled anything yet.

'So she still thinks you shouldn't marry a divorced woman?' The sub lieutenant shrugged. 'I can understand her reasons. And to be brutally frank I reckon she's right. The Navy can be a very intolerant mistress. Once the story got around you'd be *persona non grata* in every wardroom you visited.' He paused while he glanced at the gyro repeater. 'Have you heard how Woodward's taking it?'

'He's said nothing to me directly although we've natu-rally met up together on various occasions during plan-ning. That spell in hospital seems to have done him the world of good. He must be aware of the situation but he's been remarkably pleasant.'

'No point in being otherwise. Caroline certainly won't go back to him no matter what he does - she can be an obstinate little bitch when she wants to be. And he can hardly blame you because you've known her since before the war and you didn't appear on the scene until after their marriage broke up.'

Hamilton had no great desire to discuss his personal life with Mansergh and he looked at his wristwatch. 'Two minutes to go. Get down to the fo'c'sle with Dobson and stand by to release the tow. Then send Dobson below and come back to the bridge.'

The decision to tow *Rapier* across the North Sea had been taken at the last minute after tedious hours of plan-ning and sea exercises had demonstrated the dangers of trying to lift off the passage crew within range of the enemy's shore batteries. Woodward, in fact, as senior officer commanding the covering destroyer group, had been instrumental in pointing out the hazards of the orig-inal plan and Hamilton had seen no reason to disagree with him. The Captain would have more than enough problems without the additional worry of getting the passage crew off the submarine under fire. And there were other matters of equal concern.

Although the Maquis had orders to take out Zeehoven's two radar stations at Zero minus four hours there was always the chance that they might fail in their task or that the Germans had installed another scanner which had not yet been located and reported to Allied agents. As an additional precaution, therefore, the assault group was sailing in convoy rather than naval formation so that, if spotted, the enemy would not be put immediately on his guard. It was a disguise that could not be maintained for very long but even a few minutes' hesitation could mean the difference between life and death for the men involved.

Vice Admiral Winter was not a man to underestimate the intelligence of his enemy and the planning staff had devised an elaborate scheme of deception. The assault group, operating under the coded call-sign usually allocated to a coastal convoy, was routed out of Newcastle and down the east coast in accordance with standard convoy procedure. At the same time a second dummy convoy was assembled in the Thames estuary ready to sail north. At the appropriate moment the admiral's staff had arranged for an 'incident' to take place off the Essex coast - a report that German aircraft had been seen dropping mines between the Nore and Sunk light vessels. This particular signal was to be sent *en claire* by a patrolling motor launch. The second convoy would therefore be ordered to sail eastward of the danger area while a signal was to be dispatched to the Newcastle convoy ordering it to steer south-east from the Galloper Shoals in order to avoid the danger of collisions with the northbound group of ships. And to add verisimilitude to the exchange of signals the Admiralty was to add a priority warning to the Commodore of Convoy NX-65—the assault group—reminding him that the alteration of course would take him dangerously close to the Belgian coast and that he should therefore be on the alert for enemy inshore patrols.

The signals were all to be dispatched in accordance with standard convoy routine and Winter had little doubt that German wireless operators would monitor the messages and pass them on to the appropriate authority. It was, of course, a gamble. The Naval C-in-C Gruppe West might decide to send an E-boat flotilla out to attack the diverted convoy as it approached the coast and, as an added precaution, an MTB patrol had been assigned to intercept such an attempt if made. But if the enemy accepted the signals as genuine the presence of a convoy steering towards the Belgian coast would arouse no undue alarm and the Germans would merely observe and log its progress in the usual way.

Hamilton reflected that Admiral Roger Keyes had needed to make no similarly elaborate cover plan when his miniature armada of ships had sailed against Zeebrugge in 1918. In those days, without radar and with air warfare still in its infancy, admirals were content to make use of mist and bad visibility to conceal their intentions. And, until within visual range of shore lookouts, their presence would be completely unknown to even the most alert enemy.

Raising his binoculars he searched the darkness to port as *Markham* swung onto a south-westerly bearing. The faint glow of dawn rimmed the low-lying land on the horizon and there was just sufficient light to pick out the leading marks as they closed the shore. The destroyer's skipper had done a good job. Dawn minus two. Dead on time.

'Stand by engines.'

'Engine room, aye, aye, sir.'

A new and simplified system of controls designed by the experts at Vickers and fitted by the dockyard engineers at Rosyth meant that *Rapier*'s diesel units could now be operated by only two men. And as the engines would only have to run for a maximum of thirty minutes there was no need for any maintenance staff.

'Engage clutches. Start both engines.'

'Clutches in, sir.' A cloud of black oil smoke erupted from the exhaust trunks abaft the conning-tower as the diesel units started but as Harding trimmed the injector valves it quickly thinned to a fine shimmering haze. 'Engines running, sir.'

Hamilton picked up the telephone link to the destroyer and, at the same time, leaned forward over the bridge screen and pointed a small hand-torch towards Mansergh and Dobson on the bow casing.

'Stand by to take in tow,' he told *Markham*. 'Releasing cable—' his thumb jabbed the button-switch twice, — *now!* He leaned over the voicepipe. 'Half ahead both.' Then, after checking that the destroyer was moving to starboard, he nodded to Ernie Blood. 'Steer one-seven-zero, Cox'n.'

Blood acknowledged the order and eased the wheel to port to clear *Markham's* stern as the submarine gathered speed. 'End of mole in sight, sir,' he reported calmly as if he was guiding *Rapier* into Portsmouth harbour at the conclusion of a day's exercises in Stokes Bay. 'Starboard bow - about forty degrees.'

'Keep at least one cable clear. But don't go too far to port. The Germans haven't completely dredged the entrance yet.'

Mansergh came up the rungs on the outside of the conning-tower, swung his legs over the coaming with practiced agility, and joined Hamilton at the for'ard end of the bridge. Everything had gone smoothly so far. The tow had been released on receipt of the double green flash from the torch and, almost immediately, the destroyer had swung hard a'starboard to give the submarine adequate sea-room.

'All okay, sir,' he reported cheerfully. 'Where's all this action you kept talking about?'

Hamilton searched the darkened mole for signs of movement. 'If you enjoy sitting on top of a gunpowder barrel waiting for some damn fool to strike a match I suppose you could say everything's okay,' he said drily without taking the binoculars from his eyes. 'But once the Boche realizes what's happening you'll get all the action you want.'

The steady throb of the diesels, the smoothness of the sea, and the mocking quietness of the shore, reminded Hamilton of the night he had taken *Rapier* down through the straits between Hong Kong island and Kowloon to shoot up the Japanese troop concentrations waiting to make their final assault on the colony. At least on that occasion, despite the risks involved in operating close inshore in shoal water, *Rapier* wasn't packed to the gunwales with nearly a hundred tons of high explosives.

And she still had her ability to dive out of danger once they reached the open sea.

In the circumstances his pessimism was understandable. Although he could sink the submarine to the bottom by flooding the ballast tanks he had neither the blowing capacity nor crew to bring her back to the surface again. Once she was down she would stay down - forever. In addition, *Rapier* no longer carried the 3 in deck gun which had done such good service in the Far East and without a reliable weapon Hamilton felt a little like Daniel entering the lion's den. Admittedly they'd fitted a couple of Oerlikons for close-range defence but, as a realist, he had no great faith in the submarine's capacity for survival if they came under fire. Once *Rapier* closed within range of the shore batteries she would have the life expectancy of a barrel of gunpowder thrown into a furnace!

When *Campbelltown* had destroyed the lockgates at St Nazaire her demolition charge had consisted of twenty- four Mk VII depthcharges each containing three hundred pounds of Amatol - a total of three and a half tons of high explosives. A cold shiver ran down his back as he contemplated the results of his mental arithmetic. *Rapier* was carrying *thirty times as much!*. And, loaded to the limit of her stowage space, the necessary reserve of buoyancy had only been achieved by dispensing with ninety per cent of her oil bunkerage. Even so she was running awash and she wallowed clumsily through the water like an overfed whale as Blood steered for the entrance to the harbour.

The sky ahead was already growing lighter and Hamilton stole an impatient glance at his watch. Dawn plus three. Only two minutes to zero! He turned his glasses on the seaward end of the mole which was now less than a hundred yards away but there was no sign of any activity. It was too damned quiet. What the hell was the Boche doing? Surely they'd been spotted by the enemy lookouts - they couldn't *all* be asleep!

Mansergh was standing at the after end of the bridge keeping watch astern. A light mist hung over the horizon but as it shifted and swirled in the morning breeze he glimpsed the shadowy shapes of the assault group moving in.

'The Commandos are on time, sir. Landing craft in sight.'

Hamilton made no comment. He was concentrating

on a small concrete pill-box situated on the very end of the mole. A few moments earlier he had seen a German army officer running towards it. Then a door had opened and he had disappeared inside. *Rapier's* skipper wiped the drizzle from his binoculars and waited.

'Line your sights on that pill-box, Phillips,' he warned the starboard Oerlikon gunner. 'There's some sort of gun emplacement just below the parapet and it's my guess the Boche will come out onto the mole and make for their weapons when the alarm sounds. Hold your fire till I give the word.'

Phillips swung the barrel of the pom-pom towards the end of the mole and wedged the recoil pads into his shoulders. He knew exactly what the skipper meant. Pick the bastards off one by one as they came out - like shooting ducks on a fairground rifle range. He wondered whether he'd win a coconut if he knocked them all down.

'Aye, aye, sir.'

Dawn plus two. Where the hell were the fighter bombers? Any attempt to penetrate the harbour without air support could only lead to disaster but *Rapier* was too deeply committed to pull out now. Trust the bloody RAF to be late!

'Here they come, sir,' Phillips reported. He passed the warning in a hoarse whisper as if afraid of being overheard.

Hamilton focused his glasses and saw three soldiers in field-grey uniforms scrambling hurriedly down the stone steps leading to the gun emplacement while another soldier, holding a portable signaling lamp, climbed up onto the parapet closely followed by an officer in a great-coat. A sequence of sharp pin-points of light flashed through the rain and Hamilton read off the morse-code letters one by one . . . *H-E-A*. He grinned complacently. The Allied agents had certainly done a good job - the interrogative signal exactly matched the cipher group predicted in the final operational briefing issued the previous day. *And*, even better, Intelligence had supplied him with the appropriate reply. Lifting the Aldis lamp out of its waterproof locker he raised it to his shoulder, aimed the sighting 'scope at the two men standing on top of the mole, and began flashing the initial identification letters of the reply.

'*Aircraft astern!*'

Mansergh's warning shout was drowned by the ear-splitting roar of the Packard-built Rolls Royce Merlins as the first wave of Mustangs hurtled towards the mole at zero feet and Hamilton instinctively ducked behind the plastic armour of the reinforced bridge screen. Above the deafening scream of the engines he heard the soulful wail of the alarm sirens ashore followed by the sharp crackle of aircraft cannons and the strange hissing roar of the rockets. A series of violent explosions echoed across the water and, raising his head cautiously, he peered over the top of the screen.

The gun emplacement at the end of the mole had been reduced to a charred and smoking skeleton following a direct hit by one of the rockets and there was an enormous hole in the side of the concrete pill-box. Moving his binoculars to the left Hamilton could see the top of the mole strewn with lifeless bodies. And, as he examined the chaotic results of the attack, one of the figures suddenly rose to its feet, hesitated as if uncertain what to do, and then took to its heels down the mole as if all the devils of hell were in pursuit.

'Permission to fire, sir?' Phillips asked anxiously.

'Carry on, gunner.'

The staccato bark of the single-barrelled pom-pom hammered Hamilton's ears with the intensity of a pneumatic road drill. Phillips zeroed a line of tracer shells on the fleeing figure of the officer and chips of shattered concrete flew in all directions as they burst against the parapet wall. Gernheim sheltered behind an iron bollard in a desperate attempt to find cover but the Oerlikon pursued him with relentless zeal. A shell crashed into the base of the pillar and the officer was hurled back against the wall of the parapet like a rag doll by the force of the blast. Gernheim stared at the blood oozing from a dozen splinter holes in his uniform but the stunning force of his impact against the hard concrete had numbed all feeling of pain from his torn body. He slid slowly down the wall into a sitting position, made one last agonized effort to get to his feet, and then pitched forward on his face into a puddle of dirty rain water.

'POSITION X! Two points to starboard! Keep the island to port, Cox'n!'

Blood spun the helm in response to Hamilton's order and *Rapier's* bows swung to the right as the submarine passed clear of the mole. The humped profile of the Ile d'Or lay ahead on the port bow quarter and a bright sparkle of flame rippled from the barrels of the 88 mm battery ranged along its base. Having spent many hours studying a scale model of Zeehoven and its harbour the scene looked unexpectedly familiar and Blood scarcely needed the skipper's steering instructions as he followed the prearranged course and guided *Rapier* in a long sweeping curve that would take the submarine safely past the island ready for the final four-point turn towards the E-boat pen.

Hamilton had complete confidence in his coxswain and, leaving Blood with the responsibility for steering the boat towards the target area, he concentrated his attention on the broader aspects of the battle as the harbour was swept by bursting shells and tracer bullets. It seemed impossible for anything to survive the barrage but, somehow, *Rapier* continued unscathed and steamed serenely through the hail of red-hot steel with the confident assurance of a ju-ju priest walking over a bed of burning charcoal. A motor launch sped down the port side pouring thick black smoke from the cylinders on its stern as it laid down a screen to hide the submarine from the shore batteries on the northern side of the harbour and Hamilton glanced anxiously astern to see if its flotilla mate was moving into position to lay smoke to starboard.

'Where the hell's 537?' he shouted to Mansergh.

'Mills bought it just outside the mole, sir. Direct hit on the wheelhouse. The boat went out of control and smashed into the breakwater.'

'Is anyone else coming up?' The charts of the base showed a floating battery moored just inside the elbow of the mole directly opposite the island and Hamilton knew he would need smoke cover before *Rapier* came within range of its guns.

'There's another Fairmile coming up fast, sir. Should just get into position before we come abreast of the floating battery.'

Hamilton could see a flurry of spray in the distance as the motor launch approached from seaward. The skipper was trying - but he was going to be too damned late. He leaned over the voicepipe.

'Full ahead both engines!'

Rapier wallowed awkwardly as Harding turned up the power and, lacking in buoyancy, she thrust her bows into the sea as if preparing to dive. Within seconds the entire fore-casing was awash and the water was already lapping the base of the conning-tower as she floundered to remain afloat. From his vantage point on the bridge Hamilton decided that only a miracle could save them. And the miracle, when it happened, came from the least expected source. A salvo of shells from the 88 mm battery on the lie d'Or burst close under the bows and the blast lifted the stem clear of the surface. Hamilton clung to the bridge rails as the submarine rolled to starboard and had only just regained his balance when a second salvo landed astern and kicked *Rapier* to port. For one horrifying moment he thought she was going to capsize but the violent motion shifted the water in the ballast tanks and, with a creaking groan, she regained her stability although she was still rolling sluggishly through loss of buoyancy.

'I think we're making water in one of the aft compartments, sir,' Mansergh reported from the rear of the bridge. 'That last salvo has started a couple of hull plates just abaft the starboard hydroplane.'

A sharp whistle through the voicepipe brought quick confirmation from the ubiquitous Harding. 'We have some leaks in the motor room, sir,' he reported calmly. 'Starboard side close to Number Eight bulkhead.'

'Serious?'

'Difficult to say, sir. The depthcharges are in the way so I can't check the damage. I reckon it'll be okay if the other plates hold.'

'Very good, Harding. Keep an eye on them and let me know if we start making too much water.'

'Aye, aye, sir.'

Hamilton swore to himself as he straightened up from the voicepipe. He had been strongly opposed to the idea of removing the submarine's motors to create additional storage space for the depthcharges but had been over-ruled by Winter. And now his objections had been justi-fied. Without electrical power *Rapier* was unable to operate her pumps to clear the water leaking into the stern compartments. And with only ten men aboard, manual pumping was out of the question.

Under normal conditions a minor leak would have been of no great importance but, overloaded and danger-ously unstable, even the slightest loss of buoyancy could bring disaster and Hamilton forced himself not to think too deeply about what *might* happen. Despite his inner fears he seemed outwardly unconcerned as he resumed his usual station in the centre of the bridge.

A forest of shell splashes mushroomed around the submarine as the German gunners found the range, but Hamilton ignored them and concentrated on the vital task of conning *Rapier* onto the next leg of her perilous course through the inferno of shot and shell now enveloping the harbour. He was, in many ways, a fatalist and he knew there was nothing he could do to avoid the enemy's guns. His purpose was to get the submarine into the E-boat pen and he consoled himself with the thought that if one of the shells scored a direct hit he would know very little about it. 'Wireless mast on port beam, sir!'

Hamilton spotted the landmark and watched the gird-ered skeleton of the high-powered transmitting aerial slip past on the port side. He waited until it was bearing exactly ninety degrees.

'Position Y! Steer one-eight-zero, Cox'n!'

Blood kept his eyes on the gyro repeater as he picked up the new course. Another near-miss struck the sea just ahead of the bows but he did not allow it to divert him from his path and the men on the bridge were drenched with water as *Rapier* plunged through the towering fountain of spray thrown up by the explosion.

'I told you I ought to have brought my umbrella, sir,' Mansergh grinned. 'At least we didn't get wet at Corryvreckham!'

'Concentrate on your duties, Sub,' Hamilton told him coldly. It was impossible not to admire Toby's coolness and a feeling of envy compounded the asperity in his voice. 'What's happening astern?'

'The Commandos have landed on the mole,' Mansergh reported. 'I can see old Cooper legging it along the parapet like a wing-half at Twickenham. I bet the old bugger's never run so fast in all his life.'

Hamilton knew he was referring to 98 Commando's commanding officer, Colonel Leonard Cooper, whose ample proportions were hardly suited to hurrying. Rumour had it that he'd bribed the MO to get passed fit for the raid. But stories like that were commonplace and Hamilton had taken it with the proverbial pinch of salt. Glancing to port he saw a Fairmile motor launch putting down a smokescreen to cover the submarine from the unwelcome attentions of the shore batteries on the eastern side of the harbour and he waited impatiently for the remainder of Mansergh's report.

'Second ML now only two cables astern, sir. Coming up fast on starboard side.'

But not bloody fast enough, Hamilton reflected sourly as the guard ship moored inside the elbow of the mole added the weight of its guns to the barrage as *Rapier* came into its arc of fire. The submarine shuddered as the first salvo crashed into the sea uncomfortably close to the vulnerable starboard ballast tanks and Hamilton gritted his teeth as he waited for the next. The sudden roar of aircraft engines drew his attention skywards and he was just in time to see two Hurricane fighter-bombers appear through the clouds and dive on the floating battery. The squat black bombs slung beneath their wings fell away with slow deliberation and dropped in a gentle parabolic curve. The guardship loosed another salvo that rocked *Rapier* to port and then a violent explosion tore the air as the bombs struck the enemy vessel amidships, penetrated her unarmoured decks, and detonated the magazines. An enormous sheet of flame towered into the air and tiny fragments of steel, splintered wood, and human flesh fluttered down from the sky in a gruesome confetti of death. As the smoke and spray blew clear all that remained of the unfortunate ship was a large black scorch mark on the side of the concrete mole.

Distracted from the main objective by the unexpected appearance of this new enemy the flak gunners shifted their sights from the submarine and hurled their venom at the two aircraft. The leading Hurricane, having completed its bomb run, climbed safely clear of the barrage and headed out to sea but its less fortunate companion was caught in the deadly cross-fire. Leaking glycol trailed from its damaged radiator as the aircraft wobbled and clawed for altitude and Mansergh watched the streams of tracer bullets converging on the crippled fighter with the mesmerized fascination of a small boy gaping at his first firework display. Suddenly a red glow appeared low down in the tail-plane and the fire, quickly gaining in strength, moved rapidly forward along the fuselage before erupting into flames. Mansergh saw the pilot throw back the canopy of the blazing cockpit and reach up a gloved hand to haul himself out of his seat. Then, without warning, there was a blinding flash and the aircraft exploded into a million pieces. The sub lieutenant looked away in horror and, with the characteristic complacency of the professional sailor, decided he was glad he'd joined the Navy. Submarines were a bloody sight safer than aeroplanes.

Few people would have shared Mansergh's conclusions as *Rapier* emerged from behind the lee of the island to become the target of every available weapon in the enemy's armoury. Within seconds she was engulfed by exploding shells, whining bullets, and brightly coloured tracer, but maintaining speed, and with the spray curling whitely from her bows, the submarine thrust through the storm of fire as Hamilton held course with dogged determination. Jagged lumps of red-hot steel scythed the air like angry bees and the water thrown up by the bursting shells cascaded over the exposed bridge with the fury of a tropical storm. But nothing the Germans could do seemed able to halt *Rapier's* headlong rush through the harbour.

Deafened by the noise of the barrage and blinded by the flash of the guns stabbing the murk from literally every point of the compass Hamilton clung tightly to the bridge rails and wondered how long their luck could last. The ugly thud of 40 mm cannon shells striking the hull abaft the conning-tower and a sharp involuntary shout of pain made him turn his head quickly and he saw Mansergh stagger backwards with bright red blood running down his left arm. The young sub lieutenant looked white-faced and shaken but, ignoring the wound, he resumed his battle station and passed a damage report back to the skipper.

'We've got at least a dozen holes in the outer casing, sir. And it looks like the pressure hull's been punctured.' He paused for a moment to check what other damage had been done. 'The starboard folboat's been hit as well!'

Hamilton was not unduly worried about the state of the hull but the boats lashed to the deck casing behind the conning-tower were a different matter. Without them *Rapier's* crew would have no means of escape after the submarine had been blown up inside the E-boat pen.

'How's the motor boat?' he shouted above the crashing din of gun-fire and exploding shells.

Mansergh gritted his teeth with pain as he clung to the rails and peered over the stern. The small tender with its outboard motor was still happily bobbing up and down in the surging wash that frothed from the submarine's fantail. 'All secure, sir! No damage!'

'Oil jetty two hundred yards ahead, sir,' Blood warned his skipper as he jerked the helm in a violent zig-zag pattern to spoil the aim of the enemy gunners. 'We're coming up to the turn any time now.'

Ignoring the din of battle raging on all sides Hamilton acknowledged the Cox'n's warning, estimated the distance from the oil jetty, checked the bearing of the railway shed at the landward end of the mole, and glanced quickly to the left at the gaping mouth of the E-boat pen.

'Position Z! Port your helm, Mister Blood! Take her straight in - the door's open.'

Mansergh, his left arm hanging uselessly at his side, joined the skipper at the for'ard end of the bridge as

Rapier swung her bows towards the entrance of the great concrete shelter.

'I can't see the welcome mat, sir. Perhaps we've called on the wrong day.'

Hamilton shrugged carelessly. 'I wouldn't know, Toby. I forgot to read the invitation card.'

The sudden change of course seemed to throw the enemy defences into confusion and it was apparent that Kommandant Pohl and his senior officers had not appreciated the primary objective of the attack. Without telephone communications and cut off from contact with other nearby commanders, Pohl had assumed that the dawn assault was no more than a tip-and-run raid by British commandos and now that the truth finally penetrated he panicked and ordered the battery commanders to sink the submarine before she reached the pen.

It was, as it happened, an unwise decision. Many of the heavy batteries were unable to depress their weapons sufficiently to hit the target at such short range but, responding to the insistent demands of the Kommandant to keep firing, the artillery commanders obeyed unquestioningly and the light flak guns flanking the approach to the concrete shelter were rapidly overwhelmed by their own heavy guns shooting across the harbour.

Hamilton was quick to sieze the opportunity created by the confusion. *Rapier's* own Oerlikons added to the chaos and carnage ashore and the ignition of the smoke-floats on the submarine's fantail served to compound the Kommandant's total loss of control by creating even more uncertainty.

'Steady as she goes, Cox'n. Toby, get below and start checking the fuses. I'll join you as soon as we're safely inside the pen.' He leaned over the voicepipe. 'Stand by to open flood valves. Stand by to stop engines.' Stepping back from the speaking tube he glanced up as the over-hanging parapet of the concrete roof loomed towards the submarine and, for some unaccountable reason, a picture of Jonah being swallowed by the whale flashed into his mind.

A machinegun emplacement carefully concealed on top of the E-boat shelter opened fire as *Rapier* pushed her bows into the black maw of the entrance and Hamilton ducked behind the armoured bridge screen as a hail of bullets ripped the deck plating. There was a brief pause as the machine-gunner swung his weapon onto another part of the target and the respite was followed almost immediately by another long burst. Hamilton looked up as the starboard Oerlikon stopped firing and he saw Phillips collapse to the deck with blood pouring from his chest. Getting to his feet, he seized the silent gun and aimed it upwards towards the hidden machinegunner on the roof. But nothing happened when he squeezed the trigger and, glancing down, he saw that the breech mecha-nism had been smashed.

'Leave it to me, sir! I'll get the bastard!'

Leading Seaman Mullins heaved the port Oerlikon round so that it was pointing towards the bows and tilted the barrel skywards. It was impossible to aim accurately and the overhang of the roof made it difficult to see the target but Mullins did not allow the difficulties to deter him. He sprayed the parapet of the shelter with tracer shells as if he was directing a hose-pipe onto a fire and jagged lumps of masonry cascaded over the exposed bridge like petrified confetti. The angry chatter of the machinegun faltered momentarily and then stopped and, as Hamilton looked up, he saw a large black object tumble from the sky and land on *Rapier's* foredeck with a heavy thud.

He stared blankly at the field-grey uniform and, semi stunned by the concussion of the Oerlikon hammering relentlessly a few inches behind his head, wondered vaguely where it had come from. Mullins removed his finger from the firing button.

'That's brought the buggers down out of their nest, sir,' he grinned with modest satisfaction. 'I always did fancy myself as a poacher!'

Rapier glided slowly through the entrance into the black void of the concrete cavern like a train coasting gently into a railway tunnel and, as the dank gloom of the vault closed over the submarine, Hamilton groped for the voicepipe in the sudden darkness.

'Stop engines! Open vents and flood main ballast!' He raised his head from the voicepipe and as his eyes adjusted to the dim light inside the half-completed E-boat pen he could just make out the shapes of the other two men on the bridge. 'Get the boats launched and stand by.'

Rapier was already settling deeper into the water and Hamilton shinned down the conning-tower ladder in record time. Mansergh and the remainder of the crew were in the control room waiting for orders.

'Well done, lads. Now get the hell out of here all of you. The starboard folboat's been damaged so you'll have to take the tender. There won't be room for the lot of you so Dobson better go in the folboat with the coxswain. Up you go!' He turned to the sub lieutenant. 'And that includes you, Toby. I can manage the rest of the fuses on my own.' Mansergh hesitated as if reluctant to leave his skipper alone in the slowly sinking submarine. Assuming that Hamilton was not aware of the danger he jabbed his thumb towards the depth gauge.

'We're down five feet already, sir. The old girl's submerging quicker than we expected. You won't have time to check them all - I'll look after the stern section if you take the bow compartments.'

With *Rapier* going down more than twice as fast as they had calculated there was no margin of time to argue and Hamilton knew that Mansergh was right. Obviously the damage in the stern was more serious than he had anticipated. He nodded his agreement.

'Okay - but get up that ladder as soon as I give the shout. And if you haven't finished - hard luck!'

He saw the needle of the depth gauge inching towards the 7 ft. mark and, hastily grabbing a torch from the emergency rack, he ducked through the for'ard hatch into the fore ends. It was completely dark in the bow compartment but with the aid of the torch he quickly located the carefully stacked depthcharges. Each weapon was connected in series to the others with cordtex, an instantaneous waterproof fuse and, working in the dim glow of the torch, he meticulously checked where the junctions and connections were as he worked his way slowly back along the central cat-walk to the control room. He found Mansergh standing at the bottom of the ladder as he emerged through the hatchway. The sub lieutenant's face was a ghostly white in the darkness and he grimaced with pain as he held his injured arm.

'All secure aft, sir.'

Hamilton nodded and bent over the main fuse. 'Well done, Toby. Now take yourself topsides and get your party away. Use the motorboat - I'll manage with the folboat. See you in Harwich. And if you're still in one piece I'll buy you a drink.'

'Promises, promises,' Mansergh grinned weakly. He shone his torch on the depth gauge as Hamilton began setting the mechanism of the delay fuse. 'She's down to twelve feet, sir,' he reported anxiously.

'*Will* you get up that damned ladder, Toby!' Hamilton snapped impatiently. 'I've plenty of time yet. And having got this far I don't intend to cock everything up by hurrying.'

The sub lieutenant recognized his tone of voice and he knew it was no use arguing. Grabbing the ladder with his good arm he climbed awkwardly up through the lower conning-tower towards the upper hatch. If the skipper didn't get his skates on *Rapier* would go under leaving him trapped inside - but perhaps that was his intention. The final gesture of bravado. The captain who went down with his ship.

Mansergh hauled himself out of the hatchway and found the motorboat lying alongside. Mullins reached out a hand to help him aboard and the sub lieutenant slid down into the tender. He looked back at the water lapping against the top of the conning-tower and watched it sinking lower until it was barely showing above the surface. The hatch was still open and the gentle rolling motion of the motorboat was sufficient to send tiny ripples of water spilling down into the gaping orifice. He shivered and looked away.

'Cast off! Mullins - take the tiller. And everyone keep their heads down. There'll be all hell waiting for us outside!' The spluttering beat of the inboard engine echoed against the bare walls of the concrete shelter and he waved a warning arm at Ernie Blood waiting patiently in the stern of the folboat.

'Don't hang about too long, Chief,' he shouted. 'Shove off as soon as she goes under. If the skipper's not clear by then he'll never make it. And remember to keep the island to starboard. Good luck!'

Mansergh glanced back almost despairingly as the motorboat headed towards the entrance. The conning-tower was now barely an inch above the surface of the black turgid water and the upper hatch was still open. But there was no sign of Hamilton and, as he turned his head away, the sub lieutenant shrugged.

Perhaps that was the way he wanted to go.

TEN

As the urgent throb of the motorboat's Morris Marine engine faded into the distance the silence inside the deserted E-boat shelter was broken only by the soft lapping of the water against the concrete walls and the vulgar gurgling sound of the sea flooding into the opened Kingston valves of the submarine. Ernie Blood shone the beam of his torch towards the conning-tower hatch and anxiously checked his watch. The motor launches lying off the mole and waiting to pick up *Rapier's* survivors had been ordered to clear the harbour by Zero plus sixty and time was running out.

The Chief Petty Officer considered the problem with stoic detachment. The long return sweep through the harbour would take at least ten minutes even in favourable conditions and he was uncomfortably aware that the little boat would be under heavy fire from the moment she emerged from the entrance to the pen. He looked at his watch again. Zero plus fifty-one. If they didn't leave immediately the rescue launches would have disappeared from the scene by the time they reached the mole. And, assuming any of them were still alive, that meant spending the rest of the war in a German prison camp. He glanced round the boat to confirm that everyone was aboard before making the decision. Jack Phillips, the starboard gunner, was dead and his place was vacant, but Harding, the Stoker PO from the engine room, was in the bows and Charlie Dobson was sitting on the thwarts amidships. Only Hamilton was missing.

Cocking his head to one side the coxswain heard the enemy guns open fire on the survivors in Mansergh's motorboat as it ran clear of the entrance and emerged into the fight of day. They'd been bloody lucky so far. Only one man dead and the skipper missing. But how long could it last?

An unexpected swirl of water suddenly rocked the folboat as the surface gave a violent heave and *Rapier* vanished quietly from sight. A long bubbling sigh echoed back from the walls as the air trapped inside the submarine was forced out through the open hatchway by the rising pressure of the sea and then everything fell silent again.

'Get a move on Chief! I don't want to freeze to death. This water's bloody cold!'

Blood peered into the darkness as he recognized the skipper's voice and he swung the beam of the torch towards the spot where *Rapier* had gone down. Hamilton's face reflected palely in the gloom and, treading water, he waited while Dobson seized a paddle and urged the boat towards him. Harding was crouched in the bows and, as Hamilton reached out to grab the side, he hooked his hands under the skipper's armpits and dragged him over the gunwales.

The Lieutenant Commander collapsed in a heap in

the bottom of the boat, gasping for breath and choking in a paroxysm of coughing.

'Are you alright, sir?' Blood asked anxiously.

Hamilton raised his head for a brief moment and nodded. Then another spasm of coughing racked his lungs and he fell forward again. The acrid oil scum floating on the surface of the water was burning his eyes and the darkness inside the pen made it difficult to tell whether his vision had been affected or not. His right hand hurt abominably where he had caught it on the steel rails of the conning tower and the harbour filth in the water was clogging his nose and making breathing difficult.

'What's our elapsed time, Cox'n?' he asked hoarsely without trying to move from his crouched position on the floor of the boat.

'Plus fifty-four, sir.'

'Then what are you waiting for? Start the engine and get the hell out of here!'

Blood jerked the lanyard of the outboard motor but nothing happened. He swore and tried again. At the third attempt it sputtered to life and, gripping the tiller, *Rapier's* coxswain steered the overloaded boat towards the entrance. In common with most long-service men he felt lost and bewildered without having someone in authority standing behind him giving orders. But, as the senior man he was in command until the skipper recovered and, like it or not, the responsibility for their survival was in his hands.

Although the worst of the coughing spasms had subsided Hamilton was still hunched in the bottom of the boat and his shoulders heaved spasmodically as he retched up the muck he had swallowed into his stomach while swimming clear of the sinking submarine. Ernie Blood looked down at him and decided he was going to be on his own for some time.

As the little craft emerged into the bright morning sunlight the Chief Petty Officer swung the tiller violently to left and right in an effort to spoil the aim of the German machinegunners and the flimsy folboat rocked precariously with its gunwales bare inches from the surface of the water. Ignoring the danger of capsizing he opened the throttle of the Seagull outboard and ran through the perilous gauntlet of bullets and tracer shells as fast as he dared. The noise of the gunfire roused Hamilton from his stupor and, heaving himself onto his knees, he stared blindly over the side. His eyes were tight shut - the lids glued together by the scum of oil sludge clinging to his face.

'Are we out of the pen, Chief?'

'Yes, sir.' Blood looked at the skipper and frowned. It seemed a stupid question to ask. Suddenly he understood. 'Harding! Get the medicine box and see if you can find the eucalyptus oil.' He waited while the Stoker PO dragged the box from under the thwarts, opened the lid, and rummaged inside. Harding delved into the contents and produced a small bottle triumphantly. 'Good lad! Put it on some cotton wool and wipe the skipper's eyes.' The coxswain ducked as a stream of coloured tracer bullets whined over the boat. 'And keep your head down, sir!' he yelled.

'How's the sub lieutenant doing?' Hamilton asked as the stoker bent over him with the cotton wool and dabbed gently at the oil sludge.

'He's run clear of the island, sir,' Dobson reported

from the bows. 'Just turning to starboard. He's going like a bloody bat out of hell!'

Hamilton winced as the softness of the cotton wool irritated the raw skin of his left eyelid. At least young Toby was going to make it. He wasn't out of trouble yet but if Dobson's report was accurate the motorboat must be halfway to the mole by now. Harding eased the left lid open carefully and Hamilton shook his head with pain as the bright sunlight stabbed the damaged eye. Everything was blurred and the stoker was no more than a vague shadow in a silver mist. He turned his head slightly so that the petty officer could treat the other eye and bit his lip as the folboat rolled sharply to starboard pressing the weight of his body on his injured hand.

'How's the time, Cox'n?'

'Fifty-seven minutes gone, sir.'

'Where are we?'

'Coming up to the oil jetty, sir. About two hundred yards to go.'

Hamilton focused a mental map of the E-boat base in his mind as Harding continued to dab his eyes gently with the cotton wool pads. Once past the jetty they would be in open water and under fire from the shore batteries ranged along the mole. The prospect was not encouraging but there seemed no alternative. The odds were stacked firmly against them and they had little hope of reaching the pickup area before the motor launches were withdrawn at Zero plus sixty. Harding's careful treatment was working but although the right eye was now open as well his vision was too blurred to see what was happening and he cursed his disability. Pushing the Stoker Petty Officer aside he scrambled across to the starboard side of the boat and stared blindly towards the island.

'Feeling better, sir?'

Hamilton could sense the relief in the coxswain's question. Realizing that Blood needed someone to take the responsibilities from his shoulders, he nodded.

'Can you see that passage between the mainland and the island, Chief?' he shouted.

'Yes, sir.'

'Steer for it! The Germans have no shore batteries on that side. We'll probably have to face small-arms fire but it'll be better than the heavy stuff.' Keeping the map firmly focused in his mind he calculated that the short cut to the east of the island might just bring them up with the motor launches before they were withdrawn.

The coxswain hauled back the tiller and the folboat swerved sharply north towards the narrow strip of water separating the island from the coast. Hamilton was staring confidently ahead over the bows and Blood had little doubt that the skipper could see the passage as clearly as he could. He offered up a quick prayer of thanks that the Old Man was in command again. Any lingering doubts he had previously entertained about their chances of survival vanished.

The noise of the gun barrage on the western side of the harbour attracted Hamilton's attention and, moments later, the sound of a violent explosion thundered across the water. He kept his face turned towards the island as if intent on guiding them safely through the narrow strait ahead. He could see absolutely nothing but he was thankful for an excuse not to reveal his blindness by failing to see the cause of the explosion. And Charlie Dobson's incredulous exclamation gave him the opportunity to find out what had happened.

'Good Gawd Almighty!'

'What's the matter, Dobson?'

'It's Mister Mansergh's boat, sir. The Boche have scored a direct hit!'

Hamilton managed to conceal his fears as he maintained the pretence of staring ahead. 'Are the lads alright?' he asked tightly.

Dobson peered into the smoke hanging like a pall over the middle of the harbour. It was impossible to see what was going on and he began to stand up to obtain a clearer view.

'Keep your bloody head down, Dobson!' Blood shouted from the stern. A burst of Spandau fire reinforced the coxswain's warning but Charlie took no notice. A strong breeze was carrying the smoke away to the west and he strained his eyes to penetrate the murk.

'There's no sign of anyone in the water, sir,' he reported. 'The boat must have blown up. There's nothing there.'

'If you don't get your bloody head down *you* won't be there much longer, my lad,' Blood told him sharply. 'Stay under cover. Me and the skipper can manage quite well without your bloody help!'

Hamilton smiled to himself as he listened to the exchange. No matter what the situation a Chief Petty Officer never changed his spots. He decided the coxswain needed moral support. 'The Chief's right, Dobson. No point in giving the enemy a sitting target. Keep out of sight. There's nothing you can do to help the poor bastards.'

The worst of the firing died away as the folboat came under the lee of the island. The main batteries fell silent and only the occasional chatter of the machineguns pursued them. The din of battle still reverberated to seaward and Hamilton guessed that the supporting warships were still heavily engaged with the batteries on the mole. He decided to take advantage of the respite to reinforce his bluff.

'There's a causeway linking the island to the shore, Chief,' he told Blood. 'According to the charts there should be six feet clearance at high water. We're about midway between tides at the moment so it'll be touch and go. Can you see it?'

Blood tucked the tiller under his arm and peered ahead. 'There's a line of broken water dead ahead, sir. I reckon that must be it.'

Hamilton shaded his eyes with his hand as he pretended to check and confirm Blood's observation. He wondered how long it would be before the other men in the boat discovered his blindness. *And,* when they did, what effect would it have on their morale?

'You've got it okay, Chief. Now keep her on full power and go straight at it.' He crouched on his knees so that only his head showed above the level of the gunwale. 'Keep down you two - and hang on tight,' he warned Harding and Dobson. 'There'll be a hell of a bump when we hit the bar.'

The caution had hardly left his lips when a violent jolt shuddered through the boat and threw all four of them in an untidy heap on the bottom boards. Hamilton heard the slithering rasp of gravel beneath the keel followed by the sharp snap of breaking steel. Almost simultaneously the outboard motor screamed to impossible revolutions and, with an ear-splitting bang, the con rod slammed through the side of the sump and the motor rattled to a stop.

'The propeller's gone,' Blood reported dispassionately. 'The blades must have hit the bottom as we went over the bar.'

Hamilton reacted without hesitation. 'Grab the paddles! Harding - you take the port bow. Dobson take the starboard position. The cox'n and I will back you up from the stern. Come on – *move!'*

The folboat rocked violently as the men scrambled into their seats and, hoping that everyone was too busy to notice, Hamilton fumbled behind his back to locate the aft thwart. Having found it he began groping blindly in the bottom of the boat for one of the paddles. He was suddenly conscious of a movement at his side and, a moment later, a firm hand guided the handle of a paddle into his grasp.

'Here you are, sir,' the coxswain whispered hoarsely. 'Keep it up - the other two haven't guessed yet.'

Hamilton gripped the handle tightly and plunged the paddle over the side into the water. Thrusting it back, he lifted the paddle clear, and as he pushed it down again for the next stroke he wondered how long the chief had been aware of his secret. He concluded that he should have known better than to try and bluff Ernie Blood. Gritting his teeth he paddled blindly and hoped they were going in the right direction.

'Come on, me lucky lads! Put your backs into it! You're not on the bloody Serpentine now!'

Hamilton heard a sharp crackle of rifle fire from the direction of the shore as Blood urged the folboat's crew forward and he forced himself not to duck as the first bullets whined overhead. If he was to extricate *Rapier's* survivors from the holocaust he needed information. But how could he question the coxswain without the other two guessing the truth? Blood seemed to read his thoughts.

'I see the motor launches are pulling out, sir,' he grunted conversationally as he dug his paddle into the water. 'The smoke's making visibility difficult - I suppose they haven't spotted us. In any case they won't be expecting us to come this way.'

Hamilton's crushed hand was agony as he gripped the handle of the paddle but he steeled himself to withstand the pain. Getting the boat to the mole was a team job and he was determined to shoulder his share of the burden.

'They're a minute later by my watch,' he told the coxwain. It was a subtle touch and the two men crouched over their paddles in the bows had no reason to doubt that the skipper was well in command of the situation. He paused for breath as he thrust the paddle into the sea. 'How far would you say it was to the entrance, Chief? Three hundred yards?'

'More like five, sir,' Blood informed him. 'It's difficult to tell with the smoke. You could be right.'

Hamilton digested the information. His arms were aching and his injured hand was giving him hell but he kept paddling as he worked out their position on the mental map in his mind. Still five hundred yards to go! That meant they were barely clear of the island. And if the motor launches were pulling out what the hell were they going to do when they reached the entrance. His thoughts were rudely interrupted by a sharp crack from the shore to his right followed by the sobbing moan of a shell in flight. There was an ear-splitting crash as it burst some ten yards beyond the boat and he felt the spray thrown up by the explosion on his face. The coxswain's hoarse whisper quickly him of the new hazard.

'They're bringing up a battery of mobile field guns, sir. I can see a couple of them on the coast road just in front of the radar mast.'

Hamilton nodded. 'Okay, Chief. I think I've got the picture. There's not much we can do about it. We'll have to push on and hope for the best.'

Two more explosions following in quick succession rocked the folboat and Charlie Dobson glanced anxiously over his shoulder as a second battery of mobile guns hurried onto the scene. The skipper had guts - but what was the point of going on. The Boche guns were so close they were firing over open sights and the next few minutes would bring them within range of the machine-guns and pom-poms on the mole. He thrust his paddle into the water and tried not to think. They had travelled another fifty yards when Harding's excited shout sent his pulse racing.

'The bloody Navy's here! They ain't forgotten us after all!'

'One of the destroyers is coming inside the mole by the look of it,' the coxswain explained in a undertone. He sounded puzzled and Hamilton turned his sightless eyes in the approximate direction of the entrance.

'I can't see properly from this side,' he reminded Blood in an effort to obtain information without revealing his secret to the others, 'but it can't be a destroyer - there's no room to turn it round.'

Ernie Blood peered anxiously through the confusion of smoke and spray obscuring the entrance. 'It's approaching from the north-west, sir.' He paused and clung to the side of the boat as two more artillery shells exploded close to the stern. 'It looks like *Boxer* - and, by God, she's coming straight in!'

Hamilton said nothing. He felt sure that, for once, the coxswain was indulging in wishful thinking - a not unusual occurrence when a man was close to physical exhaustion. The timetable for Operation Tenfold had been precise and unambiguous. All ships would withdraw at Zero plus sixty without regard to stragglers or survivors who might be left behind and he could not imagine Winter departing from the plan. With the lives of a thousand men at stake the Vice Admiral would not allow sentiment to cloud his judgement.

In any case it would be an act of utter madness to try and bring a two-thousand-ton destroyer inside the mole. Even the world's worst gunner couldn't miss such a target at point-blank range. And there was another more cogent reason. *Boxer* was Woodward's boat. And although the Captain had mellowed considerably since his unfortunate breakdown Hamilton could not imagine him risking his neck or his ship to pick up a bunch of submariners.

The deafening crash of a heavy shell exploding uncomfortably close under the stern put an effective stop to any further thoughts and Hamilton clung grimly to the gunwale as the cockleshell craft bucked violently in the aftermath of the blast. He was soaked to the skin and his ears were ringing painfully from the concussive pressure of the explosion while the continual whine of bullets from all sides gave him the impression that he was sitting in the middle of a wasps' nest. Their situation was deteriorating with every passing minute and yet, with the prospect of rescue seemingly so close at hand, he knew it needed only one last determined effort of leadership to bring them to safety. Hamilton clenched his hands in frustration at his inability to see what was going on. Just thirty seconds of God-given eyesight was all he needed. But even that brief miracle was denied him.

'Shit!' Dobson swore in the bows. 'Now I've lost my bloody paddle!'

'Grab the bailer,' Blood told him quickly. 'Use it as a paddle - we've only got another hundred yards to go.' The CPO dug his own paddle deep into the water to gain extra impetus and lowered his voice as he turned to Hamilton. '*Boxer's* right inside the mole now, sir. They're dropping lifelines over the side for us.' The thunderclap roar of two more bursting shells drowned his words but *Rapier's* skipper could just make out the coxswain's closing comment. 'The poor sods are taking a proper pasting and no mistake. Must be bloody 'eroes!'

Hamilton was inclined to agree but it was hardly the appropriate time for considering the relative merits of bravery. A new sound had attracted his attention - a sound that was beginning to superimpose itself over the rumbling thunder of the battery guns on the mole. Listening carefully he identified it as the heartening bark of the destroyer's quick-firers answering the defenders in kind. Clinging grimly to his paddle he thrust it blindly into the water and concentrated on the only thing that mattered - survival. For once in his life he could no longer rely on himself alone. And it was a galling thought for a man of Hamilton's self- reliant disposition. He was now no more than a cog in a machine. Whether he lived or died depended on the skill and courage of his trusted coxswain and the determination of a man who had once tried to kill him. In any other circumstances it would have seemed an odd combination.

A blinding flash seared the fog of blindness clogging his eyes and the bows of the boat lifted sharply as if a giant hand were trying to pluck it out of the water. Stunned by the blast of the exploding shell he fell backwards into the bottom of the folboat, grasping for the paddle as it was torn from his grasp. Lying sprawled on the keel-boards and trying to recover his breath, he could hear the sea pouring into the boat through the jagged hole in the bows. A strange, almost unearthly, silence followed the explosion and, hanging on to the thwarts with his good hand, he tried to drag himself upright. His groping fingers touched the motionless body of the coxswain and he shivered. He felt suddenly sick but, fighting back the urge, he forced himself to concentrate. Somewhere ahead in the dark void of his blindness he heard Charlie Dobson's tightly controlled groan of pain.

'Are you alright, Dobson?'

'I think my leg's gone, sir,' Charlie reported weakly as he tried to staunch the flow of blood. 'How about you?'

'The flash has blinded me for the moment - otherwise I'm okay.' Hamilton was relieved to share his secret. 'What's happening? I can't see a damned thing.'

'We're going down fast, sir. I think Mister Blood's dead. And I haven't seen Harding since the shell hit us. He must have been blown over the side.' Dobson broke off suddenly as a spasm of pain engulfed him and he was glad the skipper couldn't see the tears in his eyes. 'What do we do now, sir? I can't swim with my leg in this mess.'

'How far away is the destroyer?'

'About fifty yards to starboard, sir. I doubt if we can make it.'

Hamilton shared his pessimism. He listened to the bullets thudding into the wooden bulwarks as the sinking folboat drifted helplessly in the current. Dobson couldn't swim. And *he* couldn't see. Individually neither of them stood a dog's chance once the tiny boat went down. But together . . .

'Grab hold of me,' he told Dobson sharply. 'I reckon I can keep you afloat. And,' he added with unnecessary brutality, 'I'll need you to tell me which way to swim. A blind man's no use without a guide-dog!'

Hamilton found himself treading water as the folboat sank gently beneath his feet and, moments later, he felt Dobson's arms clutching tightly around his waist. Twisting onto his back, he crooked his arm protectively round Charlie's neck and lifted his mouth clear of the water. His damaged hand was still painful and his body was exhausted but he somehow found the strength to kick out with his legs and drag the young seaman with him.

'That's it, lad,' he whispered encouragingly. 'Take it easy and leave it to me. You won't come to any harm while I've got you. Just keep your eyes open and tell me if I'm swimming in the right direction.'

CAPTAIN GERVAISE ST JOHN WOODWARD could not explain the mysterious impulse that had prompted him to make one last sweep of the harbour entrance. It seemed a futile gesture in the circumstances and it was in direct disobedience to orders. Yet something or someone had made it impossible to ignore the animal instinct that drew him irresistibly back towards the mole.

He had already seen Mansergh's boat disappear in a sheet of flame and, like everyone else in the Support Group, he had concluded that *Rapier's* other boat had been lost as well. Certainly there was no sign of it as the commandos withdrew to their landing craft and headed out to sea; nor was anything visible when Vice Admiral

Winter had signaled the assault force to pull out at Zero plus sixty. And yet there remained this inexplicable urge to continue the search.

Boxer had already paid dearly for his rashness. The hatches and Carley floats abaft the funnel were blazing furiously and the fire-party was having its work cut out to bring the flames under control. B turret on the fo'c'sle was a blackened shell as the result of a direct hit that had killed every member of its crew. And the bridge and superstructure was riddled with more holes than a discarded colander. But peering through the smoke he had finally spotted the little folboat coming through the narrow strait on the eastern side of the Ile d'Or. He knew it should not be there - the detailed operational orders had routed the survivors to the west of the island where the motor launches were to wait - but, equally, he knew it could only be Hamilton; breaking the rules as usual by seeking the sheltered lee of the island before making his final dash for safety across the open waters of the harbour.

The destroyer was now within yards of the two exhausted men in the sea and Woodward watched anxiously as the life-lines snaked over the side. The German gunners seemed to have redoubled their efforts in the last few minutes and he was eager to complete the rescue before *Boxer* was too badly damaged to make her escape.

'Lower the scrambling net, Number One! They're not bloody fish coming up for bait!'

Four members of the destroyer's crew clambered down the netting to help the two exhausted submariners to safety and, ignoring the bullets, they gently helped them up the swaying lattice of ropes towards the deck.

Woodward made sure there was no one else in the water and turned to the quartermaster.

'Full astern both!'

The destroyer shuddered as if stirring from a long sleep. Deep down in the engine room the stokers turned up the sprays and black oil smoke erupted from the funnel as the propellers began to move - slowly at first and then faster until the sea beneath the counter was a frenzy of boiling foam. *Boxer* hesitated as if reluctant to leave and then started to glide gently out of the harbour stern-first with her battle flags fluttering defiantly in the off-shore breeze.

Urged on by the sailors clinging to the scrambling net, Hamilton hauled himself over the side rails and, lacking the strength to support his weight, crashed headlong to the deck like a sack of potatoes. He struck the unyielding plating with bruising force and, partially stunned by the impact, tried to orientate himself. The eucalyptus oil which Harding had used to bathe his eyes had begun to take effect and his involuntary swim had also helped to wash much of the oil sludge and grime from his face. The figures hurrying forward to help him to his feet were still only blurred shadows but even partial sight was better than the horrors of total blindness and, ignoring the pain of his broken hand, he lifted himself up.

One of *Boxer's* sick berth attendants bent over him and pulled a pad of cotton wool from his first-aid pouch but Hamilton pushed him roughly aside.

'I'm alright for the moment - look after Dobson.'

Leaving two men to stand by the injured officer the SBA led the stretcher party to the rails and helped the fo'c'sle hands to lift the wounded sailor gently over the side before carrying him behind the temporary cover of the upper- deck bridge supports. The guns on the mole, firing at point-blank range, kept up a merciless barrage throughout the rescue operation but, undeterred by the bullets, the destroyer men worked with selfless devotion to bring the last survivor to safety.

Charlie was barely conscious. His left leg had been shattered just below the knee by an 88 mm shell and the remains of the limb was a horrifying mess of blood, splintered bone, and torn flesh. A boy seaman, scarcely fifteen years old, took one look and was violently sick on the spot but the sick berth attendant steeled himself to his unenviable task and set to work. Taking a length of rubber tubing from his bag he looped it quickly around Dobson's upper thigh, pulled it tight, and secured it firmly.

'How is he?'

The SBA had just finished tying the tourniquet when *Boxer's* Surgeon Lieutenant arrived on the scene to examine the wounded submariner. 'I've stopped the bleeding, sir. But he's in a bad way.'

'Morphine!'

The orderly who had followed the doctor on deck from the sick bay opened the case and handed him a ready-filled hypodermic. Emmerson checked it quickly, pulled back Charlie's sleeve, and plunged the needle into his arm. 'Right! Get him down to the sick bay and prepare him for amputation. I'll start operating as soon as I've attended to the other one.'

But the 'other one', it appeared, had different views on the matter. By the time the Surgeon Lieutenant had reached him, Hamilton was back on his feet and he gestured the doctor away impatiently.

'I'm okay, Doc. Just some oil in the eyes. It's beginning

to clear. You get down to the sick bay and look after young Dobson - he's due to get married next month.'

He tried to push past but Emmerson grabbed his arm and stopped him. 'You *must* have your eyes attended to, sir,' he told Hamilton firmly. 'Oil is corrosive. It will burn out your bloody eyeballs!'

'And balls to you too, Doc! You take care of Dobson first. I promise I'll report to the sick bay as soon as I can. But I must see the Captain.'

The Surgeon Lieutenant shrugged. He knew he was wasting his time trying to argue with Hamilton. And if he wanted to save the other survivor time was all important.

'Very well, sir. I'll leave it to your good sense. But if you don't have your eyes washed out inside the next ten minutes you'll find yourself signing on at St Dunstan's when you get ashore. And it won't be my fault.'

Hamilton knew that Emmerson was making no idle threat. But despite his exhaustion the old streak of truculent obstinacy continued to burn bright. He flattened himself against the superstructure as a burst of machinegun fire stitched a neat line of bullet holes in the bulkhead just above the doctor's head.

'What's our elapsed zero time, Doc?'

Emmerson checked his watch with the casual calm of a man waiting for the last train home. 'Plus seventy, sir.' Hamilton peered cautiously around the screen in the direction of the E-boat pen. The huge concrete shelter was hidden behind the rocky hump of the Ile d'Or but he knew it was there somewhere beyond the grey mist clouding his eyes. The fuses of the depthcharges had been set for a twenty-minute delay which meant that *Rapier* would go up in three minutes precisely. And after all he had been through he had no intention of missing it.

'Ten minutes will suit me fine, Doc.' He turned to one of the sailors waiting in the background. 'I want to get up to the bridge. Will one of you lads show me the way?'

A hand tightened on his arm and Hamilton obeyed meekly as the leading seaman guided him across the unfamiliar deck towards the bridge companionway. He was aware of vague shapes hurrying past and he felt the destroyer shudder each time another shell slammed home. The noise of battle was awesome in its intensity and the concussion from *Boxer's* own guns threatened to split his eardrums. The acrid smell of smouldering wood and burning rubber mingling with the sickening stench of scorched flesh and fresh blood reminded him of a visit he had once made to a slaughter-house on a damp November evening.

'Good God, Hamilton! Why the devil aren't you in the sick bay?'

Hamilton recognized Woodward's voice even though he was unable to distinguish his features. The leading seaman guided his hand onto the rail of the companionway and he felt for the bottom rung with his foot.

'I wanted to see the fireworks, sir. I've promised the Doc I'll go down for treatment as soon as the charges detonate. I'd like to make sure we made a good job of it.'

He paused as the Captain took his arm and began leading him up to the destroyer's bridge. 'You didn't have to come looking for us, sir. It was strictly against orders.'

'You're a fine one to talk about breaking orders, Lieutenant Commander,' Woodward said gruffly. 'Let's just say I was repaying a debt I owed you.'

Hamilton knew it was Woodward's way of apologizing for Corryvreckham and he made no comment as the Captain guided him up the ladder with gentle concern. They emerged on the bridge at the exact moment a fresh enemy battery opened fire and *Boxer's* captain pushed him down on the deck without ceremony as the first shells moaned overhead and exploded in the sea fifty yards beyond the destroyer.

'You stay there and keep out of the way. I don't want any more casualties.' Woodward joined the Watch Officer at the compass platform. 'I reckon we're nearly clear now, Jenkins. Hard a'starboard, Mister Quartermaster!' 'Starboard wheel on, sir.'

Woodward leaned over the side of the bridge as the twin $4'5$ in guns of the after turret opened fire on the new target. His face was grimed with smoke and his tin hat was wedged firmly on his head. A thin trickle of blood ran down his cheek where a splinter of steel had cut his face. But he was happy. He saw the flash of the destroyer's shells bursting short of the German battery and he beat the rail excitedly with his fist.

'Up fifty, Mister Gunner!' He glanced quickly towards the bows. 'Midships helm. Full ahead together. Hard a'port, Quartermaster. Make smoke!'

A blinding sheet of white flame engulfed the bridge as a heavy shell struck the chartroom abaft the steering position. Crouched in his corner, Hamilton heard the deafening roar and felt himself lifted bodily from the deck plating by the force of the blast. Stunned by the violence of the explosion, he groped his way forward through the dust and smoke in the vain hope of doing something to help and he was dimly aware of men doubling up the ladders to the charnal house of torn metal and splintered wood to clear the casualties and regain control.

'Take over the steering, Hoskins! Maintain course and speed!' *Boxer's* executive officer seemed unconcerned by the surrounding carnage. He passed his orders calmly and without fuss as he strove to restore order from chaos. 'Davis, check the communications. Tell 'em to send stretcher parties to the bridge to evacuate the wounded and then tell the bo's'n to report to me.'

Woodward had been standing alongside the chart-house and he had caught the full blast of the explosion. As the acrid smoke dispersed he found himself under a pile of debris and, struggling clear, he crawled painfully towards the after end of the bridge so that he did not impede the men taking over. His uniform was torn and covered in dust, and blood was soaking through the front of his shirt where a fragment of red-hot steel had pene-trated his ribs. Reaching the shelter of the port bulwarks he paused, caught his breath with sudden pain, and started coughing. He waited until the paroxysm passed and then dragged himself into the corner where Hamilton was lying.

'Only another sixty seconds, Lieutenant Comman-der,' he managed to gasp. 'And then you'll be hearing the biggest bloody bang you've ever heard in your life.'

He started to cough again. His vision was fading but he was aware of a sick berth attendant leaning over him and wiping the blood from his lips. With his last reserves of strength he pushed the man away. 'Don't waste time on me, Johnson. I've had it. Get the Lieutenant Commander to the sick bay—' He turned his head towards Hamilton as two ratings lifted the submariner onto a stretcher. 'Give my love to Caroline when you see her.'

Hamilton signaled to the stretcher bearers to wait. Reaching out with his hands he tried to ease the captain into a more comfortable position against the bulwark.

'I'll do that, sir,' he promised quietly.

Woodward raised his head. Blood was running from the corners of his mouth and his eyes were beginning to glaze. By a supreme effort he forced his lips into a grin. 'Good luck to both of you - I suppose that when Caroline's a widow there's no reason why you shouldn't marry her, eh?' His head fell forward on his chest as the thunder of the demolition charges echoed across the harbour. But the sound of success came exactly ten seconds too late for him to hear it . . .

CHARLIE DOBSON PUT down his cup of tea, leaned back on the settee in front of the fire, and rested the stump of his left leg on the cushion. Picking the newspaper up from the carpet, he opened it at Page 3, and read the story again:

VC WEDS WIDOW OF NAVY HERO Lady Caroline Woodward, whose husband Captain Gervaise Woodward was killed in action during the raid on Zeehoven last year, was married to Commander Nicholas Hamilton, VC, DSO, DSC, at Caxton Hall yesterday. The bride was given away by her stepfather, Admiral Sir John Keble-Hampshire, the 6th Sea Lord, and amongst the many distinguished guests at the ceremony were: Vice Admiral Mansergh, whose only son was tragically killed in the same raid; Vice Admiral Sir Charles Winter; and Viscount Cavendish. The reception was held at the Savoy Hotel and the couple later left for a Scottish honeymoon in the ancient and romantic castle of Lord and Lady Davidson.

Commander Hamilton, who was temporarily blinded during the Zeehoven raid, has just been appointed to command a submarine flotilla . . .

Dobson put the newspaper down and stared at the fire. His wife glanced at the headline as she came into the room and stooped to look at the photograph beneath it.

'She looks nice, doesn't she, Charlie?' She paused to read the story. 'Wasn't Mr Hamilton the captain of that submarine you were on?'

Dobson nodded. 'That's right. It's funny, you know. He said something to me when he came to see me in hospital. I couldn't make head nor tail of it at the time but I reckon I know what he meant now.'

'Why, what did he say? You didn't tell me about it, love.' 'It wasn't that important, Thelma.' He grinned at the memory. 'He just said: Dobson, take my advice. *If you can't beat 'em - join 'em!*'

A LOOK AT: DIVING STATIONS, NICK HAMILTON BOOK 4

1941: Lt. Hamilton, commander of the only British Submarine in the Far East, relies on his own unorthodox daring to deal the Japanese a savage blow.

Available January 2019 from Edwyn Gray and Wolfpack Publishing

ABOUT THE AUTHOR

AUTHOR EDWYN GRAY specialized in naval writing, and has occasionally written short stories.

Born in London, Gray pursued his education at the Royal Grammar School, High Wycombe. After reading economics at the University of London, he went on to join the British civil service.

Gray began his career as an author in 1953, writing for magazines. His first novel was published in 1969, and he became a full-time writer in 1980.

www.ingramcontent.com/pod-product-compliance
Lightning Source LLC
Chambersburg PA
CBHW031211260626
47169CB00007B/2010